# ABSENCE

OF THE

# HERO

# Charles Bukowski

# ABSENCE

## OF THE

# HERO

## UNCOLLECTED STORIES

### AND

## ESSAYS, VOLUME 2: 1946–1992

EDITED AND WITH AN INTRODUCTION BY

David Stephen Calonne

CITY LIGHTS : SAN FRANCISCO

Cover design: Jeff Mellin www.bigblueox.net

Library of Congress Cataloging-in-Publication Data

Bukowski, Charles.
Absence of the hero : uncollected stories and essays, volume 2: 1946–1992 /
by Charles Bukowski ; edited, with an introduction, by David Stephen Calonne.
p. cm.
Includes bibliographical references.
ISBN 978-0-87286-531-0
I. Calonne, David Stephen, 1953— II. Title.
PS3552.U4A6 2010
811'.54—dc22
2009049106

Visit our website: www.citylights.com

City Lights Books are published
at the City Lights Bookstore
261 Columbus Avenue
San Francisco, CA 94133

# CONTENTS

# ACKNOWLEDGMENTS

*Absence of the Hero* is a companion volume to my earlier book of uncollected Bukowski writings, *Portions from a Wine-Stained Notebook*, and I am indebted again to many of the same cool humans who sustained me in that earlier effort. I am grateful to Ed Fields, University of California at Santa Barbara, Department of Special Collections, Davidson Library for permission to include the unpublished manuscript "Ah, Liberation, Liberty, Lilies on the Moon!" Claude Zachary of the Doheny Memorial Library, Specialized Libraries and Archival Collections at USC, was helpful in solving last-minute bibliographical mysteries. Thanks to Roger Myers and Erika Castano of the University of Arizona Library, Special Collections, where I discovered the unpublished essay "The House of Horrors." I thank Julie Herrada, Head of the Labadie Collection, Special Collections, University of Michigan, Ann Arbor, as well as the Interlibrary Loan staff at Eastern Michigan University. Bukowski's letter to Curt Johnson is from the Brown University Library. Jamie Boran was a helpful correspondent when I began my work a decade ago. I am grateful to my friend Abel Debritto, whom I finally had the pleasure of meeting last summer in Spain. Abel generously sent me several fine stories and essays and I have also learned a great deal from his pioneering Ph.D. thesis. Roni Braun, head of the *Charles Bukowski Gesellschaft* in Germany helped with my request for *Jahrbücher* and was a wonderful host during my time in Andernach. Deep gratitude to Henry Corbin, who keeps me straight among the angels. Thanks to my inspiring, courageous, vital, and joyously literary eighty-nine-year-old father, Pierre Calonne, who reads to me from Montaigne, Plutarch, LaRochefoucauld, E.M. Cioran, and Thomas Wolfe and shares with me his latest Chinese recipes. Thanks to my brother Ariel Calonne and his wife Pat and my nephews Alexander, Nicholas, and Michael. Thanks as always for everything to Maria Beye. At City Lights I have received help and encouragement from Elaine Katzenberger, Stacey Lewis, Robert Sharrard, and especially my hip, sensitive, brilliant editor Garrett Caples. Thanks to John Martin for believing in my work and to Linda Lee Bukowski for her thoughtfulness and many kindnesses.

# INTRODUCTION

Charles Bukowski composed a sequence of six stories between 1944 and 1948, including "Aftermath of a Lengthy Rejection Slip" (1944) in *Story*, "20 Tanks from Kasseldown" (1946) in *Portfolio III*, and the quartet appearing in *Matrix*: "The Reason Behind Reason" (1946), "Love, Love, Love" (1946–47), "Cacoethes Scribendi" (1947), and "Hard Without Music" (1948).[1] "The Reason Behind Reason"—although decorated with Bukowski's first published drawing, depicting a baseball player comically reaching out to catch a fly ball—is pervaded by an eerie sense of disquiet. The main character Chelaski is puzzled, enigmatic, muted, withdrawn; he sees no reason to perform his appointed role in the game because, like the game of life, it is an absurd one. Bukowski pays close attention to the oddly-observed disconnected small detail and demonstrates his early mastery of fictional craft: "fire on things sticking in mouths" of the spectators; "the thick veins in the red neck" of Jamison; a rhythmical, lyrical flash of erotic mystery from the girl in the grandstand with "a green skirt, and a pleat in a green skirt, shadow-like, and leaping."

Like Roquentin in Jean-Paul Sartre's *La Nausée* (1938), who experiences the world as "out there" and is made ill by the chestnut tree's horrible quiddity, so too Chelaski feels "different," adrift in an indifferent universe where "things don't set right" and "even the sun looked a little sick, the green of the fences too green, the sky much too high" and a weird recurring bird "skipped through the air, up and down, somewhere, very fast." The title "The Reason Behind Reason" suggests an inscrutable riddle occluded behind the reasons we invent to interpret our experience. Whatever meanings there might be are so unreasonable that they are best passed over in silence. It is the individual, questioning poet who is lost, while the crowd "all hung together in a strange understanding." This is the solitary mystical zone where nothing and nobody connect; we should remember that one of Bukowski's favorite novels was Carson McCullers' *The Heart is a Lonely Hunter*.[2]

"Cacoethes Scribendi" concerns an editor/writer who seeks an assistant for his literary magazine. Again the mood is uncanny, with strange perturbations in the atmosphere, the abstruse word choice purposely jarring: "suzerain," "diacritic," "acephalous," "zebu," "argute." The title is taken from Juvenal's *Satire* VII and may be translated as "an incurable endemic writer's itch," which precisely describes Bukowski himself since he was a hard-working, ceaselessly productive writer, constantly submitting poems, stories, and essays to virtually every literary magazine in the United States (and several in Europe).[3] Indeed, contrary to the myth fostered by the author himself, he did not fall silent after 1948, the period of his infamous "ten-year drunk" when he claimed to have written nothing. In fact, he submitted poems to *Poetry (Chicago)* between 1953 and 1956 and published the poems "The Look" in *Matrix* in 1951, "Lay Over" in *Naked Ear* in 1956, "These Things" and "You Smoke a Cigarette" in *Quixote* 1956, "Poem for Personnel Managers" and "As the Sparrow" in *Quixote* 1957, and "Mine" in Wallace Berman's *Semina 2* in 1957.[4]

"80 Airplanes Don't Put You in the Clear" (1957) is noteworthy as the first work in which the narrator is named "Hank," while in "Love, Love, Love" the main character is "Chuck" and in "The Reason Behind Reason" he is "Chelaski." Bukowski would finally settle on Henry ("Hank") Chinaski (derived from his given name Henry Charles Bukowski, Jr.) as his literary alter ego. This story marks a return to the more whimsical tone of "Aftermath" and the tale is built around D.H. Lawrence's biography: his failed attempt to found the colony of *Rananim* with his friends, his wife Frieda von Richthofen, and her kinship with "The Red Baron," Manfred von

Richthofen. The allusion to the Red Baron returns us to Bukowski's literary beginnings; one of the first stories he invented as a child concerned the German World War I fighter pilot.[5] Richard Aldington, Homer, Shakespeare, Twain, Stevenson, Huxley, Confucius, and Beethoven are all invoked during a night of playful drinking and womanizing. *Wein, Weib, und Gesang*—wine, women, and song, or alcohol, sex, and poetry/music—would become Bukowski's obsessive thematic holy trinity; if one exists in his narratives, the other two will surely be present.

Bukowski's transgressive sexual writing begins with "The Rapist's Story." Though it was published in *Harlequin* in 1957, Bukowski had actually submitted it to *Story* in 1952, thus predating Vladimir Nabokov's *Lolita* (1955) by three years.[6] It is clear from a psychoanalytic perspective that the cycle of stories about violation ("The Fiend" from 1970 is a later example) are replayings of Bukowski's own terrorized childhood at the hands of his violent father. His unpublished essay "Ah, Liberation, Liberty, Lilies on the Moon!" illustrates his compassion for the victims of child abuse as well as his sensitivity to animal cruelty. Later, in his "Notes of a Dirty Old Man" columns, he would continue to experiment with explicit erotic themes, and when he quit his position in the Los Angeles Post Office in 1970 to begin his career as professional writer, he began to consciously create increasingly sexual and violent narratives in order to successfully market his work to adult magazines.

Bukowski alternated between composing fiction and poetry, but when he wrote essays, they were most frequently devoted to literary polemics. He often seemed particularly concerned to distinguish himself as a solitary creator separate from the various "schools" of American poetry: Imagist, Confessional, Objectivist, Black Mountain, Deep Image, New York, Beat. In "Manifesto," he takes aim at the "university poets," a familiar target throughout his career. The essay is perhaps a parody (the vocabulary—"nosography," "censorious dictum," "heuristic," "steatopygous," "hierophants"—is obviously outrageous) of the genteel literary criticism of his day, which he enjoyed reading in the *Kenyon Review* or the *Sewanee Review*. In opposition to the pampered ivory tower boys, Bukowski is at pains to remind us that he lived by the Aeschylean dictum *pathei mathos*: through suffering comes wisdom, inspiration, creativity. In "He Beats His Women," he asserted: "The gods were good to me. They kept me under. They made me live the life. It was very difficult for me to walk out of a slaughterhouse or a factory and come home and write a poem I didn't quite mean. And many people write poems they don't quite mean. I do too, sometimes. The hard life created the hard line and by the hard line I mean the true line devoid of ornament." A more concise statement of Bukowski's poetics would be difficult to find.

In another of his essays on the writing life, "The House of Horrors," he makes sarcastic observations about poets who "are quite comfortable with TV sets, air coolers, loaded refrigerators, and apartments and houses by the sea—mostly at Venice and Santa Monica, and they sun themselves in the day, feeling and looking tragic, these male friends (?) of mine and then at night, lo, perhaps they have a bottle of wine and a watercress sandwich, followed by a wailing letter of their penury and greatness to somebody somewhere." It is a Romantic conceit, but for Bukowski many poets were mild-mannered reporters who did not honor Nietzsche's mighty apothegm in *Also Sprach Zarathustra*: "Of all that is written I love only what a man has written with his blood."[7] And he would agree with Charles Péguy, who remarked: "Un mot n'est pas le même dans un écrivain et dans un autre. L'un se l'arrache du ventre. L'autre le tire de la poche de son pardesssus." "A word is not the same with one writer as with another. One tears it from his guts. The other pulls it out of his overcoat pocket."

The subject matter of Bukowski's writing is very frequently

writing itself: his constant effort to define the act of composing in relationship to an authentically lived life, his theories of creativity and poetics, his admiration for other writers, as well as his connections to editors. His essay "The Outsider," which appeared in 1972 in *The Wormwood Review*, is his tribute to Jon Edgar and Gypsy Lou Webb. Marvin Malone's *Wormwood Review*, Douglas Blazek's *Ole*, and in Germany Carl Weissner's *Klactovedsedsteen*—all were central in slowly establishing the readership that would launch Bukowski to world fame.[8] Yet most important of all would be John Martin's Black Sparrow Press; one of Bukowski's several portraits of Martin appears in his 1981 story "East Hollywood: The New Paris." And Bukowski himself edited two little magazines: *Harlequin*, with his first wife Barbara Frye and later, briefly, *Laugh Literary and Man the Humping Guns*, with Neeli Cherkovski.

Indeed, Bukowski's involvement with the underground press both as contributor and editor put him in the direct line of combat during the contentious struggle for free speech during the '50s, '60s, and '70s. As early as 1957, Wallace Berman was raided by the Los Angeles vice squad.[9] In 1966, Steve Richmond, who had published Bukowski in his magazines *Earth* and *Earth Rose*, had writings from his bookshop in Santa Monica confiscated.[10] d.a. levy, the dynamo of the "mimeo revolution," published Bukowski's poem *The Genius of the Crowd*, which was seized by the police: "levy was arrested and jailed along with Jim Lowell (proprietor of the great Asphodel Bookshop, a welcoming home for new poetry for over thirty years) on charges of distributing obscene material in Cleveland."[11] When John Bryan asked Bukowski to edit *Renaissance 2* in September 1968, he solicited a story by Jack Micheline titled "Skinny Dynamite," about "a red-haired New York girl who liked to fuck," which resulted in Bryan's arrest.[12]

Thus as a creature of the underground and as an advocate of freedom of speech, Bukowski had always been in sympathy with the ideals of the counterculture. And as we see from his anti-war essay, "Peace, Baby, Is Hard Sell" (1962), at the beginning of the Sixties Bukowski was in accord with pacifism and love, although he put on the outer mask of the tough guy misanthrope to hide his essential tenderness. It should come as no surprise, then, that Bukowski would have deep links with the Beat writers. Although the nature of his connection to the Beats has been a matter of some controversy among literary historians, he read their work closely and appeared with them in many of the same publications, such as *The Outsider, Evergreen Review, Beatitude, Transatlantic Review, City Lights Anthology, Klactovedsedsteen, Acid: Neue Amerikanische Szene, Unmuzzled Ox, El Corno Emplumado, Semina, Hearse, Wild Dog, Naked Ear,* and *Bastard Angel.* And as the Sixties progressed, an increasing number of significant writers in Beat circles came to appreciate his work; Kenneth Rexroth would positively review Bukowski's *It Catches My Heart in Its Hands* in the *New York Times* on July 5, 1964.[13]

Bukowski had corresponded with Harold Norse and his tribute to him, "The Old Pro," appeared in 1966 in *Ole,* an important "mimeo revolution" publication edited by Douglas Blazek. The two poets met when Norse moved to Venice, California in January 1969.[14] Bukowski reviewed Allen Ginsberg's *Empty Mirror* in *Ole* in 1967 and at the beginning of 1968 encountered Neal Cassady ("Dean Moriarty" in Jack Kerouac's *On the Road*), who became the subject of one of his "Notes of a Dirty Old Man" columns.[15] In 1969, Bukowski would appear with Norse and Philip Lamantia in *Penguin Poets 13.* City Lights published *Erections, Ejaculations and Other Tales of Ordinary Madness* in 1972 and Lawrence Ferlinghetti sponsored Bukowski's first reading in San Francisco at the City Lights Poets' Theater in September 1972 and also reprinted *Notes of a Dirty Old Man* in 1973 following its initial appearance in 1969 under the Essex House imprint.[16] And in November 1974, Bukowski read with Ferlinghetti, Snyder, and Ginsberg at the Santa Cruz Poetry Festival.[17]

Thus Bukowski's writings derive their power not only from his boisterous, energetic, autobiographical voice, but from the fact that they are vivid chronicles of the Sixties counterculture. For example, Gregory Corso is affectionately portrayed in "I Just Write Poetry So I Can Go to Bed with Girls." Jack Micheline becomes a lively "Duke" in a "Notes of a Dirty Old Man" column from 1973, while d.a. levy, who committed suicide in 1967, was the subject of two essays: "The Deliberate Mashing of the Sun" and an article in *The Serif*, the literary magazine of Kent State University. Leroi Jones (Amiri Baraka) is the subject of one of his "Notes of a Dirty Old Man" columns, while Robert Creeley is pilloried in the *Literary Times* essay "Examining My Peers." It is clear then—his own many disavowals to the contrary—that Bukowski's career was in many ways inextricably bound to the Beats.

One area of common ground with the Beats was Bukowski's development of his own style of "spontaneous prose composition," which sought to depict everything about the human body and imagination normally ignored, shunned, and rejected as "vulgar." In "The Absence of the Hero," Bukowski struggled to record violent, scatological, fascinating, grotesque images as they emerged unbidden in convulsive patterns from the depths of the unconscious. Here the words seem to be energetically thrown upon the page randomly but nevertheless they fall into a vital pattern. He records discrete perceptions, even noting the passage of time—"3:24 A.M."—in diary-like fashion as if to catch the very movement of fragmented consciousness through time. The story also illustrates Bukowski's alternating use of lines of capital and lowercase letters, the use of jagged line spacing, lists of capitalized sentences—all as if he is attempting to paint or draw with words. He experimented frequently in his prose with punctuation, type size, ellipses, idiosyncratic spellings, and repetitions—some of his narratives were entirely composed in lower case, thus transporting into prose some of e.e. cummings' poetic typographical playfulness.

This emphasis on the appearance of the text—he often illustrated his stories, poems, and letters with cartoons and drawings, while his early stories were actually combinations of words and illustrations—shows that Bukowski frequently strove to make the text itself into an image. He was actually ahead of his time, anticipating the current craze for "graphic fiction" since he obsessively joined text to image in his hand-printed stories from the mid- to late '40s.[18] As we see in "East Hollywood: The New Paris," Bukowski devoted a serious amount of time to his drawing and painting, and many of the deluxe editions of his work are accompanied by original art. So too the text of "The Absence of the Hero" reveals that Bukowski was a kind of Action Writer: he tried to make words perform, act out their meaning in a quasi-visual way in the same fashion that Jackson Pollock performed the spontaneous act of creation by "randomly" yet accurately flinging paint on canvas.

Bukowski would develop a hard, comic, lyric realism, a toughness, but underneath an abiding sensitivity and a photographic, documentary fidelity to everyday horrors. In his "Notes of a Dirty Old Man" columns, he records the humdrum facts of city life: drivers in Los Angeles, a confrontation between Nazis and Marxists, joyous nighttime sessions with his drunken landlady and landlord. He often writes the prose equivalent of William Carlos Williams' "This is just to say," telling you precisely what is in front him without commentary. He addresses the reader directly, removing any barrier between writer and audience. And he strengthened his vulnerable, hurt self by muscling it with irony, by a subversive, mocking, irreverent sharpness of observation. Bukowski's prose became more accomplished with time and his narratives more skillful: he would begin *in medias res* with an outrageous opening scene to hook readers and draw them into the story, as in "The Cat in the Closet." This story is also a marvelous example of the ways he casts his alter ego as a comical, self-deprecating, helpless character lost in a universe where things just happen.

The unexpected references to Stravinsky, Mahler, Hemingway, Camus' *The Stranger*, Maxwell Bodenheim, and Berlioz against the backdrop of graphic sexuality and comic drunken self-abasement are typical examples of a literary device Bukowski frequently employs. These surprising, sudden allusions to cultural figures serve to "equalize" "highbrow" and "lowbrow" culture to comic effect and are a kind of "winking" by the narrator to the reader, signaling that our hapless anti-hero may be a clown, but he is smarter than he lets on. So too Bukowski seeks to entertain us by playing the fool; he gives us our existential lesson, but with a knowing smile. His characters do not grow, achieve epiphanies, or reach enlightenment. Rather, as the Buddha said in the Diamond Sutra: "I obtained not the least thing from complete, unexcelled awakening, and it is for that very reason it is called complete, unexcelled awakening."

With increasing fame, Bukowski began to give poetry readings throughout the U.S.: in California (Los Angeles, Santa Cruz, San Francisco), New Mexico, Washington, Utah, Illinois, New York, and Wisconsin as well as in Vancouver, Canada, and Hamburg, Germany. He also made a rambunctious appearance on the famous television talk show hosted by Bernard Pivot in Paris, *Apostrophes*. And as always, life fed his art as he began to chronicle his life on the road in his poems, stories, essays, and novels. He became a "literary hustler," and he satirizes himself, and depoeticizes and deromanticizes poetry; he turns the lofty poetry reading into a ritual in honor of the god Dionysus, complete with rivers of wine and ecstatic maenads.[19]

The sexual revolution of the Sixties coincided with Bukowski's own raw and direct confrontation with his own sexuality. Due to his *acne vulgaris* and tortured childhood, Bukowski had never experienced a "normal" adolescence and he spent 1970–1977 playing catch-up for all the delights he had missed as a Southern Californian teenager. In "The Big Dope Reading," for example, we see Bukowski at the height of his powers, engaging in multiple levels of irony and self-parody. The title itself may carry a double entendre: "dope" as in marijuana, but also the Big Dope equals the Poet as Clown. Bukowski gives his readers a hilarious moment of deadpan self-parody when Chinaski quotes two of the most famous Bukowski apothegms—"Genius . . . could mean the ability to say a profound thing in a simple way" and "Endurance is more important than truth"—which are in-jokes for devoted Bukowskians. Here too there are complex moments when he is at once parodying erotic writing, himself, and the convolutions of sexual/romantic "relationships" (he would have been allergic to such a psychobabble word). Bukowski often plays at the "meaning" of "relationships" in a teasing, Zen way which recalls Jacques Lacan's gnomic apothegm: "There is no sexual relationship." He stripped himself down to show his vulnerability, his wounds, trying to recover through love what was lost in his childhood yet, at the same time, poking fun at the effort to find salvation through love and sex.[20] Yet Bukowski is also of course really a romantic who could write of falling in love in his June 24, 1974 "Notes of a Dirty Old Man" column: "I walked about and it felt as if the sun were inside of me." And as one of his favorite poets, e.e. cummings, wrote: "unlove is the heavenless hell and homeless home . . . lovers alone wear sunlight."[21]

Bukowski's "defense mechanism" to ward off psychic anguish is of course laughter. Wit, an unerring sense of comic timing, and a driving inexorable energy power his writings; his beloved Renaissance brothers in manic extravagance were François Rabelais and Giovanni Boccaccio.[22] He could also be sardonic, which was in perfect accord with the *Zeitgeist*: black humor would mark the counterculture of the '60s and '70s. *Who's Afraid of Virginia Woolf* (1966),

*One Flew Over the Cuckoo's Nest* (1975), and *Eraserhead* (1978) were among his favorite films—humor and madness in close and delicate counterpoint.[23] So too, Bukowski's writing is poised between despair and lyricism, moving forward with a vigorous power that virtually always redeems his writings from nihilism. His admiration for the genius of Robert Crumb (who illustrated several Bukowski works) shows that for Bukowski there is a nexus between pain, laughter, and quasi-German-Expressionist extreme states of emotion.

After he tendered his resignation at the post office at age 50, Bukowski demonstrated that he could be a practical working writer and he maximized his productivity by reassembling his plots in differing contexts. He not only recycled favorite narratives in stories and novels, but he even recast them in both story and poem: "Fooling Marie" exists in both forms. Furthermore, sections from *Post Office*, *Factotum*, and *Women* all appeared initially in his "Notes of a Dirty Old Man" column in the *LA Free Press* as separate stories. Chapter 30 from *Women* appeared in two installments and in comparing the story and novel versions, one can see how much he altered and revised; in this case, many splendid passages were left on the cutting-room floor as he shaped his prose into novel form. This method of composition made perfect sense, since Bukowski's fiction had always been episodic, constructed out of brief sections strung together. His novels are in a way a series of connected brief tales, which enabled him to detach sections for submission to magazines as separate short stories as he composed them. And there was yet another mode of literary proliferation: Bukowski's work was circulated among many underground publications under an agreement with the United Press Syndicate (UPS) which allowed articles to be reprinted by all members of the organization.[24]

As suggested above, perhaps due to both the loosening of censorship restrictions during the '60s and '70s as well as his own desire to explore more fully the darker reaches of his imagination, Bukowski would begin to experiment more dramatically with direct portrayals of violence.[25] Films such as *The Wild Bunch* (1969), *Easy Rider* (1969), and *A Clockwork Orange* (1971) laid the groundwork for a story such as "Christ with Barbeque Sauce," in which Bukowski used an actual newspaper account as the source for his narrative.[26] In later stories such as "The Invader" (1986), Bukowski traces the sudden incursion of terror into the banalities of everyday life: tales of ordinary madness. This story also recalls his earlier apocalyptic portrayals of the human inability to fathom primal wildness in stories such as "Animal Crackers in My Soup."

Bukowski's late, lovely cycle of poems about his cats reveals them to be creatures who preserve the style, poise, and lack of pretense that are so sorely lacking in human beings. And in one of his very last essays, Bukowski asserts that most people lose their magic at a very young age. In "Playing and Being the Poet," he returns to his musings about the life of the poet: "Poetry comes from where you've lived and from what makes you create it. Most people have already entered the death process by the age of 5, and with each passing year there is less of them in the sense of being original beings with a chance to break through and out and away from the obvious and the mutilating." For Bukowski, living life poetically is in fact the only way to really live.

### NOTES

1. "Aftermath of a Lengthy Rejection Slip," "Twenty Tanks from Kasseldown," and "Hard Without Music" may be found in Charles Bukowski, *Portions from a Wine-Stained Notebook: Uncollected Stories and Essays, 1944–1990,* ed. and with an introduction by David Stephen Calonne, San Francisco: City Lights, 2008. The early stories are remarkable not only for their style and approach, but also because they encapsulate virtually all of the major themes that would preoccupy Bukowski throughout his career: his romantic and erotic quest, sense of alienation, troubled family history, discovery of alcohol, struggles to be a writer, and love of classical music.

2. See "Carson McCullers" in *The Night Torn Mad With Footsteps*, Santa Rosa: Black Sparrow Press, 2001, p. 35.

3. Juvenal, *Satires* VII, ll. 50–52: "Nam si discedas, laqueo tenet ambitiosi/consuetudo mali, tenet insanabile multos/scribendi cacoethes et aegro in corde senescit." "You can't escape [you're caught up in the noose of bad ambitious habit]; there are so many possessed by an incurable endemic writer's itch that becomes a sick obsession." Juvenal, *The Sixteen Satires*, trans. Peter Green, London: Penguin Books, 1998, p. 56. On literary creativity and hypergraphia, see Alice W. Flaherty, *The Midnight Disease: The Drive to Write, Writer's Block and the Creative Brain*. New York: Houghton Mifflin, 2004.

4. For Bukowski and the little magazines see Abel Debritto, *Who's Big in the "Littles": A Critical Study of the Impact of the Little Magazines and Small Press Publications on the Career of Charles Bukowski from 1940 to 1969*. Ph.D. thesis, Universitat Autònoma de Barcelona, 2009.

5. Charles Bukowski, *Ham on Rye*. Santa Barbara: Black Sparrow Press, 1982, Chap. 34, p. 146.

6. Debritto, *Who's Big in the Littles*, p. 118. Debritto also reveals that Bukowski corresponded with Burnett from 1945 to 1955, again dispelling the myth of his dropping out of the literary world during his "ten-year drunk."

7. Friedrich Nietzsche, *Thus Spoke Zarathustra*. Harmondsworth: Penguin, 1983. p. 40.

8. Carl Weissner's translations led directly to Bukowski's success in Germany and Europe. For Bukowski's connection to Germany and Carl Weissner, see Jay Dougherty's interview with Bukowski, "Charles Bukowski and the Outlaw Spirit" in Charles Bukowski, *Sunlight Here I Am: Interviews & Encounters 1963–1993*, ed. and with an Introduction by David Stephen Calonne. Northville: Sundog Press, 2003, pp. 231–235. On Bukowski's German reception, see Horst Schmidt, *The Germans Love Me For Some Reason: Charles Bukowski und Deutschland*. Augsburg: MaroVerlag, 2006.

9. Maurice Berger, "Libraries Full of Tears: The Beats and the Law," in Lisa Phillips, *Beat Culture and the New America 1950–1965*. Paris/New York: Whitney Museum of American Art/Flammarion, 1995, pp. 122–137.

10. See Barry Miles, *Charles Bukowski*. London: Virgin, 2005, pp. 152–153 and Howard Sounes, *Charles Bukowski: Locked in the Arms of a Crazy Life*, New York: Grove Press, 1998, pp. 83–84.

11. Steven Clay, Rodney Phillips, and Jerome Rothenberg, *A Secret Location on the Lower East Side: Adventures in Writing 1969–1980*. New York: Granary Books, 1998, p. 48. On d.a. levy, see *d.a. levy & the mimeograph revolution*, eds. Larry Smith and Ingrid Swanberg, Huron, Ohio, Bottom Dog Press, 2007. For Bukowski's essay in support of Lowell, see *Portions from a Wine-Stained Notebook*, pp. 61–62. On the underground, see Jean-Francois Bizot, *20 Trips from the Counter-culture: Graphics and Stories from the Underground Press Syndicate*. London: Thames and Hudson, 2006; Diane Kruchkow and

Curt Johnson, eds., *Green Isle in the Sea: An Informal History of the Alternative Press, 1960–85.* Highland Park: December Press, 1986; Roger Lewis, *Outlaws of America: The Underground Press and its Context: Notes on a Cultural Revolution.* Harmondsworth: Penguin, 1972.

12. Jack Micheline, *Sixty Seven Poems for Downtrodden Saints.* San Francisco: FMSBW, 1999. See Miles, p. 160; Sounes, p. 93. Micheline on Bukowski, *San Francisco Beat: Talking with the Poets,* ed. David Meltzer, pp. 226–227. San Francisco: City Lights, 2001.

13. Kenneth Rexroth, "There's Poetry in a Ragged Hitch-hiker," *The New York Times,* July 5, 1964. Bukowski on Rexroth, *Screams from the Balcony: Selected Letters 1960–1970,* ed. Seamus Cooney. Santa Rosa: Black Sparrow Press, 1993, p. 165, p. 330. On Bukowski and the Beats, see Jean-François Duval, *Buk et Les Beats: Essai Sur La Beat Generation.* Paris: Editions Michalon, 1998. English edition, trans. Alison Ardron, *Bukowski and the Beats.* Northville: Sun Dog Press, 2002.

14. Harold Norse on Bukowski, see *Memoirs of a Bastard Angel: A Fifty-Year Literary and Erotic Odyssey.* New York: Thunder's Mouth Press, 1989, pp. 420–422; 424–426; and "Laughter in Hell," in *Drinking with Bukowski: Recollections of the Poet Laureate of Skid Row,* ed. Daniel Weizman, New York: Thunder's Mouth Press, 2000, pp. 91–96.

15. Bukowski's fine memoir in *Open City* of his meeting with Neal Cassady and Cassady's death in Mexico is anthologized in Ann Charters, *The Portable Beat Reader.* New York: Penguin 1992, pp. 438–444; David Kherdian, *Beat Voices: An Anthology of Beat Poetry.* New York: Henry Holt, 1995, pp. 120–123; and in Jeffrey H. Weinberg, ed. *Writers Outside the Margin.* Sudbury: Water Row Press, 1986, pp. 94–96. Charters also included another of Bukowski's "Notes" columns in *The Portable Sixties Reader,* New York: Penguin, 2003, pp. 436–439.

16. On Bukowski and Ferlinghetti, see Lawrence Ferlinghetti and Nancy J. Peters, *Literary San Francisco: A Pictorial History from Its Beginnings to the Present Day.* San Francisco: City Lights Books and Harper and Row, 1980, p. 210, p. 221; also see Barry Silesky, *Ferlinghetti: The Artist in His Time.* New York: Warner Books, 1990, pp. 177–178; Bukowski's poem "The Bard of San Francisco" is an homage to Ferlinghetti; see *onthebus* Issue 14, Vol. VI, No. 2, 1997, pp. 30–32, collected in *Betting on the Muse: Poems & Stories.* Santa Rosa: Black Sparrow Press, 1996, pp. 233–235.

17. See Sounes, pp. 140–141.

18. See Debritto, p. 214, 330.

19. Bukowski remarked, "I give poetry readings—for money. Strictly survival. I don't like to do it but I quit my job last January 9 and now I've become what you'd call a literary hustler. I do things now that I wouldn't have done before. I don't like to do it at all." See *Sunlight Here I Am,* p. 47.

20. Bukowski's obsessive returning to the site of his traumatic wounds also recalls

Lacan's conception of the unconscious. Slavoj Zizek declares that "the unconscious is not the preserve of wild drives that have to be tamed by the ego, but the site where a traumatic truth speaks out. Therein lies Lacan's version of Freud's motto *Wo es war, soll ich werden* (Where it was, I am to become): not 'The ego should conquer the id,' the site of the unconscious drives, but 'I should dare to approach the site of my truth.' What awaits me 'there' is not a deep Truth that I have to identify with, but an unbearable truth that I have to learn to live with." Slavoj Zizek, *How to Read Lacan*. New York: W.W. Norton, 2007, p. 3. Bukowski often uses humor to live with that unbearable truth.

21. e.e. cummings, *A Selection of Poems*. New York: Harcourt, Brace and World, 1965, p. 155.

22. On Rabelais see Bukowski's "he died April 9, 1553" in *The Night Torn Mad with Footsteps: New Poems*. Santa Rosa: Black Sparrow Press, 2001, pp. 218-19. And in an interview from 1981 he explained: ". . . the *Decameron*, Boccaccio. That is what influenced *Women* a great deal. I loved his idea that sex was so ridiculous, nobody could handle it. It was not so much love with him; it was sex. Love is funnier, more ridiculous. That guy! He could really laugh at it. He must have really gotten burnt about five thousand times to write that stuff. Or maybe he was just a fag; I don't know. So, love is ridiculous because it can't last, and sex is ridiculous because it doesn't last long enough." *Sunlight Here I Am*, p. 179.

23. For Bukowski's favorite films, see *Sunlight*, p. 230. On black humor, see Morris Dickstein, *Gates of Eden: American Culture in the Sixties*, New York: Basic Books, 1977, "Black Humor and History: The Early Sixties."

24. On the UPS, see Bizot, pp. 6, 226–227.

25. For a superb study of Bukowski and violence, see Alexandre Thiltges, *Bukowski ou Les Contes de la Violence Ordinaire*. Paris: L'Harmattan, 2006. Thiltges' monograph, unfortunately not yet translated into English, is the best single work of Bukowski scholarship to have appeared to date.

26. Bukowski had submitted the story to Curt Johnson, publisher of *Candid Press*, to whom he wrote a letter dated December 3, 1970: "Just glad I could curve one by you guys. That $45 check didn't bounce anyhow and allowed me to get some repairs on my old '62 Comet to get it running again so I could get around to my chickenshit poetry readings where I read half-drunk and hustle up a few more bucks. Now listening to Haydn. I gotta be crazy. Enjoyed writing the story, though. Read in the paper where they had caught some cannibals somewhere—Texas I think—and when they pulled them over this gal was just cleaning the meat off the fingers of a hand, nibbling. . . . I took it from there." Uncollected letter, Brown University Library.

# ABSENCE

OF THE

# HERO

# THE REASON BEHIND REASON

CHELASKI, CF, .285 (AB-246 H-70) felt a little ... felt a little ... different out there. There are days when you feel a little different. Things don't set right. Like now, even the sun looked a little sick, the green of the fences too green, the sky much too high, and the leather of his glove too much like ... leather.

He took a few steps forward and beat his fist into his glove, trying to shake everything. Did he have a headache or what? He felt *potential*, as if he were about to scream or to leap up or to do something that shouldn't be done.

Chelaski was a bit frightened and looked over at Donovan, LF, .296 (AB-230 H-68) but Donovan looked very comfortable. He studied Donovan carefully, trying to draw strength from him. His face was very brown, and Chelaski had never noticed the pot belly before. Such an ugly bulge, so unselfconscious. Even Donovan's legs seemed thick, tree-like, and Chelaski stared straight ahead again, feeling worse.

What was wrong?

The batter connected and it was an outfield fly ... to Donovan. Donovan moved forward a few steps, moved his arms leisurely, and caught the ball. Chelaski had watched the ball in its long, slow arc through sun and sky. It had seemed pleasant enough, but somehow unrelated, unattached to anything. The next man hit an infield single that he didn't have to handle. One out. One on. What was the inning? He turned to look at the scoreboard and saw the crowd. His eyes didn't focus on them. They were just bits of movement, cloth, and sound.

What did they want done?

It ran through his mind again: what did they want done?

Suddenly he was terrified and didn't know the reason. His breath came hard and the saliva ran in his mouth; he felt dizzy, airy.

There was Donovan . . . standing. He looked again at the crowd and saw everyone, everything, all together and separately. Glasses, neckties; women wearing skirts, men wearing pants; there was lipstick . . . and fire on things sticking in mouths . . . cigarettes. And they all hung together in a strange understanding.

And then it came . . . an outfield fly . . . to him. An easy one. He was worried. He studied the ball fiercely and it almost seemed to stop its movement in air. It just hung there and the crowd shouted and the sun shone and the sky was blue. And Donovan's eyes were watching him, and Donovan's eyes were watching. Was Donovan against him? What did Donovan *really* want?

The ball came into his glove. It entered his glove and he felt the strong pressure and pleasant push of the catch. He threw the ball to second, holding the runner on first. It was a good throw and Chelaski was amazed; it had seemed is if the ball had gone there because it was supposed to. His terror left a little; *he was getting away with it.*

The next man was out, short to first, and Chelaski began the long trot to the dugout. It was good to be running. He passed several opposing players but they didn't look at him. It bothered him a little, and the bother hung there in a little knob as he followed Donovan's set neck into the dugout. When Chelaski got down there, he felt somehow naked, or spotted, or something, and in an effort to act as if he were all right, he walked up to Hull and grinned down on him.

"Do you want me to kiss you? I could make you forget," he said to Hull.

Hull was hitting .189 and had been benched for Jamison, the college kid. Hull looked up at Chelaski. It was a look of absolute unrecognition. Hull didn't even answer; he got up and walked to the water cooler. Chelaski quickly moved up to the railing, with his back to the bench.

Corpenson singled. Donovan hit into a double play and trotted back down the first base line, lifting his legs high, his stockings showing, somehow all full of color.

Chelaski walked to the plate. There was the umpire, the catcher, the pitcher, the fielders, the audience. Everything waiting, everything waiting. Outside, perhaps, a man was holding up a bank; or, a streetcar full of people sitting, was turning a corner; but here it was different: it was settled, expected . . . not like *that*, outside: the streetcar, the holdup. Here it was . . . different, caught up, demanded.

He swung and missed the first pitch and people shouted. The catcher yelled something and tossed the ball back. A bird skipped through the air, up and down, going somewhere, very fast. Chelaski spit and stared at the birthmark on the ground. The ground was very dry. Ball one.

The next one came on the outside, where he liked them. He swung the bat swiftly, automatically, and the crowed screamed. It was a long drive, deep over the centerfielder's head. Chelaski watched it bounce against the wall by the flagpole. The crowd screamed louder than ever; it screamed louder than Chelaski had heard it all season. Then Jamison, who was on deck, began yelling at him.

"Run! Run! *Run!*" he shouted.

Chelaski turned and looked at Jamison. His eyes were extremely wide and burned like two flashes, cups of hot, driven things. His face was contorted, the lips turned out, and Chelaski noticed especially the thick veins in the red neck.

"Run! Run! *Run!*" Jamison shouted.

A cushion came out of the stands. Then another one. The crowd was so loud he could no longer hear Jamison. What was probably the same bird came flying back, hopping up and down, only a little faster. The centerfielder had fielded the ball. The noise was almost unbearable. Chelaski was hit by a cushion and he turned to look at the crowd. When he did, many of them leaped up and down, waving their arms. Cushions, hats, bottles, everything came down. For a moment Chelaski's eye caught sight of a girl in a green skirt. He couldn't make out her face, or her blouse or her coat. He saw a green skirt, and a pleat in a green skirt, shadow-like and leaping. Then he was hit by another cushion. It stung, cut, felt warm. For a moment he was angry.

The throw came into the second baseman, who relayed it to first for the out. The noise was volcanic, stifling, maddening. Jamison had Chelaski by the arm, pulling him from the batter's box. He noticed Jamison's face, streaked with shots of red and white, looking thick, as if several layers of skin had been added.

Chelaski walked to the dugout as the noise continued. The team was taking to the field, Hull replacing him in the outfield.

It was cold in the dugout, dark in the dugout. He saw the water bucket with the towel over its side. He walked down in there, saw somebody's hands slide nervously on the bench, somebody's legs cross.

Then Chelaski was standing in front of the manager, Hastings. He didn't look at Hastings; just looked at his shirt below the V of the neck.

Then he looked up. He saw that Hastings was trying to speak but couldn't get it out.

Chelaski turned quickly and ran down the runway that led to the locker room. When he got there, he stood a moment looking at all the green lockers.

Outside, the crowd was still shouting and some of the reporters were making their way down to Chelaski to ask him what was wrong.

# LOVE, LOVE, LOVE

I can hear my father bathing. He splashes tremendously, spews water, knocks his elbows against the sides of the tub.

"Have you noticed that I've had my teeth in all day, Mama?"

"No, I didn't know."

"They feel like my own teeth, all my life."

"Pretty soon you'll be able to eat nuts and things."

"Nuts. Ha!"

My father walks down his driveway, stops, stoops, talks to my mother, who is still in the house:

"This carrot is still alive."

"I know. Say, what's that . . . your sleeve. . . ."

"What?"

"Look, your sleeve is torn. Under the arm. Look under the arm. . . ."

I find a note on my bed. It's written on the back of an envelope, inked in my father's fat scrawl:

| | |
|---|---:|
| ½ bottle whiskey | 2.00 |
| 1 full whiskey | 3.65 |
| ½ bottle gin | 1.90 |
| 2 ginger ale | .30 |
| Laundry & Cleaning | 3.25 |
| Underwear | 8.25 |
| 1 dress shirt | 4.00 |
| Room and Board | 10.00 |
| | 33.35 |

My father walks down the hall. He wears leather slippers that knock on the floor. He walks into the bathroom. "Gosh, what's all this water on the floor? Did you spill all this water on the floor?" he asks my mother.

"What water?"

He opens the door and walks into my room. "Did you spill all that water on the floor?"

"Yes," I say, "I cupped my hands and tossed it around."

He begins to shout. . . .

My brother George tells his war experiences: "They blew the paratroop alarm and I thought, my God, the Japs are coming. Well, I thought, I've got my C-rations, I've got my .45, my dum-dums; I've got a bottle of Stateside, and I thought, well, I'm all set. I'll go down to the field and take a C-47 the hell out of here. . . ."

My brother George is missing all night and phones me in the morning: "Chuck. Chuck. I'm all cut up. I have a big scar over my eye. I've got a black eye. Blood all over me. My coat is ruined. Got drunk with a man who had scars all over the inside of his mouth from sticking pins in it. Said pain was merely a matter of control. Blacked out, don't remember what happened. I'm in Hollywood. What day is this?"

We are at the dinner table, except for George. My mother sits in her big house gown and puts a potato in her mouth.

"Chucky, your cheeks are so thin. I will make your cheeks so big they will hang over your jaws. It's a shame, the way you are. You have such a lovely profile."

"That's true," says my father.

"Already you've gained," says my mother. "If only you'd stop drinking. . . . Why do you keep your eyes on your plate? Why don't you look at people? Look at me. . . . Do you want some more potatoes?"

"No."

"More meat?"

"No."

"More celery?"

"No."

"Do you want some more coffee?"

"No."

"More peas?"

"No."

"How about some bread?"

"No, NO! Goddamn it, if I want anything, I'll *ask* for it!"

"Now what's the matter with *you*?" yells my father. He throws his napkin across the table, slams his chair back, and rushes into the front room, his slippers knocking on the floor.

"Chucky," says my mother, "you have no idea how you hurt us. You have no idea how we try to please you. Your father loves you. You come here. You start George drinking. You are twenty-five years old. There is still time. Father wants to teach you to drive the car. No, you say. You don't want a library card, a free movie. Just drink, drink, drink, and your eyes in your plate. Have you any money left?"

"No."

"What are you going to do?"

"Chucky, answer me, your mother."

I heard the typewriter and rang the bell. He came to the door.

"I heard your typewriter," I said.

He was a huge man, large-boned, tall, wide, somehow fortified. I glanced at his face and didn't find it particularly striking. There was a little mustache, untrimmed, the hairs standing out separate and uneven; the forehead was flat and low on the large, oval head; there was a scar extending from the right side of a too-small mouth, and the eyes were not unusual.

His writing was mostly a tautology of the popular mode, though sometimes he worked with abstraction, and because the others *weren't* doing it, it did give his stories a clean, fresh ring, a ring, I thought sometimes a little too valiant with experimental pageantry. But what the devil, he *was* trying.

I followed the big shoulders and head into the little house. The front rooms were dark and as I followed him to the back, we passed a red-haired woman stretched out on a couch. I judged her to be his wife, but he plunged ahead without an introduction. I smiled down at the lady and said Hello. She smiled back and said Hello. Her eyes came up out of the dark, clearly amused, and I liked her immediately.

We pushed ahead, past a swinging door and into the kitchen. He motioned a big hand at a miniature yellow table: "Sit down. I'll make some coffee."

The lights were uncomfortably bright, and I felt all unveiled in my pressed suit, clean shirt, tight and polished shoes. His shirt was open at the throat and he wore grey, musty pants. On the table was a typewriter, sheet inserted, partially done up in small, very black type. Other sheets were stacked to one side, and there were pretzels, a bulging pile of them, in a high, white bowl. I couldn't help thinking that I had been invited to a ham dinner, but I was somehow relieved that it wasn't so.

Against the back wall of the kitchen was a homemade closetlike affair without a door and strung across with shelves. It was well-stacked with those writer's magazines that give the markets and other to-do of literary journalism. They were placed neatly even, according to size, and no doubt in chronological order. From this shelf in the kitchen, and other hints, I had my open book on the suzerain of the little house.

The coffee was set up and he dropped down across from me, behind his typewriter. He looked half-ritually at his sheet a moment, the eyes becoming round, dog round; the little glitter funneled to his reading. Then the spherical head came up.

"Have a pretzel," he said.

I reached to the high, white bowl, sensing he was going to launch an analytical look, so I let him have full sway. I came back with my pretzel and bit off half of it.

"I thought you were a younger man," he said.

"I'm twenty-five," I answered, "but I've led a hard life."

"Still, you look the way I thought you would. I can always tell the way you fellows will look."

I knew what he meant: darkly sophisticated and strung up on a rather sharp edge. I stood up, took off my coat, threw it over a chair and loosened my tie. I would have taken off my shirt, too, but I wasn't wearing an undershirt. I sat down and took another pretzel. The coffee began to boil.

"Say, where's the bathroom?" I asked. He gave me directions, and I set out. It was a surprisingly large bathroom for such a little hut . . . probably a Russian architect or an acephalous Irishman . . . but I went ahead with good intentions. I heard a sound and looked around: the door had opened a notch and a big hand was sticking through the notch with a towel. I took the towel from the hand.

"Thanks," I said. There was no answer. The big hand withdrew and the door closed.

When I returned, the coffee was ready, and he suggested that we go to the bedroom. We picked up our cups and walked carefully so the coffee wouldn't spill. There wasn't a table in the room, but we went over to a desk. He held his saucer waist-high, lifted the cup, dipped the oval head, the vagrant yellow mustache, and sipped. Then he put his cup down on the desk and left the room.

There were clippings and photographs all over the walls. On the floor was a wooden box filled with empty brown envelopes, written upon, the stamps cancelled, the brass clips twisted away. On the desk was a paper book. There was a pencil drawing on the cover, not exceptional, and the book was entitled *The Collected Stories of K_____ M_____*. I ran a thumb through the typewritten pages, then pushed the book away. I felt close in the room, as if I were being examined for assassination.

He came back with his high, white bowl of fourscore pretzels and set them before me. I obliged and sipped at my coffee. He stood in the center of the room.

"You know who that is, don't you?" He was pointing to a magazine clipping, a photograph of somebody, pinned to the wall. I left the desk to examine the clipping.

It was a woman, looking diacritic, argute, behind thick-rimmed glasses. She looked like a teacher of upper algebra.

"Who is it?"

"Read underneath."

Martha Foley, it said.

I went back to the desk, sat down, and ate another pretzel.

"I didn't make it this year," he said. "I think I'll make it next year, though. She was lucky to get a book out this year . . . moving . . . she lost some of her things. I had to send her two extra copies of the magazine . . . the one with your story in it. I have letters from her. Do you want to see them?"

"No, it's all right. . . . Look, let's go catch a drink."

"I don't drink," he said.

"How about a beer?"

I heard him rumbling about in the closet, and turning in the swivel chair, I saw his buttocks working in the musty grey pants as he bent over looking for something. Perhaps a bottle of wine?

I got up and went to the window. I saw a grassless backyard surrounded by a profusion of lots. Well, he was alone, at any rate. There was a tire back there, an incinerator, a box of cans. It was all I could make out in the moonlight, and it was enough.

He came out of the closet with a paper shoebox. He stood next to me and lifted the lid. For the first time, he smiled at me, at last coming out of his hoop of seriousness, and I felt warm and glad. His faced looked so much more honest when he smiled; the small mouth widened and the scar pulled just a little on the chin.

"Letters," he said.

I looked down into the shoebox. He withdrew one, then another. "*Accent, Circle,* all of them. You know, ones that *just* missed. They write you about them."

I made some comment and he put the lid back on the shoebox and returned it to the closet. He came out of the closet looking grave again. I was back at the desk, at the high, white bowl. He stood there a moment, silent, looking very huge, the zebu.

"I've decided," he said, "that I can't use you as an associate editor. You may not believe in such things—I doubt if you do—but sometimes God speaks to me, and last night I had a vision, and I was told you wouldn't do."

I left soon after that, and he insisted on driving me the two miles to the streetcar line, saying that the buses probably didn't run out there at that time of night, and if they did, it was probably at hour intervals.

I stood out on the porch with the red-haired lady who was probably his wife, as he went back to the garage to get the car.

"He's really a nice fellow," I said.

She stood there, her arms folded, with that beautiful, clearly amused smile. It was then that I remembered it was Sunday night and she had been alone for hours.

"We've been married almost twenty-five years."

"Yes?"

"And it was all right until this writing thing started."

The car came down the drive backwards . . . about a 1928 model; thick steel body and enormous headlights, like the eyes of a monster, a great steel monster refusing to die.

He opened the car door and looked out at me. The red-haired woman opened the door of the little house.

"Goodbye," I said.

"Goodbye," she answered.

He drove toward the streetcar terminal and we discussed Sherwood Anderson. Arriving, we shook hands, said the parting words, and he helped me with the door handle. I got out. The monster chugged once, almost stopped, and then charged off into the night. . . .

I am in another town now, but he has written me. It was a short note, typewritten on a piece of small yellow paper. I understand he has given up abstraction. He says his job there is done. He has agents in New York and London. Also, he writes, he has given up the magazine to devote himself fully to his art.

# THE RAPIST'S STORY

I never knew I'd be one.

And I still don't feel like one. Or maybe I do. I don't know how they feel. I only know how I feel.

You know, I'd read about them in the newspapers now and then, and that was it.

I'd get to thinking, for just a minute, now why in the hell would a guy do anything like that? There's so much of it walking around.

But I never tied *myself* in with it at all.

I guess that's the way it is: one minute you are walking around just being a person and then all of a sudden you, yourself, are accused of being a rapist, an attacker, a ravisher, and people everywhere are opening up newspapers and reading about you.

And somebody's thinking, now why in the hell would a guy (meaning *me*, this time) do anything like that?

There's so much of it walking around.

I guess they just figure that a rapist is some guy who has been running around peeking into windows with a bunch of dirty pictures in his pants pocket. Then he gets some kind of chance he has always been waiting for, and he goes ahead with the rape.

That's what *I* thought.

Now, I only know myself.

Well, all this talk is not telling the story of how I got into this jam.

I don't know exactly how to begin. If you just list down what happened and what you did, it doesn't come out right. By that, I mean the question and answer sort of thing that goes on in courts. It isn't right. They make you wrong. They just add up a set of question and answer figures and you flunk out on the total. It's too automatic.

Hell, they ought to let a man lean back in court and explain everything at his leisure, if he is able to.

You know as well as I do, there is all that stiffness, and the judge, and the look of the place. You sit there just a minute or two—not even that, maybe 30 seconds—and you can feel where your shoelaces are tied across your feet and the way your collar runs around your neck.

You can't breathe right and are nervous as hell.

And why?

Because you know that justice has nothing to do with it. Maybe you'll see a couple of guys marching around with paper in their hands. They are nervous too. Even the judge is nervous, even though he tries not to be and goes through with it every day.

Some of them even try to smile and joke a little, especially in cases of minor concern. Those, I feel most sorry for, even if *I* am the case of minor concern.

Yes, I'll have to admit I've been in plenty of courts.

But mostly only on drunk and vag raps.

But listen, what I'm getting at is that there is nothing you can say, don't you see?

You were drunk?—O.K., guilty.

You were a vag?—also, O.K., guilty.

They don't ask you *why* you were drunk or *why* you were a vag. A man gets drunk for a damn good reason and a man is a vag for a damn good reason. There's nothing "guilty" about it.

No more than being guilty because you've got brown hair or 8 fingers and two thumbs.

O.K., they say I'm a rapist.

An attacker.

A ravisher.

In fact, they've got me up for two counts of rape, child molestation, breaking and entering and everything else.

Well . . . as they say. . . . I'll begin at the beginning.

1 4 / THE RAPIST'S STORY

The whole mess started like this: I was in the cellar picking up the old cardboard Mrs. Weber (she is the woman I am wrongfully accused of raping) said I could have.

I knew where I could sell it for a little money, maybe for a little wine—which was mostly what a little money meant, anyhow.

I saw the cardboard one time when the cellar door was open and I was walking down the alley.

One time later when I saw Mrs. Weber (the woman who I am accused of ravishing) I asked her if I could have this cardboard that was laying around unused in her cellar.

She said, "O.K., Jerry boy, anytime you want it, it's O.K. with me. It's not doing me any good the way it is."

Mrs. Weber said it just like that, without even hesitating.

It took a lot of nerve to ask her. You see, I am pretty nervous from drinking and run down from living in that shack on the lot. I'm all alone and do a lot of thinking. All this thinking has sort of pressed into my mind and I'm not relaxed anymore. I feel so dirty; my clothing is old and torn.

I don't feel like I used to some years back. I'm only 32 now but I feel like some sort of animal outcast.

Christ, it seems not like too long ago when I was going to high school in a clean blue sweater, carrying books on geometry and algebra, economics, civics, and all those things.

I sort of thought of that when I asked Mrs. Weber for the cardboard and it helped a little. She was a big woman, a clean, big woman just this side of being fat. She had on a different dress every day, bright new colors, and she made me think of soap suds and soft, cool things.

I thought of when I had been married, of the four years with Kay, the various apartments, the lousy factory jobs.

Those factories got me down and I began hitting the bottle at night—at first now and then, and after a while, most of the time.

I lost job after job and then I lost Kay, and I thought of it all as I asked Mrs. Weber for the cardboard.

I hadn't always been a wino and a vag.

As Mrs. Weber walked away I looked at the backs of her legs, the sunshine hugging the nylons. Her arms, and the hair like something to make you sing.

Don't get me wrong. I know what I'm accused of. But I'm honest, and also I think I'm innocent of this rape charge, and I know I'm getting this mixed up but I'm trying to get it down so you can see what I mean. I don't want to miss out on anything.

A rapist, that's what they call me.

After Mrs. Weber went into the house, I looked down on my dirty and stained hands.

The neighborhood was used to me in my paper shack, a little sorry for me and a little amused with me.

But I was harmless.

I am harmless.

I'm no rapist, on the bible or anything you want.

I wouldn't *dare* touch Mrs. Weber—she was so far above me, such a different creature entirely, that the thought neither occurred to her or to me or to anybody else.

It was impossible. . . .

Well, one day I was moseying around and I noticed the cellar door open. I had a little hangover of a sort and nothing to drink, and I thought, well, might as well be doing something, might help me forget my sorrows. It was one of those cloudy days when it looked like rain but it never did and you almost went crazy waiting for it but it just hung there and your mind kept saying, *well, come on, come on, rain*, but it never did. It just hung there.

I went down there and found an electric light. Click, it went on, and it stank the cellar-stink down there. It made you think of wet gunnysacks and spiders or say a human arm buried somewhere in the mud, a human arm with some of the sleeve around it, and if you lifted it out of the mud, a bunch of water bugs would run up and down its side, scurrying past each other in direct line paths, with now and then a bug or two shooting out of the constellation.

*Constellation!*

You didn't know I knew a word like that! You see, I am not just an ordinary vag. It's just that the grape has me down.

Well, anyhow, the cardboard was very wet and I figured I wouldn't get anything for it at all, but I decided to drag it all up out of there because maybe Mrs. Weber would pay me just to get rid of a mess like that.

I was afraid of spiders, though. I have always been afraid of spiders. It's a funny thing with me. I've always been afraid of them and hated them. When I see a spider with a fly in the web, and the spider moving about swiftly, weaving like something mad and evil and dark, that movement there—I can't explain it. Oh God, I'm getting off the track. I am accused of this rape. I'm accused of raping a ten-year-old girl and I am accused of raping her mother, and here I am talking about spiders.

It all began in that cellar with the cardboard. You'll just have to believe me. I didn't know that Mrs. Weber's little girl was down there in the cellar with me. I didn't know until she spoke. When she did, I was so scared I jumped up into the air like a sand flea.

"What're you doing down here in this cellar?" I asked her right away. I could make out a red dress and white bloomers. As I said, she was about nine or ten years old. She was just like her mother: clean and plump, a real little lady, an apple dumpling. But I was scared of her almost like I was scared of her mother, but I was more scared not to act like an adult, and since I didn't know much about little girls, I tried to act like an adult to sort of fool her, you see.

She didn't answer my question. She just sat there in her red dress and white bloomers, looking at me. That's the way kids are, I guess. I got kind of nervous then. The adult thing wasn't working.

"I asked you," I repeated, "what you were doing down here!"

"Nothin'."

"Nothing? Aren't you afraid of spiders?"

"Naw! I'm bigger'n they are."

Well, I hadn't thought of that. People often make me feel silly like that: I'd say something I'd think was sensible and then they'd say something that would take all the sense out of my statement, and then I couldn't answer.

I couldn't answer the little girl either, so I bent over and went ahead with stacking my cardboard over by the steps so I could drag it out. I didn't want to stack too much of it against the steps, though, because then me and the little girl would be trapped down in that cellar together all alone. I didn't want that to happen on account of the spiders and things.

"You're a pretty man but you're awful dirty. Don't you have a place to wash?"

Well, I'm telling you, that made me feel sort of funny. It was the first time anybody'd said anything like that to me for a long time. It gave me a real lift, somebody saying something like that.

Of course, I'd always imagined I was handsome in my way, and the little girl had seen it too.

"I don't have any place to wash. I just live in a paper shack," I told her.

"Why don't you use our house?"

"People don't do that, little girl. Everybody uses their own place and my place doesn't have any water."

"But I'll let you use our house. We got water upstairs. And soap. Green soap, pink soap, white soap, towels, washrags . . . everything."

"Well, thanks a lot little girl but I have to refuse your offer. And besides, your mother wouldn't like that."

"My mother has gone downtown."

"You mean, you're all alone by yourself, little girl?" I asked her.

Though I called her a little girl, she looked like a little woman. A little woman in a short dress with white clean legs and white clean bloomers. She was just like her mother.

"How long's your mother been gone?"

"She just left."

"How long does she usually stay downtown?"

"She always stays all day."

"And you're sure you're all alone?"

"Sure I'm sure."

"Well, that's all right, but I got no right in your mother's place."

"But she'd never know. And you're so dirty I feel sorry for you, mister."

"And you'd never tell on me, no matter what happens?"

"No matter what happens."

"Promise? Word of honor?"

"I promise. Word of honor."

"You're a nice little girl," I told her. "A real nice little girl. . . ."

Well, we went upstairs and I walked into the bathroom and took off my shirt and let the hot water run into the washbowl. It was real funny to see tile again. It made me feel sort of strong and good again.

There was no reason I couldn't have those things again. There was no reason I couldn't have anything I desired. Maybe it was my lucky day.

I began to sing the song "Happy Days Are Here Again." The steam from hot water rose off the bowl and I let it float against and around my face like a big hand cleaning the dirt out of me, cleaning the misused life out of me. It wasn't too late. I was only 32.

Some people even considered me handsome.

"Say, why don't you get into the bathtub?" the little girl asked me.

"The bathtub?"

"*Sure!* All people do! Go on, get into the bathtub!"

"Well, O.K.," I said. "Why not?"

I put the plug in the tub and let the water run in, meanwhile taking off my shoes and the rest of my clothes. I stood there and looked down at the warm, clean water. It was my lucky day.

"Oh," screamed the little girl, "you got a *worm, a worm!*"

Well, I knew I was pretty dirty but I'd never had any worms before, and I couldn't for sure feel any on me.

"Oh no, I haven't," I said.

"Sure! I can *see* it!"

She said it like she meant it. I got a little scared. "Where's it at then?"

"In *front* of you! In *front* of you there!"

"Oh," I said.

"That's no worm," I said.

"What is it?"

"It's what I go to the bathroom with."

There was no need to say any more about it. She didn't ask any further questions, just stood there looking at me.

I got into the tub and sat down in the water. It felt pretty good. It was my lucky day. Yes sir, it was. I felt real funny in a good sort of way. I was just about relaxed when the little girl screamed again.

She was a screaming kid, that one.

And I'd like to make that clear. The neighbors claimed later that they heard the little girl screaming almost all the time that it was established I was in that house.

Of course, they didn't know I was in there then.

But they tied up that screaming, later, to mean in their minds, that I had been molesting her all during that time.

Well, I'm telling you what really happened, so don't pay any attention to them.

I would have no more of touched that little girl than I would have touched her mother, and you can believe that. She was just like her mother, only just a little lady in a very short skirt with clean white bloomers.

Just then, the little girl screamed again, and you could see I wasn't doing anything to her. How could I when I was laying in that bathtub? As man to man, brother, I wanted to get clean. Kids don't interest me. Though I understand in Mexico, they start pretty young. It's the hot climate.

"What's the matter, kid?" I asked her. "You mustn't scream. If you scream the neighbors will hear you and they'll find out I'm here with you and you wouldn't want that to happen, would you?"

The little girl screamed again. "You'll *drown* the worm!" she screamed. "You'll *drown* the worm!"

"Please go away in another room somewhere, and please stop screaming and let me bathe in peace," I told the little girl. "This was your idea, after all."

(You can see here, by the way I talked to the girl, that I wanted absolutely nothing to do with her.)

"But the worm will drown."

"No, he won't," I assured her. "This worm likes water."

"No, he *don't*! No worms like water, not water *that* hot. You'll *kill* him!"

"Believe me, kid," I said, "I wouldn't kill this worm for anything in the world."

I guess the little girl didn't believe me.

The kid began to cry.

She began to make a hell of a noise. (And I guess this is part of what the neighbors mentioned later that they heard.)

I began to think of the neighbors too. I knew, though I was

innocent, it would look bad if I were caught there—so, in desperation, I tried to keep her quiet.

"Look," I said, "he won't drown. I'll hold him out of the water. See?"

She came and watched and at last she was quiet. I felt sort of foolish washing with one hand, but it was worth it.

"O.K.," she said, "now I'll hold him up out of the water so you can have both hands to wash."

"Nothin' doin'!" I said.

The kid stood back, clenched her fists at her sides, and began screaming all over again.

I got scared. It was more than I could take. I kept thinking about the neighbors.

"O.K.," I said.

So she held him up and I began to use two hands to wash. It was a little awkward but it was my first in years and the kid was keeping quiet, so it was worth it. I guess it was my lucky day.

I was just about calm again when the kid let out another screech: "Hey, he's moving!"

"Worms move," I said.

I kept on washing.

"I'll wash the worm," the little girl said and grabbed an extra piece of soap and began rubbing.

I began to wish I had never listened to the kid. It all really began when the little girl had called me a pretty man. I thought of her mother downtown, moving up and down shady department store aisles, touching things, buying things, moving around. I was just some sort of animal, some sort of animal outcast. I had no rights. The Mrs. Webers were not for me. Yet, I couldn't help thinking about her.

"Hey, he's *growing!*" screamed the little girl. "He's growing real *big!*"

I rinsed the soap off of myself, pulled the plug, and stepped out of the tub. I began to dry myself off and the kid was drying off the worm when, so help me, Mrs. Weber stepped into the bathroom. I hadn't heard her come in at all.

Of course, she'd never seen me that way before. And I didn't have time to explain.

She just stood there and began to scream just like the kid had screamed, only better—I mean, worse: louder and with a trill that sent whirlings up and down my spine.

I ran up to her and put my hand on her mouth to try to keep her quiet while I explained. I could feel the texture of her new dress against my skin. It felt funny. It felt like another animal or something.

But under the texture was Mrs. Weber and I was frightened. She bit my hand as I tried to hold it over her mouth and she began to scream again.

I had to hit her. I knocked her down.

I felt real sorry for Mrs. Weber as she lay there on the floor, her new dress mussed on the wet, steamy floor. I could see where her rolled stockings ended and the flesh began.

I was going to help her up but then the little girl began to scream. I ran to the little girl and grabbed her and tried to keep her quiet.

But then Mrs. Weber began. Then, all I could do, was run back and forth, back and forth, grabbing and hitting, grabbing and hitting, hardly knowing what I was doing.

And now, I'm in this goddamned jail and I never did get my cardboard.

I never even got a little drink of wine out of the whole thing.

They've got me up for two counts of rape, child molestation, breaking and entering, and everything else.

The doctors claim that both of them had been raped. Maybe so.

I hardly knew *what* I was doing, trying to keep them quiet, trying to keep them from screaming.

I say not guilty. It wasn't my fault. I never did get my cardboard or even a little drink. I have shown you how it wasn't my fault. Do you believe me? Or don't you believe me?

I keep thinking of myself in high school in a clean blue sweater. I used to have a friend named Jimmy. We would listen to the high school orchestra in the auditorium sometimes during homeroom period. We would go around singing songs later that the orchestra had played. Songs like "Ave Maria" and "When the Deep Purple Falls Over Sleepy Garden Walls" and "God Bless America."

Don't you believe me? Doesn't anybody believe me?

# 80 AIRPLANES DON'T PUT YOU IN

# THE CLEAR

When I was a young one, I used to read *The Collected Poems of Richard Aldington* to my friend Baldy while we were drinking. To me, there was no greater honor (to Aldington) than to sing his things out over wine, under the bright electricity of my cheap room. Baldy did not rise to my enthusiasm—and I could never really understand; Aldington was a clear poet: clear, emotional, and forward. I think he has affected me more than the greater-rated poets, but my friend Baldy never praised R.A., never rejected. He simply sat and drank with Bacchus.

He praised not Aldington (which I was trying to get him to see) but me. "Jesus," he'd say the next day, "Hank was really drunk last night! He got out the old book of poetry. He can really read that stuff too! I never heard *any*body read poetry the way Hank does!"

Baldy happened to say just this one day to Helen, a woman who cleaned the rooms.

So, following with the informality of the situation, I put forth: "How's about a little snip, Helen?"

She didn't answer. They had the damnedest people around there. They never said anything when they were supposed to.

I poured a goodly portion and she snatched it up off of the dresser.

"I really got to clean the rooms," she said.

Then *I* had a spot. "Aldington knew Lawrence," I said. "D.H. Lawrence. Now there was a guy. That son of a bitch could really *spin* it!"

"Yes," Baldy said, "Lawrence."

"Out of the coal mines," I said. "Married Richthofen's daughter.

You know, the guy who shot down 80 airplanes. Or maybe this guy was her brother. Though Lawrence wasn't exactly out of the coal mines. It was his father."

"Do you have another spot of that stuff, honey?" the housecleaner asked.

I poured her a little refresher.

"What kind of stuff is this? It tastes so different."

"Port."

"Port, eh?"

"Yes," I said. " I used to drink muscatel but it dried me up. They put too much sulphur in it."

She knocked off her glass. "Ya know, you're *nice* boys. I don't mind drinking with *you* boys. You're different."

Well, that made me feel pretty good, so I poured a big one for myself and a big one for Baldy and a big one for Helen, to sort of celebrate.

"This Lawrence and this Aldington buddied around together," I continued.

At that moment there was a thunderous knock on the door. Like a Beethoven climax. "Hank! Hank!"

"Come in, Lou."

It was the ex-con and ex-hard-rock miner. He had a bottle with him. Port. Good for the stomach.

"Sit down, Lou. We were just talking about a guy whose relative shot down 80 planes."

"See you got company, Hank."

"Yeah, Lou."

"Here, have some of my stuff folks."

"Pour away, Lou!"

"I really *should* clean the rooms, but you boys are *so* nice."

"Where's your husband, dearie?"

"Oh, he sailed away in the Merchant Marine and when he came

back he wasn't worth a damn. He'd gotten all these women and he was never satisfied anymore."

"But you still got me, Helen," Lou said, putting his hand on her knee. "What's say you and I—" He leaned over and finished the sentence in her ear. He might as well, of course, have spoken it aloud.

"You *bastard* you, why can't you be nice like these *other* boys? *They're* not that way! Why can't you be *nice*?"

"But I *am* nice, baby! Wait 'til you get to *know* me! Wait 'til you see what I *got*!"

"For Christ's Sake, Lou!" I screamed. "Keep your *pants* buttoned!" (I was sensitive in those days). "This is a *literary* discussion!"

Everybody settled back for a moment then and I rose and went about replenishing their glasses.

"One time this Lawrence wanted to form a colony, a colony just of his friends. You know: start a new world somewhere. I thought it was a pretty good idea, myself. If I hadda been there I would have shoved off with him right away and considered it a great honor. But all these people turned him down. He asked them one at a time: 'Are you coming with me to this island or not?' And everybody backed down. Except Aldington. No, maybe it was Huxley. Anyhow, Lawrence got disgusted and he got drunk and sick and the whole thing fell through."

"Where was this island?" the ex-con asked. "Maybe there was nothing to eat there. And maybe they couldn't take women. You can't tell. There might have been something fishy about this Lawrence guy."

"No, no," I said, "it was straight. They were to colonize, to make a new world."

"How about the grub? How about the broads?"

"Everything was set," I said. "Everything was worked out beforehand."

"And they still wouldn't go?"

"No."

The ex-con turned to the scrubwoman, hand on knee. "Helen, would you go to an island with me? I could show you something you'd *never* forget."

"Lou," I said, "stay in line, please."

"That's right, Hank, keep the bastard off me! I'm just here for a friendly drink."

"But I'm tryin' to be friendly, real friendly," protested the ex-con.

"Take it easy, Lou."

"Sure, Hank, sure."

"Hank," Baldy woke up, "who do you think was the greatest writer of all time?"

"Shakespeare," the ex-con said.

"I think Robert Louis Stevenson or Mark Twain," said the scrubwoman.

"What do you think, Hank?"

"Well, I don't know, Baldy."

"Shakespeare, beyond a doubt," the ex-con maintained, draining his glass. "Nobody could touch old Shakey, but *nobody!*"

"Some claim Shakespeare died in a barroom brawl," I disclosed.

"*Sure!* Shakey was a *man!*"

"Dearie," the scrubwoman asked me, "could I have a bit more port?"

"Let's sing something!" Baldy suggested. "The Gypsy Song. You know: *sing gypsy, laugh gypsy, love while you may.* I like that one."

"No," I said. "I've had multitudinous warnings about the gypsy song already."

"Keep your hands *off* me, you *bastard!*"

"Lou!" I shouted. "Anymore of that and I'm kicking you out!"

"You're not *man* enough!"

"I'm *warning* you, Lou."

"I used to be a hard-rock miner. Once I fought a guy with pick-handles. He broke my left arm with the first blow and I still went on to kill the son of a bitch with one hand! Go on: you hit *me* first! You get first knock! Go on, Hank buddy! I *like* you, Hank! You're a man, a *real* man! Let's fight! Let's you and me *fight*, Hank!"

"Calm down, Lou. I don't want to get kicked out of here."

"Maybe you'd better read some poetry," the scrubwoman suggested.

"This Lawrence, what'd he write about?" Baldy asked.

"Well, he probed around a lot. Like a lot of us he wanted to keep the Inner Man as unpolluted as possible. He was preoccupied, much of the time, with sex."

"Who the hell *isn't?*" the ex-con stood up. "We're *all* that way, ain't we, baby?" He stood there swaying, looking down at the scrubwoman. "*Ain't* we, baby? Huh? *Ain't* we?"

"Look, Lou, these boys are talking about *literature.* Can't you be decent?" the scrubwoman asked.

"This Lawrence guy's got nothing on *me*! *I* know why he wanted to go to this island with all those people and I know why those people wouldn't go! Because they were *crazy-afraid* of this Lawrence, *that's* why! They could see it in his *eyes*, it showed all *over* him! . . . Wanted to take a bunch of broads and *colonize*! COLONIZE! Just because this guy shot down 80 airplanes, it doesn't put him in the clear!"

"No, no, Lou," I said, "that wasn't Lawrence. That was Baron Manfred Von Richthofen."

"Well, he was probably worse than Lawrence! Each time he shot down a plane he probably got his—"

"You mean," I interrupted Lou, "each victory represented a Sexual Symbol?"

"*You* know what I mean!" he snarled.

"Well, it's been a nice evening folks," I said, "and I bid you all a fond farewell."

"Ya mean we gotta *go*?" the ex-con asked.

"That's about the content of it," I replied.

"Well, to hell with that *fish*! I'm goin' down to the bar and finish it off right! Comin', doll baby?" he leered at the scrubwoman.

"No, thank you, Louis."

"O.K., you old *bag*!"

The door slammed.

"Maybe it was Homer," I said.

"Homer what?" from Baldy.

"Homer who was the greatest."

"See you tomorrow night, Hank?"

"Sure, Baldy."

"How about Confucius?"

"That's good. He was right in there, all right. . . ."

"Just another spot, my dear boy," the scrubwoman said.

"All right, Helen."

"You know you have the most *lovely* hands, like a violinist."

"It's nothing. It's really nothing at all."

"You been to college, haven't you?"

"Yes, but college can never make a man intelligent. It can only educate him."

"Do you write stories and poetry and stuff?"

"Well, yes."

"Ya had anything printed?"

"Not yet, Helen. I'm still developing, you see."

"Develop'ng?"

"Yeah. You see, a writer's got to go through a period of development."

"Ya mean, ya gotta shoot down airplanes or something first?"

"Not exactly. But it helps a hell of a lot."

"Will you write a story about me, sometime?"

"Maybe. Maybe I will."

"You see, I was born in Pittsburgh, PA. My father was a doctor but he drank too much and they took away his license—"

The next morning as I turned over in bed, my freedom of movement was blocked by a very substantial mass of humanity: the scrubwoman.

"Good mornin', honey boy!"

"Oh . . . hello, Helen."

"Ya *sure* had a load-on, Hanky. The minute I began tellin' you my life story, you began pourin' it down left and right."

"And then what happened?"

"Don't tell me you don't *remember*, honey boy?"

I leaped out of bed and began donning my clothing.

"Where ya goin', honey boy?"

"Down to a bar. Down to some bar somewhere."

"Ya comin' back, honey boy?"

"Not for three or four days, at least."

I moved toward the door with some acceleration, opened it, and then—

"Ya know somethin', honey boy?"

"What?"

"Ya know who the greatest writer is?"

"I said 'Homer' but I really haven't given it much thought."

"*You* are, honey boy, and ya don't need any more *development*! I never met this Homer guy, but I know he can't hold a candle ta YOU, honey boy!"

I closed the door and went bar-ward to seek the solace of my ex-con friend. *He* could have it: Homer and Helen, Helen and Homer, and all the development it implied. With D.H. Lawrence thrown in.

# MANIFESTO: A CALL FOR OUR OWN CRITICS

The insurgency of criticism from a nosography on poetics to a censorious dictum by certain university groups who write the laws of poetry, and spawn, with sumptuous grace and style, their own puppeteers—these, and their half-brethren and their purlieu, form a most deadly and snobbish poetic fixation. They create, record, and argue their own history, charmed with the largesse of their chosen circumference.

What the university critics have lost in pulling down the blinds around their little ivy world they have gained in direction and prestige. To the remainder of us, the unwashed, the loiterers in pool halls and back alleys, there remains a frustrated and discordant yammering. In order to inculcate a more heuristic force, perhaps a manifesto, a gesture . . . a gestation . . . is necessary. It is difficult for a single poet to stand against the university coterie. Perhaps we too must invent our own history and choose our own gods if our portion of American literature is to receive a hearing on some tomorrow.

Our writers should acquaint themselves with the claustral intent and exorcises of the campus groups—and let us be fair here: many of our imprint are not only pretty well unwashed but rather damn shoddily read as well (damn shoddily read as readers and damn shoddily read as writers). Our saving factors are our lack of monstrous clannishness and a more hybrid emergence. Yet this eminence should be both shaped and amorphous, with its own critics guide-wiring and giving form and numerical integration, cultural insertion, to our writers. This does not mean confirmation or confinement but a transelementation of mixed voices into a more *visible* shape. The fresh air of a new culture, the magnetism and meaning and hope, the exactness of our energies—these things haven't, in any sense, been harnessed or realized. And until they are . . . five or six old men, craggy and steatopygous in university chairs, will be the hierophants of our poetic universe.

# PEACE, BABY, IS HARD SELL

Dear John Bryan:

. . . Look, on the war-thing, I can give you nothing in poem form since I just wrote something about how I ducked the shells (WW2) for another magazine and rolled off with banana leaf and used car oil off a duck's back, and now, after this, my pecker hangs limp. If you keep poeming about the same thing and in the same way, you become the same thing and the same way, which is—nothing.

I can bullshit you a little about the subject, though. (There's nothing like the oscillation of the balls in quiet complication.) How do you begin? I imagine it hurts like hell to be torn to pieces and die for something different . . . every century, every 50 years, every 20 years. I read someplace where Man will eventually be replaced by robots he builds that will be more intelligent than he. It about figures: all they've got to do is stay out of the rain and the lightning and replace the parts as they wear . . . they don't have to worry about toothache or hemorrhoids, or fucking. They'll just go on walking around the place looking for things to do, and there won't be much to do because they won't have to worry about eating and they won't be stupid enough to pay rent, and if they make the drunktank, they'll be smart enough to enjoy it. But I wonder if these babies, these unlamentable babies who will not know pain, pity, tenderness, the meaning of a lover walking away and into the arms of another, I wonder if these babies will be *intelligent* enough to avoid *war*? I'd like to think so—that these tin shadows of our past could sweep out the last disease. But I don't know why—I've got pictures of these grappling masses of tin . . . crushed electric eyes . . . beautiful silver brains spread amongst their copper flowers. . . . Christ, what's wrong? What's wrong?

Now, I'll start right off and try and tell you why I have this vision and why it is so hard to stop *war*. This mainly being the rusty side of the coin, the portico of recant, and it works badly, always has, *because it is hard as hell to get emotional about peace*, or religious about it, or sexual about it, or wave it around on the end of a flag, or whatever. You furnish the words; I am tired. I mean, padre, *peace* is as propitiatory as a Sunday bell. They don't write national anthems about *peace* and girls don't strip in front of you for *peace*, and you don't see countries and waters and hills and sunsets and whores that you never would have seen, and you don't get drunk in some tongue that is a town you do not speak and pinch the mayor's wife because you've got nothing to lose. *War* even makes *art*. Without *war*, Hemingway would have been a wine-drinking pink-eyed picador for a fat and farting matador. *War* gave him the golden gate to point up some fairytale about guts for the cockeyed bats of the occident. Salique seems *peace*. *Peace, baby, is hard sell*. Why, why, why, why, hell, why???? Adjust your jock, and I'll tell you. People don't *know* what *peace is* because people (most people) have never had *peace* in times of so-called *peace*. Figure it yourself. Take a kid, a child. As soon as he gets so he can walk around pretty good, they shove him to a school while his brain is still soft and *they get to him*—they tell him that *his country is the country*. If he lives in Mexico, Mexico is the country. The beans are hard to take, but better things are coming. If he lives in Brazil, O.K., Brazil, what the hell ya think they're going to tell him: Bermuda? They need their jobs. Germany equals Germany. Russia means Russia. Despite world ideology . . . Russia means to be the head, the rest the legs. . . . Just as we mean, through monetary control of other national industries. . . . We give them their *freedom* by letting them *work* for us. But let's let go of this for awhile. Let's get back to the punk kid. The nail we're driving home that will end up in a juice joint slavering into a mirror wondering where he went. Next, the church grabs his soft little ass and tells him about *The Man Above*. Friend, this is a pretty frightening thing. Most of us have to go with it . . . strictly on under-the-table percentages . . . but on top of the table we spread our cards and call it *faith*. Now, then, this child, this kid, baby, small chunk of bologna is already spun out into the open plateau where they've got him dizzy, hardly a chance . . . he's, frankly, out of the *peace* area altogether: his loyalty is sanctioned and his spirit is set along the rails where it is *supposed* to go. (You can shoot a barracuda between the eyes and it won't go to hell because it doesn't know where or what hell is. On the other hand, we've fixed ourselves fine. Finely. Fuck it.)

I'm trying to tell you while I am laying here in bed at 3:55 A.M. in the morning, writing this in pencil in an Empire Wire-Glo notebook with a green cover and lined paper (price 49¢)—out of cigarettes and lighting short butts out of a teacupful on the old chair near the bed, I am trying to tell you that it is difficult to canonize and adore the pity of no-blood; I am trying to tell you why *peace* is so hard to sell, this mainly being because so very very very few so few so few dear christmice and rabbits running in moonlight *know what peace is*!!

Let's get back, if you're not asleep, to our bastard kid. They teach the kid math. They tell him Washington crossed the Delaware. A fine thing, I'm sure. They have separate toilets for boys and girls. They hit his head with Brahms, Schubert, and that great steel fist Beethoven while he's too small to seize it, and he remembers this, these large punches against his unprotected frame and he later goes to jazz in rebellion. It is easier to go to jazz in rebellion than it is to go to another country or another god. It's safer, it's cheaper, and there's hardly any risk at all. They know this; it's planned; they let them have the jazz. If they gave our bastard kid jazz *first*, he'd go to Beethoven later and then they'd have a mess on their hands, a danger. Baby, they know what they're doing. There has been no such thing as *peace*. Now they let him out on a football field and tell him to knock somebody down. They teach him some more crap to narrow him down a niche and then rush him off to *work*—which is not *peace* either. They give him a couple of hours in which to sleep, eat, buy things, and mainly time to fuck, make more babies to keep the thing going, and then back to *work*.

The mind has never been given a chance. You ask the average man, "Do you want *war* or *peace*?" and he'll tell you, "I want *peace*, of course. War is stupid."

*He says he wants peace but he doesn't know what peace is. He's never had it.*

He's bred for *war*, he's shucked into it, he's shacked with it like a golden-legged whore who keeps reaching into his back pocket when his ass is to her face. O, my, he'll go *passionate for war*, he'll *scream* for *war*!! but he won't fall in love with *peace* because he's never had it from the moment he started wobbling on his tiny man-legs. It's a christ-awful fishbowl pity and makes me so angry sometimes that I just smash my whiskeyglassfuls against the walls instead of drinking them; I often curse Man and his scab-blindness, his smallness, his monkey-sucking away of Everything. . . . But I'm wrong. What chance has the poor fuck?? And who am I to take his measure? O, demolished and demon-drained idiot, he argues with his old lady who gets a roll of fat around her gut and wears those flat-heeled shoes after the second kid. He gets fired 2 or 3 or 6 times, he gets scared. He drives with air in his brain and gets in a couple of automobile accidents. He's taxed until his balls ache. No matter how much money he makes, he never has any money. He can never breathe free from day to day. Always a herd of horns ready to slash him into some back alley where they sit and split a wine bottle, unless he talks fast and fancy. Is this *peace*? Is he supposed to get excited about *this*? Then, sick with thin light and lying, he comes home early one night and finds his *wife* (rolls of fat and all) in bed with the gas-meter man . . . *peace*?—he's never had it.

He'd been geared like a bull to ram into somebody or something or somewhere from the start.

What's the answer? Well, I only know I am out of jail right now (which is good, *and* selfish); but not being a master of phrenology or even a master of the pooltable as is one of my dear friends out of the South who writes poetry like an exalted bull examining fire, the only answer is a breakdown of our normal educational concepts of upbringing into a vaster plane that excludes *less* and gives more choice . . . of gods, leaders, countries . . . music, loves, sports, hilarity, liquors, liqueurs, lectures . . . what I mean is the sea washing down to our ankles and with us . . . with time . . . to think of other things . . . beside fast bread, easy pussy, acquisition, ;;;;I think it's too late for that . . . it's almost too late for this . . . maybe this H. Bomb is *big enough* to scare the shit out of us, all of us, and may we realize that things like *honor* and *country* don't mean anything— dark hymns in an empty chapel, and that we are letting the *tin men* in, the *tin men* of our minds, the *tin men* of a possible future, if we keep letting go to this *war*-thing as we have been trained to do.

It's time we learned to walk and talk like this big thing inside us tells us to do. It's time for better and bigger miracles and talking about them, seeing how we have been wrong for so long . . . this is a beginning, not a *begging*. *Peace begs nothing but realization.*

going now,
peace on you,
Charles Bukowski

# EXAMINING MY PEERS

All right:

The poets who are getting it done are David Pearson Etter, Irving Layton, Al Purdy, Larry Eigner, Genet.

The Ginsberg-Corso-Burroughs circle has been swallowed by the big whale of adulation and they have never quite recovered. But, alas, we have learned that the difference between an artist and a *performer* is the difference between God and a necktie salesman. Yet it is difficult for most of us not to take the bait of a *lifetime* erection. We are given the chance of dancing easily in the lights before the fools or going back to work as a dishwasher. Unfortunately, one can learn more by washing dishes than one can by debating with James Dickey, Jack Gilbert, Nemerov, and T. Weiss at 92nd St. and Lex Ave.

*Poetry Chi*, once the thumper of the land with a young Ezra as European editor, has now diminished into the bones of its reputation; you can see one in any library, safely shining, saying nothing, heralding the same safe names. It is much like going to a Friday night concert: they open with the overture to *La Gazza Ladra*, follow with *L'Après-midi d'un Faune*, slug them with Beethoven's 5th, and then send them home happy with some *Water Music* by good old Handel.

And now that I've buried *Poetry Chi*, let's move on. Another particular bone in the poetic throat is the work of Robert Creeley. I have been told by professors of English (those with "Dr." appended to their names) that Robert Creeley is the miraculous confessor of all of our talents. Me, I have tried Creeley again and again. And it was always much like falling asleep at the beach the time I tried to read Steinbeck's *The Wayward Bus*. Try this for your insomnia.

But back to R.C. Usually as I return the books to the good

professors with some such acidulous remark as: "It appears very thin. Nothing here." Or: "What the hell are they trying to sell me?" I would always get the tender kindly smile through the beard, the hand-on-shoulder bit: "Oh, come now, he's not *that* bad!" Which all infers that *they* understand, they understand something which such a crude one as I does not. (The niceties, you know, the pure unadulterated phrasing, etc., etc.) But the bearded Dr.'s in Creeley-shadows are good souls after all: they will forgive everything but their own convictions.

And then too—I might be a bitter old man because I somehow get the feeling that they are *afraid* of Creeley. Why this should be, I do not know; but perhaps it is because I am closer to washing dishes than I am to teaching in any University.

Creeley is just one of the horrors and outcroppings of the poetry-political powerhouses: "The School." But The Age of the Bomb has taught us more than the mushroom; it has taught us not to swallow pap. "School" is out. The days of schools are over. Thank God, or whoever is up there. It is kind of intensifying in a banal sort of way to think back to the good old days when the "Imagists" drew up their manifesto with blood-stained fingers. But most schools are invented by the critics, or by photographers from *Life* magazine. Or by stodgy old men teaching English in Midwestern Universities while being driven mad by the knees and thighs of 19-year-old girls who do not pull their skirts down because they'd like to "make" a B in English; and, of course, the talk about Allen Tate, Dr. Williams, Wallace Stevens, Y. Winters, and John the Crow bores them.

The state of American poetry? U.S. poetry? Well, I've named you 2 Canadians and a Frenchman as good workmen. . . . But maybe somewhere on the farm there's a boy working over a calf who might later do it for us with a hot typewriter. Right now, U.S.-wise, there's about as much guts showing as at a tea for the Retired

Ladies of the Auxiliary to Chase Phantoms out of the Closets of Dog Catchers. Whatever that means. Ah, right now a beer and a dose of salts. Chicago, where's your Sandburg? The brave teeth and big hand of Mencken? Sandburg, where's your banjo? Christ, christ, we need some music!

# IF I COULD ONLY BE ASLEEP

We are in bed. I am reading the racing charts and she is reading *Russian Icons from the 12th to the 15th Century*. She turns a page.

—See the Saint?

No.

—See him?

Yes.

—If I could only be asleep.

What?

—Everything would be all right.

Why?

—I see pretty pictures. Don't you see pretty pictures when you dream?

No.

—The Ascensions . . . look, who went into Heaven?

Christ, I don't know.

—What does the door mission of the Virgin mean?

I don't know.

—Ooh . . . isn't she *pretty*? You don't like her?

No.

—You don't like her because she can see into your soul.

That's enough. Sometimes I think religion is a giant Sadism.

—See that?

Yes, it's a guy with a hole in his chest and another guy in the hole.

—*That's* the Virgin Mary and the infant Christ is represented by a medallion. Tretykov Gallery, Moscow. About 1200. It's a painting of the Yaroslav school which wasn't in Moscow.

I see, I see.

—I keep seeing pictures of people stealing babies. What does it mean?

I don't know.

—That's St. George and the dragon.

I see.

—Look at the tiny little legs; that's the Novgorod School. Late 14th century, kinda nice. That's a cute dragon.

Goodnight, dear.

—Oh, LOOK, there's God!

Goodnight.

—Plate 6. No, that's Elijah. I'm sorry, it isn't God.

Goodnight.

—Here's somebody in a red teddy-bear suit. Hey, look at those wigs!

The book sells for 95 cents, MQ 455, introduction by Victor Lasareff. Keep your wife away from it.

# THE OLD PRO

a kiss for a good and talented fucker
getting old and older
and only recognized by a few of the
living, and so
the closed eye in the sky
marks us for our words—

If you are lucky, you might see him, someday, if you hurry—this stocky myth, this ¼ immortal.

If you are lucky you might see him in the streets of Athens, just after nightfall. He will be dressed in an old trenchcoat with buckle undone, belt dangling like a limp and lost elephant's cock—he will be prowling the streets, owl-eyed, in search of his necessaries

in search

of the ghost, the god, the way, the luck.

Harry Norse. Hal. American bum slipping through Europe, year after sad mangled year, slipping on through the shadows of dead cities. Cities bombed dead, rebuilt dead, lived dead. Dead cities, dead people, dead days, dead cats, dead volcanoes, living grief, living madness, living dullness, living butchery—all our lovely ladies grown old, roses shot to shit, the works. Hal. Writing poems and getting by. Just.

He sleeps on a bed 6 inches off the ground and the fleas cry *hallelujah* as he waits for his check from *Evergreen* or the invisible hand slipping off the thighs of Mars. Meanwhile, he sleeps in fits and spurts, living under a temporarily inactive volcano (the rent's cheaper there) which one of the best Greek geologists claims is on an eruption timetable of tomorrow morning. (You've met these Greeks in steambaths; they are not entirely to be ignored.)

Sweet christ, you must know that a man will go further for any poem than for any woman ever born.

Harold Norse. He can punch it out quietly. In style. Upside down. In grit. In fire. On fire. Tooth on tooth, hard. The smell of our butts. The cock of our shame. Light. Rabbit dream. The whole Bomb inside the head whistling Dixie.

Norse. American bum:

>                    overheard
>                 on the bridge
>        trucks are speeding under angels

>
>            . . . . on the riverbank two people
>            are breaking laws with their hips

Most people, almost all people do not know how to write, say, including Shakespeare, who wrote such terrible stuff that he fooled the whole mob, top to bottom. Other bad writers who fooled nearly everybody were E.A. Poe, Ibsen, G.B. Shaw, William Faulkner, Tolstoy, and Gogol. Today they are fooled by Mailer and Pasternak. That men do not know how to write and not only get away with it but are also immortalized is no more surprising than the length of phonies who reach the top of the cream in all areas of life and enterprise. You can find them all the way from Washington to the back room of Sharkey's.

Hal can write. Umm. I once called him a "pro" but he took it a little wrong and spit back, "Jersey Joe." That's an old fighter of the past, that's Wolcott. And I'll always remember old Jersey Joe with a touch of heart, too. The way he could land the important one.

Sometimes you've got to take a lot to land the important one. It's all an act of Art. All good men have the act of Art in them. They can be plumbers or pimps but you can spot it soon enough. It's a matter of grace and easiness and gut and Sight. I've met more good men in jails, in drunk tanks, in factories, at racetracks than I ever have in English classes, Art classes, or other writers knocking upon my door.

Just because men work with the art form, this does not necessarily justify them or purify their gut. For the same reason, priests and dwarfs or legless men and whores are not to be elevated needlessly.

When I call Norse a "pro" I only mean that he is

the right man in the right place
doing it more than properly

and that's done so little that it's enough to make a man cry.

We all exalt the cauliflower-ear belter. Norse. American bum:

dante lived here
& got kicked out
now he's worshipped
like a saint

Harold Norse: poet:

kick him in the nuts
until he leaps wildly
among the dancing couples
until he falls

unconscious
out of the dream.

Christ, have you ever been in a hospital as much as I have? as much as Norse has? Laugh with us, the bedpan mewk, the Trojan horse.

nurses/stealing my pens/&roses/snakebrained/nurses/with wrong medicine/they laugh/slamming doors/while fragile old/ladies gasp for breath/tubes stuck in their throats

Perhaps it is a mistake to give you parts of these poems for if this bit is accepted, you might get these poems in total anyhow; I am simply trying to pinpoint for you how well, how simply, how like his honor old Hotshot Jersey Joe gets it across, like Braddock got it across, coming off the relief rolls, to one fat and cocky Max Baer one night many nights ago. You know. My god:

ah go on
    bury your head
in the bug-infested blanket
    let the fleas
      bounce in yr crotch
there are no
    fuhrers of
        enlightenment
        baby

and he's right, we take it on the way in or out, sleeping under volcanoes or on park benches, it's sweet stale shit, this poeming, and it isn't that poeming is asking for sense or a chance or righteousness or $$$; it isn't really that at all.

None of us knows what it is. It's like awakening in the morning with a boil on your back and it won't go away. To ask a Patchenesque donation upon the qualities of our Art would be chickenshit—there are too many other good men with bad backs or good Art. And some with worse backs, some with Better Art.

But there sure as hell aren't any fuhrers of enlightenment, baby. And sometimes it makes for long evenings, sharp razors, accidents while cleaning shotguns.

Good writing, without fucking relent, is nothing but g.d. trying to bust through a wall of steel, and we are just not going to make it. But when I see the fade-outs, the flake-outs, the sell-outs, the chicken-livered punks of our age sucking it up, it's good to see the old hard head—the pro, Jersey Joe, still bumming the European sideroads, missing the ski meets, the Olympic games, the rich sag-tit balloon-head broads, and still hammering hammering.

the word.

I am listening to something by Wagner tonight over the radio, which is all right, and my 20-month-old daughter is asleep in the other room—the woman left her here while she went to some kind of Trotskyite meeting. And my crazy drawings are all over the walls and I am not even drunk yet. So I guess I can safely say,

> old Pro Norse
> I think that with 5 or 6 less of you
> I might not have made it this
> long.

man o man, that's enough.

—Charles Bukowski
Los Angeles, 1966

# REVIEWS OF ALLEN GINSBERG/

# LOUIS ZUKOFSKY

*Empty Mirror*. Early poems by Allen Ginsberg/Totem Corinth Books/17 W. 8th St./New York/N.Y./10011/$1.25

It is not easy being Allen Ginsberg. Nor is it easy to review him. For in spite of his romantically-avowed homosexualism, we still subconsciously look up and expect top performance. The favorite parlor games of little magazine freaks (and big magazine freaks) is to knock Allen Ginsberg, and Mailer and Albee and Capote and and and—I know. I do it myself. *Imagine, for instance, that these early poems had been written by somebody called Harry Wedge.* I'd immediately have myself a new culture hero. But since they were written by Ginsberg and introduced by W.C. Williams, my typewriter teeth are already itching for the bite. What?

Williams works around in the short foreword and I do not quite pick it up. It is a kind of a jogging through of his poetic formula of what good poetics should be and Ginsberg is his boy, "this young Jewish boy, already not so young any more." There is some talk of Dante, of G. Chaucer. Williams says that the poet must speak to the crowd in their own language yet he must disguise his lines so that they will not offend. "With this, if it be possible, the hidden sweetness of the poem may alone survive and one day rouse a sleeping world." Of course, since 1952, since this foreword was written, we have realized that no "hidden sweetness" is necessary. If Williams meant presentation (style) or humor or inventive distractions to jack-off boredom, then I will go along with him. It is possible that this is what he did mean.

The poems themselves are simple, clear, very good poems—not

yet diseased with the Whitmanesque prophet rantings of the later Ginsberg.

> I feel as if I am at a dead
> end and so I am finished.
> All spiritual facts I realize
> are true but I never escape
> the feeling of being closed in
> and the sordidness of self,
> the futility of all that I
> have seen and done and said.
> Maybe if I continued things
> would please me more but now
> I have no hope and I am tired.

There are some borrowed and overused phrases here: "feeling of being closed in," "sordidness of self," but the last 3 lines are honest enough to perhaps save the whole poem.

". . . What a terrible future. I am twenty-three," he says further on. And he was right. He had no way of knowing how he would use himself or how America would use him or make him use himself. But here he speaks of something else. Of madness. Of the feeling that his head is severed from his body. He realized it while lying sleepless on a couch.

In "Psalm I" there is some hint of the biblical line, the Whitmanesque roar-plead and act. The lines still trickle between originality and the pose. In the end, in the last line, originality loses and the pose finishes off the poem: "This gossip is an eccentric document to be lost in a library and rediscovered when the Dove descends."

While writing this, I can't help thinking how easy it is to be a reviewer, as if one (myself) held the candle of truth and was tossing light to the slobs. What horseshit, eh friends? Well, I'll do what

I can, or can't. My head hurts tonight and I am out of beer and smokes and am too lazy to make coffee. Allen, you're probably going to catch hell.

Yes, "Cézanne's Ports" is a bad poem.

> In the foreground we see time and life
> swept in a race

I am afraid that the sweetness is not too well-hidden. It gets sweet enough for toothache later on. It doesn't help me understand Cézanne nor "Heaven and Eternity" either. Ginsberg is a better writer than this. And Cézanne was a better painter. They should have met over a bottle of wine instead of in this fashion.

> When I sit before a paper
> writing my mind turns
> in a kind of feminine
> madness of chatter;

These are what I like to call perfect lines, for lack of anything else to say. I mean perfect lines to me as to content and presentation. Ginsberg lays it in your lap and there it is, as real as a kitten. Or a lion. You know what I mean.

"Fyodor" is a good poem not so much as a force but because I guess we all felt that way about Dostoyevsky, so it's charming to hear it, good to hear it, but still being somewhat snappish we wish it were better written. But let us remember that Ginsberg was young here. I wonder how Allen looked when he was young? Have you ever wondered that? All we have now is this bearded half-monk, kind of lighted with bedroom infractions and stinking of nightmares of India and Cuba and coffeehouses, this flumping spread of *hair* that is Allen Ginsberg. He'd be holy if we'd let him, but it all falls through about halfway and everybody is confused. Yet he's better to have around than not to have around. If I throw little mudballs at him it is because I can't be bothered with that cat in the Jewish Delicatessen. Allen is some kind of blessed pickle down in a fat jar full of hair and yellow seeds. You'd want to buy it but you'd end up buying something else.

"A Meaningless Institution," a kind of Kafka-dream 1948 vintage is a fair piece of work. I feel it. Especially the ending where A.G. has to wander down empty corridors "in search of a toilet." If you can't find that toilet, man, all the poetry in the world isn't worth a damn.

In "Society, Dream 1947," the poem is lighted with force and humor, genius, here is some of the stuff, the style, the bombast and flow that raised Ginsberg out of the muck. I mean this is the fore-runner of things to come, *Howl*, the whole *Howl* ruckus that made Ginsberg, and the genius that allowed Ginsberg to continue making it even after he lost a part of it.

And in "Hymn," we have the biblical fire of poetic prayer done very well. When Ginsberg is at the top of his game you might as well put down your toys and listen. It would be only the most unkind and jealous fink who would put a man down for his later showmanship when he could write as well as this early. Why must we scratch each other to pieces? The real enemy is elsewhere.

"The Archetype Poem" which begins

> Joe Blow has decided
> he will no longer
> be a fairy.

is a tragic-humorous drawing of the unworking and switched-off sex machinery. Sex is really funny as hell. We are all caught up with the damn thing and hardly know what to do. And I mean funny like slowly roasting to death might be funny—if you could watch yourself.

The book ends on "The Shrouded Stranger," which really doesn't work. Although there are some good lines that nobody but Ginsberg could have written:

"His broken heart's a bag of shit."

Ginsberg is one of the few poets trying to destroy himself with unpoetic acts yet he still has not destroyed himself. Let us say grace to his huge tank of reserve. Eliot has said it easier, Pound with more Art, Jeffers with more knowledge of forces, Auden with more precision, Blake louder, Rimbaud more subtle; William Carlos Williams had a better left jab, Dylan Thomas bigger screaming feet, this with this, that with that, but I think that Ginsberg belongs somewhere, early or late, and that without his coming through, none of us would be writing as well as we are doing now, which is not well enough, but we hang on in, watch old Allen, stare at his photos, and are still a little afraid of America, of him, of the workings of wax and sun and hangovers, we go to bed alone, finally, all of us.

*A Test of Poetry*—Louis Zukofsky, $2.50, Corinth Books, c/o Eighth Street Bookshop, 17 W. 8th Street, New York 11, N.Y.

Ah, Zukofsky, the magic name, the big name, talking about poetry! Maybe while working at the railroad yards or maybe even while fighting Sammy Zsweink behind the gym after high-school hours we heard of Zukofsky, something that might some day help us with people like Sammy or the railroad yard foreman who watched us scrub the sides of boxcars and streamliners. Damn you foreman, I've got Pound, I've got Zukofsky, I've got *Poetry Chicago*. Yeah, and thin tires on my car and flat tires. I think Sammy won the fight and Pound didn't care. I've stopped reading *Poetry Chicago*. Now we have a test of poetry.

The test of poetry, Zukofsky tells me, is the range of pleasure it affords as sight, sound, and intellection. This is its purpose as art.

Further on, L.Z. tells us, "I believe that desirable teaching assumes intelligence that is free to be attracted from any consideration of every day living to always another phase of existence. Poetry, as other object matter, is after all for interested people."

I have to read these sentences several times to make sure that Zukofsky is not pulling my leg, my ears, or any part of me. The writing is not clear; it is stodgy but I get the message. Poetry is for us, the special ones—and it's of life (almost) and yet divorced, finally, and fixed and pleasurable. To sight, sound, intellection. Well, intellection is the catch-word, the out.

Yet once I thought poetry was to keep me alive, to keep everybody alive; other people's poems, my own, paintings, stories, novels, I had thought that these things were to help me get on through so that, when I went into the cabinet to get a razorblade, I shaved carefully with it instead of going for the throat with the big slash. *A Test of Poetry* was first published in 1948 and reissued in 1964. We are living in strange and violent and unusual times. I am afraid that life has caught up and extinguished such as Allen Tate, Lionel Trilling, Louis Zukofsky. We will no longer accept dry and safe bread. Poetry is going into the streets, into the whorehouses, into the sky, into the picnic basket, into the whiskey bottle. The fraud is over—certain people will not be allowed to live while others die. At least not from this typewriter, and the action is heavy too at the universities, the alleys, the beer-halls. This type of primer is not going to fool anyone any longer. There *are* some well-chosen poems but we will not let them be put into their little cages of mechanistic and prissy explanations. Some of the explanations, let me say, are thoughtful and even make sense in the limited way of a charming circle. But I can't imagine handing this book to a man doomed to go to the chair in a month.

The true test of poetry is that it fits every man everywhere.

There are some poems like this in this book but Zukofsky talks about everything else. There goes another idol. There go another 165 well-printed pages that might have crawled with love and blood and laughter, that might have gone good with beer and salami sandwiches, that might have made the next morning better instead of that trained slippery nostalgia of horror slipping through the curtains to fall upon me like a mother-axe and make me close my eyes again and hold the mean in my belly and wonder when the living will arrive??

# BUKOWSKI ON BUKOWSKI

*Notes of a Dirty Old Man*, Essex House, paperback, 255 pgs. with an introduction by the author. $1.95. Written by Charles Bukowski, reviewed by CHARLES BUKOWSKI

I drank with a friend the other night who said or maybe it was I who said, "It is terribly difficult not to like the smell of your own shit." We spoke of staring down at our turds after an accomplishment and feeling, somehow, proud of our deed.

Now, an opener like this will give the hackers, the poison-ivy boys, the university-ivy boys all that they need, so I give it to them early in order to feed them first. Let us get the suckerfish off of our sides and begin to speak decently. I've already had enough Creeley-University nightmares to last me 44 lives and dream-lives to go.

All right. Kirby sent me a couple of advance copies. So you get the thing out of the mailbox and you look at it.

I got into bed—I like beds, I think that the bed is Man's greatest invention—most of us are born there, die there, fuck there, jack-off there, dream there. . . .

I am somewhat of a crank and a disbeliever, so I clambered into my jack-off sheets, alone, expecting that Kirby and Essex House had taken out the best, not that I knew anything about Kirby or Essex House; I was only speaking of my experiences with the world—man, I flipped on through and they had left in everything—the rants, the literary, the unliterary, the sex, the no-sex, the whole bag of warty screams and experiences.

It was honor.

I like honor. And it was cleanly set with immaculate cover, *Notes of a Dirty Old Man*, 0115.

I got into bed and read my *own* stories or whatever they were and I enjoyed them. Once I have written a poem and go back to it, I only get the sense of vomit and waste. And people quote lines to me, verily, from back poems and I don't know what the hell they are talking about. It's like when they tell me when I am in hangover, "You chased 23 people out of my house and tried to fuck my wife."

You know, it seems like a bunch of shit.

But the stories, as I laid there in bed, I rather liked. Rotten thing to say, what? I do suppose it was the gathering of experience between covers ghostly which cuckolded me. Reading the life-days and nights of my life I wondered how I could possibly still be *alive* and walking around *now*?

How many times can a man go through the thresher and still keep his blood, the Summer sun inside of his head? How many bad jails, how many bad women, how many sundry cancers, how many flat tires, how many this or that or what or what or what? . . .

Frankly I read my *own* stories in easy wonderment, forgetting who I was, almost almost, and I thought:

Ummm, ummm, this son of a bitch can really write.

I remember other writers. Being very discouraged with Chekhov, G.B. Shaw, Ibsen, Irwin Shaw, Gogol, Tolstoy, Balzac, Shakespeare, Ezra Pound, so forth. They, all of them, seemed to put literary *form* in front of the actuality and living of life itself. In other words, or perhaps more clearly, each of these men condescended that life itself could be evil but that it was all right so long as they could get by and say it in their special literary way.

Which is all right. If you like playing games.

And I do think that the professors are finding, now, that the students themselves are tired of game-playing.

All right, let's get back to *Notes of a Dirty Old Man*.

Re-reading them, stories and fantasies, I found them wondrous and flaming. I thought, Jesus, there hasn't been a short storyteller this good since Pirandello. At least since then.

It's crappy to say, but I think that the book is worth reading. And that the unborn librarian virgins, 200 years hence, will come in their flowered panties, recognizing the power, after my damned dumb skull has become a chickenshit playground for subnormal worms, gophers, other underworld creatures.

Oh, one other thing.

In ten years your $1.95 copy will be worth $25. And if you live *long* enough and the Bomb doesn't do it, you may be able to pay a month's rent with the book.

Until then, read your nuts off and

Gobble and grow what you can.

# NOTES OF A DIRTY OLD MAN

*OPEN CITY*, DECEMBER 8–14, 1967

In the Dec. issue of *Evergreen* there is a small poem by one Charles Bukowski far in the back pages, and all through the magazine there is an interview of LeRoi Jones, poems by LeRoi Jones, ads for LeRoi Jones' latest book, plus a speech by the departed Malcolm X—"God's Judgment of White America." *Evergreen* was beginning to look like *Ebony*. I read on through.

Later in the day, the woman came over with my 3-year-old child. We sat down to dinner.

"I think I'll write a poem called 'WHO'S AFRAID OF LEROI JONES?'"

"*You're* afraid of LeRoi Jones" the woman shouted. She was a very liberal white liberal liberal liberal.

"*Who's Afraid of Leroi Jones?*" I asked again, looking at my little girl.

She pointed an arm at me over her ground round and french fries. "YOU ARE! YOU ARE!"

The woman was meanwhile pantering and bantering, her voice neurotically high-pitched, explaining to me the meaning of black America and LeRoi Jones, in the way that only a very liberal white liberal female can do. I was not attacking LeRoi Jones but I had somehow stepped upon sacred ground and he was being defended, almost violently. It was nice—for LeRoi. Hell, I remembered him when we were *both* scratching to get our poetry into the little magazines; now I was *still* scratching. I was still the better poet. His plays had put him over. The fat dull whitey wives no longer getting their sex got it through Jones' black violence in his plays. "Oh Lord, honey, that man *frightens* me, but I'd *like* to see one of his plays. Oooooh, let's go see one of his plays!!!" The old man, after a hard day at the ballpoint pen office, would take her to the play. Anything, rather than try to get his dick hard.

"I don't understand," I said. "Hitler told me that the whites were the superior race and now Jones turns around and tells me that the blacks are the superior race."

"Well, who do *you* think is the superior race?"

"It depends upon who you are; if you are white, then the white race is superior; if you are black, then the black; if you are yellow, then the yellow; if you are mixed, then the mongrel. . . ."

She went on some more, sentence running into sentence. She must have spoken ten minutes without pause. A little of it was good stuff. Most of it was just religious sacrifice at the altar. Hot white liberal liberal female air. Even Jones wouldn't want to hear it.

"How many blacks have you known?" I asked.

This is always a good stopper in a religious argument. Being a common laborer all my life at poor and underpaid jobs, I had worked with more black men, known more black men, drank with more black men, fought with more black men than any theoretical liberal with books jammed between the ears. Coming up through the back streets of New Orleans in a light rain with my paper suitcase, a high yellow sitting on her porch showing leg had named me. She laughed and shouted, "POOR WHITE TRASH!" I put down my paper suitcase and looked up her legs. "Come on!" she said. "Come on, poor white trash, and get yourself a little!" I saw a curtain move just a little and behind it this black male face, eyes beautiful with murder for my 2 dollars and 20 cents. Then I laughed, feeling good in the early sun, picked up my suitcase full of poems, and moved on down the street.

"Jones got out on 25,000 dollars bail," I threw at her. Money only represents evil to the white liberal ladies—until you stop giving it to them.

"Well, *you* got out of jail. In ten minutes, *you* had bail!"

"It took 6 or 7 hours. The bail was between 20 and 30 dollars. I had it in my dresser but it took me a long time to find somebody who would trust me for it. Jones got up $2,500 in cash, if you want comparisons, plus 2 houses, friends of his parents. I don't know anybody who owns a house. I don't even have parents. I'm still poor white trash."

"Jones' house doesn't belong to him. It belongs to the Negro community."

"Oh, shit," I said. So there it was, haggling over LeRoi Jones over the french fries. To find out who owns a man's house, find out who is shitting in the crapper and who is fucking in the bed. You can bet he owns part of it. Also, if you have to ring the bell to get in, you don't own any of it.

I decided to let the conversation go but she had hold of it.

"Suppose you kept walking down the street and getting punched in the nose and told you were getting punched in the nose because of the color of your skin, how would you feel? You can't blame them for wanting Black Power. Black Power isn't anything because they don't have any power. . . ."

She went on and on and on. I didn't have any particular argument with her. She only *presumed* that I did. But I knew that if the blacks ever got total power, they would kill her long before they got around to me. So I listened and listened and then kissed the little girl goodbye and drove on down to work.

Down there, 9 out of 10 of them are black but you forget this as the years go on. It's nothing special until the female white liberal liberals make it so. We worked away. Then I said, "LEROI JONES!"

The one next to me turned, and here was the finger again. "YOU BETTER NOT SAY ANYTHING ABOUT LEROI JONES!"

"My little girl says that I am afraid of him."

"YOU ARE! YOU ARE! YOU BETTER NOT SAY ANYTHING ABOUT LE-ROI JONES!"

"What will happen if I do?"

"You'll be taken care of, that's what will happen."

"You mean mentally or physically?"

"We don't care about the mental. His boys will handle you the other way."

"You mean I can't have freedom of speech?"

"You just be careful what you say! LeRoi Jones is an INTERNA-TIONALLY-RENOWNED PLAYWRIGHT! Who are you? You just be careful!"

"Give me a cigarette."

"Hell no, buy your own. They sell them in the machines."

His friend walked over. "Hello, brother," he said.

"Hello, brother," I answered.

"You gonna invite me over to your house for breakfast?" (We work nights.)

"Sure. We're having grits and beans. Only I don't have a house."

"You got a front door?"

"Yeah."

"Well, I'm comin' to the front door in broad daylight and ring your bell. I'm not comin' to the back door so's people will think I'm some servant or trashman or delivery boy. I'm comin' to your *front* door!"

"Brother Roy, my front door is your front door as long as the rent is paid."

"Good, and I'm gonna grow me some of that shit like you got on your chin and I'm gonna get me some young hippie girl and we gonna walk down Sunset Boulevard hand in hand, right down Sunset Boulevard."

"I'd like to get me one of those nice young blonde hippie girls myself," I told him.

After some remarks about Gov. Reagan, he walked over and sat down. We worked away, while back at my place the mother of my child got ready to go to a communist party meeting. Of all white members.

A pretty fucked-up scene.

Eh, LeRoi?

Brother?

Having earlier tried to pick up a very young whore whose stockings wrinkled down like stiff skins around her dirty ankles—she didn't want me—I grabbed her ass in the alley, she *farted*, a fart that sank my soul from Singapore to Mt. Ganges, she farted and left with a wonderfully subnormal sailor. I walked out into the street and the green trees stuck their yellow teeth out at me. And their rubber cocks. I was a dead gagging finger in a sexless sky.

Sadness. Sadness becomes so much, then it becomes something else—like a beerglass. Sadness is one thing, madness another. So you go to your place, towel the shit out of your ass, decide to go mad . . . what happens?

THE DOORBELL RINGS! A woman in a dusty black hat that flops down over her half-face. She wears a green cape and you can smell her underwear . . . probably a very big pussy that always emits this kind of white mulch, I don't mean *come* I mean *mulch*, and she says, *Would you like to donate to the starving children of Bionbiona?* No, mama, no, please. . . . *Oh, you were asleep? I'm sorry.* . . . Be sorry. But I wasn't asleep, mama.

She goes away.

—the people are better than I
the stones are better than I
the dogturds on somebody's lawn are
                              better than I.

3:24 A.M. I had gone someplace, evidently, and had come back. When I opened the door, I had the feeling that there was somebody in the room. I turned on this old lamp and stood there. Then the closet door with my paintings on them, pasted to them with snot and come and gum, that closet door opened and out came a man with a face that was almost yellow; hair that was both yellow and grey; ugly teeth and he smelled like hay and barndung, old chickencoops. He ran out and hit me in the face. As he tried to run out the doorway I got a hammerlock on his left arm, bent the damn thing almost up to his neck. He began to cry and he still stank terribly. "Franky Roosevelt is dead," he wept. "Listen, ass, who gives a motherfuck?" I asked. "I do, oh, I do!" "You STINK!" I screamed at him, "TAKE A BATH!" I booted him in the ass and pushed him out the door. I heard him run down the street. I looked into the closet and there was this little pile of turds, fresh turds. I looked at them and vomited. Then I took yesterday's newspaper, some dull shit about men landing on the moon, and I gathered the whole mess together and threw it into the garbage can.

Then I went to the refrigerator, made a bologna sandwich, drank two beers, then began on the wine. Then I went to my blackboard, a large one which hung from the center of the room by ropes and was weighted with brick anchors, and I found some chalk and wrote:

THIS ONE HAS A CLUBFOOT

THIS ONE WANTS TO SUCK MY DICK

THE THIRD HAS A HEAD-TICK

THE FOURTH WEARS A WIG

THE FIFTH IS A COMMUNIST

THE SIXTH IS THE GRANDSON OF HITLER

THE SEVENTH READS DICK TRACY

THE EIGHTH CLAIMS I OWE HIM TWO PACKS OF CIGARETTES

THE NINTH IS A WOMAN WHO ONCE DANCED WITH A 9-FOOT COBRA BUT SHE WON'T FUCK ME. NO, IT WAS A BOA CONSTRICTOR! ANYWAY, SHE WON'T FUCK ME.

The doorbell rang. 4 A.M. DeJohns.

Sit down, DeJohns.

Milk-red eyes, tits enough for both of us, but, of course, no cunt.

We need the hero, DeJohns. There's nothing. Everything has dried up. What can we hang to?

Hehehehehehehe hehehe.

He was looking at the rope that held up the blackboard.

Hehehehehehehe hehe, tough, nothing but shit. Little boys playing games now. Hehe. Pretense. And *no humans anywhere*, hehehe. Birds, cats, ants, all right. Sure. We remain drunk. Jam pills. Hehe. I remember you, Bukowski, hehehe, when you were a man instead of that bag o' sick shit you are now, hehe.

Go suck a water faucet, DeJohns.

He, hehe, the time you ran round the block one morning, *twice*, 7 A.M., completely *naked*—your balls, cock, ass bouncing in the clear air. No sound. Just your feet, bare feet: pat pat pat! We clothed, 3 of us, trying to catch you. Hehehe, the time you hung by your ankles out the window of that fourth floor of that hotel. The whores in that room weeping, begging you to come back inside. Promising to suck your cock, lick the hairs of your asshole, anything. Hehe, that was good.

Go suck a hot spoon, DeJohns.

That was funny. But funnier was when you tried to lift yourself in and your legs wouldn't pull you up. You had your ankles wrapped around the wooden separator that made two windows out of one. Then you got real funny.

Yeah?

Yeah. Hehehehe. You said, o o, if I don't pull up on the next one, that's it. I'm getting weak. Whores ran up and you screamed, DON'T TOUCH ME! And how you ever pulled your whole body up by the ankles, I'll never know. You became a snail, a centipede, something inhuman. Hehehe, when you got in the whores ripped your pants down, licked your asshole, balls, cock . . . hehehhe. Then the knock at the door and you opening the door with that hard cock, YEAH?

and the landlord saying, WHAT THE HELL YOU DOING HANGING OUT THE WINDOWS BY YOUR FEET? Hehehe. And you saying, JUST TRYING TO PUT SOME LIFE INTO THIS GODDAMNED PARTY! Hehehehe. And the landlord saying, ALL RIGHT. YOU DO THAT ONE MORE TIME AND I'M GOING TO CALL THE POLICE! Hehehe.

DeJohns looked at me: "What has happened to you, Bukowski?"

I don't know, man. Tired.

I was going to do a book on your life. Now you no longer interest me.

The things I did were things I had to do. I don't need those things anymore.

FUCK YOU, MAN! YOU'RE FINISHED!

DeJohns got up and left.

My last chance for immortality.

Maybe he was right. I took a bit of whiskey to get up my nerve. Got on the phone. *Hey, baby, I have a bottle. Come on over. We'll drink. Talk some shit. Then fuck.*

She hung up.

I went back to the blackboard:

WHY WASH UNDER THE ARMS WHEN THE ROACH HAS CONQUERED MORE THAN ALEXANDRIA?

WHY RIDE A BICYCLE WHEN HENRY MILLER RIDES A BICYCLE?

WE'VE PLAYED AT SOUL—NOT HAVING ANY—WE HAVE FUCKED-UP THE SACRED ATROCITY OF BREATHING.

WE HAVE BRUTALIZED THE EARTH MORE THAN ANY ARMIES.

WHEN THE HERO ARRIVES WE WILL FIND THAT HE WAS ALWAYS HERE.

Then I sat down, lit a cigarette, took two reds, and waited.

# CHRIST WITH BARBECUE SAUCE

The hitchhiker was standing just below the gas station when they picked him up. They put him in the back seat with Caroline.

Murray was driving. Frank turned around, put his arm on the back of the seat, and looked at the hitchhiker.

"You a hippie?"

"I don't know. Why?" asked the kid.

"Well, we kind of specialize in hippies. We're used to them."

"Then you don't dislike us?"

"Why, hell no, kid, we *love* hippies! What's your name?"

"Bruce."

"Bruce. Well, that's a nice name. I'm Frank. The guy who's driving, that's Murray. And that beautiful bitch next to you, that's Caroline."

Bruce nodded and grinned. Then asked, "How far you going?"

"All the way, kid, we're taking you all the way."

Murray laughed.

"What's he laughing at?" asked Bruce.

"Murray always laughs in the wrong places. But he's our driver. He's a good driver. He drives us all up and down the coast, through Arizona, Texas, Louisiana. He never seems to get tired, but he's all right, ain't that right, baby?" he asked Caroline.

"Sure, and Bruce is all right too." She put her hand on the kid's knee, squeezed it. Then she leaned over and kissed him on the cheek.

"You had anything to eat lately, kid?"

"No, I'm pretty hungry."

"Well, don't worry. We're going to stop and eat something pretty soon."

Caroline kept smiling at Bruce. "He's nice. Real nice." Bruce felt

68

her hand slide down along his leg toward his penis. Frank didn't seem to mind and Murray just kept driving. Then she was upon his penis, rubbing it and smiling.

"Where'd you sleep last night, kid?" asked Frank.

"Under the trees. It was pretty damned cold. I was sure glad when the sun came up."

"You're lucky some animal didn't gobble you up during the night."

Murray laughed again.

"What do you mean?" asked the kid.

"I mean, under all that hair, you look like a nice juicy kid."

"Sure does," said Caroline. She kept stroking his penis. It was getting hard.

"How old are you, Bruce?"

"19."

"You read Ginsberg, Kerouac?" "Sure, but they were kind of from the Beat era. We like rock and folk music, that stuff. I like Johnny Cash too. And Bobby Dylan, of course. . . . "

Caroline had his zipper open and had his thing out. Then she had her tongue on it, was giving him the barberpole. Frank acted like it wasn't happening.

"You been up to Berkeley?"

"Oh yeah. Berkeley, Denver, Santa Barbara, Frisco. . . . "

"You think there's going to be a revolution?"

"Yeah, there has to be. There's no way out. You see. . . . "

She had his cock in her mouth. The kid couldn't talk anymore.

Murray finally looked back, then laughed. Frank lit a cigarette and watched.

"Jesus," said the kid, "o my god, Jesus!"

Caroline was bobbing. Then she got it all. It was over. Bruce fell back in his seat, pulled up his zipper.

"How was that, kid?"

"Well, real fine, you know."

"Not often you get a ride like this. And it's not over yet either. It's just beginning. Wait'll we stop and eat."

Murray laughed again.

"I just don't like the way he laughs," said Bruce.

"Well, you can't have everything. You just had a nice head job."

They just drove along for a while.

"Getting hungry, Murray?"

Murray spoke for the first time. "Yeah."

"Well, we'll stop as soon as we find a nice spot."

"Hope it's soon," said Murray.

"I guess Caroline isn't hungry. She just had lunch."

"I can use some dessert, though," she laughed.

"When did we last eat, anyhow?" asked Frank.

"Day before yesterday," said Caroline.

"What?" asked Bruce. "The day before yesterday?"

"Yeah, kid, but when we eat, we *eat*—Hey! This looks like a good spot. Lots of trees, isolation. Pull off the road, Murray."

Murray pulled off to the side of the road and they all got out and stretched.

"That's a hell of a nice beard there, kid. And that head of hair. The barbers don't take much off you, do they?"

"Nobody does, I guess."

"Atta boy, kid! All right, Murray, dig us a hole for roasting. Set up a spit. It's been a couple of days. I'm about to lose my pot gut."

Murray opened the trunk. There was a shovel in there. Wood and even coal. Everything they needed. He began carrying the stuff down in between the trees. The others got back in the car. Frank passed out smokes and handed around a bottle of scotch. A 5th. It was smooth stuff but the kid needed the water bag a couple of times.

"I really like Bruce," said Caroline.

"I like him too," said Frank. "What the hell, can't we share him?"

"Of course."

They all drank without talking. Then Frank said, "Come on. Murray ought to have it up about now."

They got out and followed Frank into the trees, Caroline holding Bruce's hand. When they got there, Murray was about finished.

"What's that thing?" asked the kid.

"That's a cross. Murray built it himself. Isn't it nice?"

"I mean, what's it for?"

"Murray believes in rituals. He's a little funny, you know, but we humor him along."

"Listen," said the kid, "I'm not hungry. I think I'll just walk up the road a bit."

"But *we're* hungry, kid."

"Yeah, but I'm. . . . "

Frank punched the kid in the stomach and as he bent over, Murray clubbed him behind the ear. Caroline made a pillow of leaves and sat down while Frank and Murray dragged the kid over to the cross. Frank held Bruce against the cross while Murray drove the large nail into the kid's left palm. Then they got the right palm.

"You wanna go for the feet?" asked Frank.

"No, I get tired of that. Too much work."

They sat down next to Caroline and passed the bottle.

"They have beautiful sunsets out here, don't they?" asked Caroline.

"Yeah. Look at it. Pink and getting red. You like sunsets, Murray."

"Sure I like sunsets. What do you think?"

"I just asked. Don't get touchy."

"Well, you people always treat me like some kind of idiot. Sure, I like sunsets."

"All right. Let's not argue. Or maybe we ought to argue. Because I've got something on my mind."

"Yeah?" said Murray.

"Yeah. I'm tired of using barbecue sauce. I'm tired of the taste. And besides, I read somewhere it can give you cancer."

"Well, I like barbecue sauce. And I do all the driving, I do all the work, so we ought to have barbecue sauce."

"What do you think, Caroline?"

"I don't care one way or the other. Just as long as we eat."

The kid was moving on the cross. He spread his legs to stand, then looked up. Then he saw his hands.

"Oh my god! What have you done to me?"

Then he screamed. It was a long, high, pitiful scream. Then he stopped.

"Keep your cool, kid," said Frank.

"Yeah," said Murray.

"Guess he don't want a head job now, huh, Caroline?"

Caroline laughed.

"Listen," said the kid, "please take me down. I don't understand. This pain—there's very much pain. I'm sorry I screamed. Please take me down. Please, please, god o mighty, take me down!"

"O.K., take him down, Murray."

"Oh my god, thank you!"

Murray walked over to the cross, pushed the kid's head back, and slit his jugular vein with the butcher knife. Then he picked up the claw hammer and began yanking at the nail of the left palm. He cursed.

"This is always the hardest part."

Then Murray had the kid down and was stripping him. He threw the clothing and the sheets to one side. Then he took the knife and ripped the kid open, starting just below the ribs and cutting down through the stomach.

"Come on," said Frank. "I don't like to watch this part."

Caroline and Frank got up and walked into the woods. When

they came back, the sun had set and Murray had the kid up on the spit and was turning him.

"Listen, Murray."

"Yeah?"

"How about the barbecue sauce?"

"I was just about to put it on. You gotta put it on while the meat is cooking to get the real flavor, you know that."

"I'll tell you what. I'll flip you for it. You game, Murray?"

"All right. Come 'ere, Caroline. You turn it while we flip."

"O.K."

"One call," said Frank. "Call it when it's in the air."

Frank flipped the coin high into the air.

"Heads!" Murray yelled.

The coin fell. They walked over and looked at it.

It was heads.

"Goddamn it," said Frank.

"Well, you don't have to eat if you don't want to," said Murray.

"I'll eat," said Frank. . . .

The next morning they were driving down the road, Frank and Murray up front, Caroline in the back. The sun was well up. Caroline was in back with a hand, cleaning the meat off of the fingers.

"That girl's got the damnedest appetite I ever saw," said Murray.

"Yeah, and she had first taste too. Almost as soon as the guy got into the car."

Frank and Murray laughed.

"You guys aren't funny. You guys aren't funny at all!"

Caroline rolled down the window and threw the hand out.

"I'm so full," said Murray, "I never want to see another hippie."

"You said the same thing 2 or 3 days back," said Frank.

"I know, I know. . . . "

"Look! Slow down! I think I see another one! Yeah, look, beard, sandals, the works."

"Let's pass this one, Frank."

The hippie stuck out his thumb.

"Stop the car, Murray. Let's see how far he wants to go."

They pulled up.

"How far you going, kid?"

"New Orleans."

"New Orleans? That'll take us 3 or 4 days, at least. Get in, kid. Get in back there with our beautiful lady."

The hippie got in and Murray was back to driving.

"What's your name, kid?"

"Dave."

"Dave. That's a nice name. I'm Frank. The guy who's driving is Murray. And that beautiful bitch next to you, that's Caroline."

"Good to meet you all," said Dave, and then he turned and grinned at Caroline.

"And we're all pleased to meet you," smiled Caroline.

Murray belched as Caroline put her hand on Dave's knee.

# AH, LIBERATION, LIBERTY, LILIES

## ON THE MOON!

It is a time of groups demanding their dignity and place under the smoggy sun. Often their demands reveal their weaknesses and cruelties, but the blinkers are on and they only see straight ahead—for themselves. Groupism can be an Al Capone gang or a ballet co. Groupism can be the Catholic Church or the men's track team at Stanford. Groupism means "win" and "win for us." Groupism means "I want mine and by God you better give it to me or else—." Groupism is a demand for Love through Threat. Love meaning a great many different things to different people. Groupism will not work. Groupism will only form counter-groupism. Groupism, in a sense, isolates more than it frees, but let's let all that go. Everybody's doing it now. But I'm thinking of some of the groups who haven't organized. Like say, the children. Can you think of any other group with fewer rights than children? They are beaten, scolded, schooled, shoved aside, primped when needed, bathed at will, fed at random, told when to sleep, awaken, talk, not talk, and on and on. The excuse being that they do not know how to do these things for themselves—long after they do.

I well remember my childhood. I was held in total slavery. Saturday was lawnmowing and watering day. Sunday was church. The other days were school, homework, and tasks. I was beaten 3 or 4 times a week by a bully of a father, a hateful man. He used a razor strop. My mother's only comment was: "Respect him. After all, he is your father."

I was a slave. I'd think, god, I'm only 3 feet tall. I can't get a job. I must stay here and take these beatings in order to have a place to sleep and something to eat. This sounds a bit humorous to me now but it wasn't then.

I read where one mother used to stick her little girl in red-hot bathwater in order to teach her to be "obedient." A father, after stomping his child with his shoes, would open a beer and look at TV. Another mother starved her baby to death. You can read horror story after horror story in your daily paper. Think of the unrepresented children, the largest slave group in the world.

If you want to go further, how about dogs and cats? Did you ever consider the atrocious food you feed your pets? It's dog food, it's cat food, you say; they eat it. You'd eat it too, if that's all you had. You give it to them because it's cheap—you can have a live slave for 12 cents a day. While you demand liberation, you enslave your children and pets. What's the matter with you?

We can even get quite extreme and say, how about roaches, spiders, flies, ants, snakes, cows, bulls, horses, mules, butterflies, steer, monkeys, gorillas, tigers, lions, foxes, wolves, pigs, chickens, turkeys, fish, seals, parrots, and the like? Come, old boy, you either control or use all these things, murder them, capture them, or profit by them. While you demand liberties, you enslave everything. What's the matter with you?

What's in the dignity of a pig, you say; he looks better as bacon and ham and pork chops. Well, maybe to you.

And the tiger, you say, if we don't kill him or capture him, he'll kill us.

Ah, same old story. When's the next war start? Is that an Indian behind that bush or a Nazi from Hoboken?

Well, you say, the bullfights may not be quite proper.

How about the boxing matches then? We put two men in the ring and hope they beat hell out of each other. If they don't, we'll let them know about it. . . .

So you see, when you speak of liberation, there are plenty of unliberated groups in the world. Now take the cockroach—

Please, Bukowski, don't get completely ridiculous.

Have you ever asked the cockroach?

I can't.

That's the point. I am hereby appointing myself founder of *The Cockroach Liberation Society.*

By god, you've got enough of them around this dump!

There, you see!

You mean?

Of course. . . .

I'm getting out of here.

You'd better. We're forming. Stronger every day. Right on, brother!

He walked to the door, slammed it, walked down the street.

The damned fascist swine!

I had been drunk for a week, and then a black girl with big innocent eyes read me one of her poems, and the poem was so bad and she was such a nice thing; I couldn't say anything about how bad the poem had been so I went into the bathroom, took the top off the water closet, and broke it on the floor.

Then I came out and stretched on the floor. I was stretched out in front of a folk singer, listening, squeezing her legs, rubbing her thighs when somebody said, "Hank!" and I looked up and there were 2 cops at the door.

I got up.

"You own this joint, buddy?" they asked.

"I rent it."

"Well, there's too much noise going on here."

"All right, we'll keep it down."

"See that you do. Because if I have to come back, somebody is going to land in the slammer."

They left. I don't remember much about the rest of the party but when I awakened I was alone in my bedroom, sick, too weak to get out of bed. The sun was well up. I had to get off the merry-go-round. I had been drunk too long.

Then the phone rang.

Oh, shit. I picked it up.

"Hello?"

"Hank?"

"Yeah, yeah. Hank."

"You in bed?"

"Yeah."

"Get up. We're going on a boat ride over the beautiful Pacific."

"Maybe you are. I'm not."

"Come on. Get out of that bed. We'll be over in half an hour."

I got up, weaved to the bathroom, and looked at my face in the mirror. I gagged, went into the kitchen, and opened the refrigerator. Not a beer in there. My hand trembled as I closed the refrigerator door. I hadn't eaten in 3 days.

I got into some clothes, sat in a chair, and waited.

An hour went by. Good, I thought, they've changed their minds.

I took off my clothes and got back into bed, pulled the covers to my chin.

I must have slept. The doorbell rang. I got into a robe.

It was Barbie and Dutch.

"Come on, come on! Get some clothes on!"

"Listen, I'm sick, really sick . . . I can hardly walk."

"Come on, get dressed. It'll do you good."

"Yeah."

Then we stopped off to pick up the guy with the motor. We drove down to the pier. While they were making arrangements I walked along the pier looking for a place to get a beer. I didn't see any signs for beer. Fresh fish. A merry-go-round. Hamburgers. But no beer.

I walked back.

I walked down the swinging gangplank that hung over the floating dock. I almost broke my leg leaping to the dock. There we were. three white guys with a beautiful black woman. We climbed into the rowboat. Again I barely made it.

I sat on a plank and said, "Shit! Oh, shit!"

"You'll get a good sunburn," said Dutch. "You're pale. You never go out in the daylight. This way you get off the booze and you get healthy."

I shook all over. "But I'm dying."

They looked at me and laughed.

"Can you swim?"

"Not today. Too weak. I'll go right down."

Clyde was trying to start the motor. It wouldn't start. He kept pulling the cord.

I might luck it yet, I thought.

Five minutes later the motor started. Dutch sat there bailing out the water from the bottom of the boat with an empty can. There were dead fish in the boat, a week old.

I staggered over and sat next to Barbie. She held my hand.

"Isn't this nice?"

The water was rough. Dutch sat in the prow and leaped up and down as the boat bucked.

"I can swim!" he yelled at me. "I can swim 5 miles!"

We passed a suckerfish floating close to the top of the water.

"Did you see the suckerfish?" Dutch asked me.

"I saw it."

We got out beyond the breakwater and headed out to sea. We had the smallest boat out there. There were mostly sailboats and one or two large engine-driven yachts.

I began to heave.

"Stick your head over the side!"

There wasn't much. I hadn't eaten in days. It was just green slime.

"What is it, Hank? Are you seasick or is it the hangover?"

"Hangover . . . yurrrp! ahhh! yoorrrrk!"

"Want us to turn back?"

"No . . . yooorrrrrk! . . . go . . . ahead."

I was finished.

Clyde kept going out to sea. We were out beyond the sailboats. I kept thinking how nice it would be sitting in a chair in my beat-up place, drinking a stout malt liquor, and listening to Stravinsky or Mahler.

"Head back!" I yelled to Clyde.

"What? I can't hear! I'm over the engine!"

"I said, 'Head back to shore!'"

"What? I can't hear!"

"He says, 'Head back to shore!'"

"Oh, we'll sail along the coast for a while. As long as you can see those hotels you know we're not too far out."

The hotels were 40 floors high.

"Shit!" I said.

"What?"

Finally Dutch and Barbie took turns steering and Clyde came and sat by me.

"Isn't this great?"

"It's stupid. Drop me off and you guys go on with it. I'll wait."

"But I thought you were the great Bukowski, the guy who bummed across the nation a dozen times?"

"A man gets tired of sticking his head into windmills. . . . "

Harry's was more like it. ". . . damn fools pulled me out of bed with a week's worth of hangover and put me in a leaky rowboat and drove 7 miles out to sea with a ¼-horsepower engine. . . . "

"But why did you say I was 5 feet tall in that story *Evergreen* printed? I'm not 5 feet tall. . . ."

". . . they are the kind of people who get on roller coasters. Essentially they are jaded and need an extreme shock to stimulate. . . ."

". . . you know what 5 feet tall is?"

"No."

He stood up.

"Five feet comes right here, bastard."

Harry put his hand right below his hairline.

"I'm 5 feet 2."

Harry sat back down. "And I wish all the things went on around here that you say go on around here—all the huge reamings and suckings."

"They do."

"And I wear a wig that slips, you said. People are staring at my hair."

Harry was writing critical articles for the *Free Press*. He explained to me the meaning of "Panic" in literature and how "Panic" created Art. He explained the root of the word "Panic." The old boy was onto something.

The Panic of Hemingway: the boxing gloves, the bullfights, the hunting trips, the rushing out to save a man while under extreme fire. And Camus' *The Stranger*. Nothing but reverse Panic.

Then Harry got onto Maxwell Bodenheim in New York City. Max was always drunk. He'd be walking along the streets of New York at 3 A.M. in the morning, nobody around, and then he would turn with his sneer on his lips and he would half spit out, half scream the words: "FASCIST SWINE!" How he bummed beers in bars and sold his autographed poems—"beautiful poems!"—for a dollar. And the man who had murdered Max had gotten his photo in the papers with this big grin on, and the caption, "Well, anyway, I murdered a communist!" Only Max hadn't been a communist.

Then Harry got into the story about the 6-foot-2 sailor who had taken so much dick he was jaded on dick and he used to go into the bars looking for guys with large hands and forearms and he'd get these guys to jam the forearm into his ass up to the elbow. Harry talked some heavy shit. How all you had to do in Arabia when you were in a jam was drop your pants and grin. They thought you were a holy man.

Then I heard Dutch's car door open 4 floors down. He never got a lube job. He used his doors as a horn.

"Oh oh. There are the sailors. I'll go down and meet them so they won't bother you."

"I don't want to be a complete shit. I'll go outside and wave," said Harry.

Harry waved to Dutch. Dutch waved to Harry.

I took the elevator down.

Then I was in the car and we were driving along.

"Well, how did it go?" I asked.

"Oh, god, it was wonderful," said Barbie.

"We went way out," said Clyde. "The waves were 7 feet tall. We turned the motor on full blast and smashed into each wave. It was great."

"Like going through brick walls," said Dutch. "We really had a time. We got in an hour late and the guy hollered at us."

"Fuck him," said Barbie. "I told him off."

"What we gonna eat?" asked Clyde. "I gotta see *Hair* at 8:30 P.M."

"Did you see *Hair*, Hank?"

"Did I ever tell you about the 6-foot-2 sailor who got so jaded with dick he took guys' arms up his ass, right up to the elbow?"

"That's pretty hard to believe," said Barbie.

"Well, you know, Catherine the Great died after being fucked by a horse."

"They say Catherine the Great had the palace guards killed after they fucked her," said Barbie.

"I wonder if they knew they were going to get killed?" asked Clyde. "Seems to me it would be pretty hard to get a hard-on under those conditions."

We drove along thinking about how hard it would be to get a hard-on under those conditions.

We stopped at a supermarket and Dutch and Barbie got out.

"Get some beer," I told them.

They finally made it back and I asked Dutch if he had gotten beer and he said, "Yes, yes," and then we were up in Clyde's $110-a-month apartment full of all the books, stereo, record player—glass doors on the shower—and I sat at a table and watched Barbie cook while drinking my beer.

"I'm pretending you are in my kitchen, baby."

She grinned.

The dinner was all right. My first food in 3 days.

Then Clyde had to make *Hair*. But first Dutch bought the boat motor from Clyde for $90.

"I'm buying this for you, Bukowski. Now we can go boating every weekend."

"Thanks, Dutch."

We left with the motor, said goodnight to Clyde, and then drove over to check out Dutch's bookstore. Nobody ever bought books there. But there was a place in back, large, where people read poetry to each other. Friday nights. And on Saturday nights, the folk singers.

So we opened the place and Dutch ran around.

"Shit! Somebody's been in here!"

I sat down with my beer and watched.

"Catfood! Somebody fed the cat! And the coffee's still hot! Shit! Who's been in here?"

I just drank my beer.

Dutch walked to the back.

"Hey! The back door's open! I know I locked the back door!"

Then Barbie found a sleeping bag on the floor.

"Shit, this ain't our sleeping bag."

Then Dutch walked to the toilet. The window was open. Somebody had crawled through the window. Sure, a chair outside there. And a *City Lights Journal*. Goddamn, somebody had been in there. But he couldn't be a bad guy because he fed the cat.

"You mean only good guys feed cats?" I asked.

"Now, Bukowski, if I place a bar across this toilet window, nobody can get in, right?"

"Wrong."

A 13-year-old kid walked in through the open back door.

"Hey, man," he said, "everybody's *spaced*! Where am I?"

"You're at the Golden Spider Bookshop," said Barbie.

"Man!" said the kid.

He walked in, sat on a chair.

"Jesus," he said, "where's all the people? Robert said this was a live joint, almost as live as Bukowski's. Where's all the people?"

"It's just on Friday and Saturday nights," said Dutch. "On Sundays we rest."

"Oh," said the kid, "well, shit, I'm on acid. Just half a tablet though."

Then I heard a cat. It was scratching and meowing.

"Dutch, what's that?"

"It's the cat, coming through the bathroom window."

"But you just locked the window. Look in that closet. It sounds like it's coming from that closet."

Dutch walked over, pulled a bench from the front of the closet and their cat walked out, just a bit pissed and indignant.

"Now, just who would put a cat in there?"

"The same guy who fed it," I said.

"Robert said this was a swinging place," said the kid.

The cat walked around with its tail straight up in the air.

Then two people walked in the back door. The girl was about 19, very hard, bulky. The guy was about 15, one of those tall thin ones.

"Come on," he said to the girl, "let's crash."

He started to walk up the stairway leading to the sleeping quarters upstairs.

"Hey, man," screamed Dutch, "if I let you go up there we'll have every teeny-bopper in town crashing here and we just won't last. I can't let you go up there. Where'd you hear of this place?"

"Robert."

"You can't stay here."

"O.K., where's Sunset and Normandy?"

"Hey, hold it," I said, "that's my place."

"Look," said Barbie to the 19-year-old girl, "I think you've got a place to stay. Why don't you take him there?"

"Because I've got a guy staying with me."

"O.K.," said Dutch, "you guys have got to go."

They walked out, both of them very angry.

"Look, Dutch," I said, "I've got to go."

"O.K.," said Dutch.

"Look," said the kid, "you going near Santa Monica and Western?"

"We'll drive you there," said Dutch.

Dutch locked the place up again and we walked out to the car, Barbie and the kid in back, Dutch and I in front.

"Bukowski, if I bar that back window it will keep them out, won't it?"

"No," I said.

I got out in front of my place. I took the beers, kissed Barbie goodnight, and waved them off. I got to the front door, managed to get it open, checked into the sack—3 beers left—went to the phone book, found the underlined number, dialed it:

"Hello. Bukowski. Yeah. You remember? O.K. Two six-packs tall, yes. A pint of scotch, you know the kind I drink. And you know I tip well. So get your boy out here and get him here fast!"

I put two beers in the refrigerator and opened the other. I turned on the radio. Berlioz *Symphonie fantastique*. Not bad. I was back in my kingdom. I sat back and waited for the delivery boy.

# NOTES OF A DIRTY OLD MAN

*CANDID PRESS*, DECEMBER 6, 1970

Sexual conquests generally happen, they are not chased down. I lived in the Suicide Hotel across from MacArthur Park in L.A. It was an old rotting place full of losers. I was sitting by the window one day holding my glass of wine when something dropped by in front of me, soundlessly. We were on the fourth floor, and this body came on by in the air, fully clothed, head down, legs following. The court-yard was cement and I heard him hit but I didn't look. That's when I named it the "Suicide Hotel." But let's get on to sexual conquests, a more pleasant subject.

I was living with a girl named May who was very good on the bed but who, like me, didn't quite fit into society. Neither of us could hold a job or wanted a job but we were continually worried about money. We lived on our luck. Money seemed to come along one way or the other. May was good at rolling drunks, and once when it was just about over for us, I found a wallet with $197 laying in the bathroom. May had been using our john that day so I walked on down to the communal john and there was the wallet. We had to be lucky or we were dead.

I was sitting in the park this day thinking about it. We were down to our last 63 cents and I was watching the ducks swim about, thinking they had it made. No rent, no food problems, no job prob-lems. The poor dumb things had all the luck. No wonder men killed themselves and went mad. I sat there thinking about how nice it would be to be a duck. I rather dozed in the sun. Hours went by. It was almost evening when I roused myself and went back to the Suicide Hotel.

I got in the old elevator, and it rocked me up to the 4th floor. As

I neared my door, I heard all the noise and laughter. What was going on? I opened the door and here was May and two of her girlfriends, Jerri and Deedee. They were well on the way.

"Hank!" May said, "Jerri just got her first unemployment check and we're celebrating. Have a drink."

I had a drink. I had a number of drinks. I had to hurry to catch up with them. Here I had 63 cents and was drinking with 3 very well-built women. Their faces could use a little help but there wasn't much more you could add to those bodies. And they dressed to advantage. They showed what they had.

A little later Jerri went out and bought 2 pounds of ground sirloin, coleslaw, and a large pack of fries and May cooked it up and we ate and drank several bottles of wine. Everybody was feeling all right. It was one night at a time for folks like us. Tomorrow would have to wait.

After dinner the girls sat around and talked about their funny experiences with men. I heard plenty. For instance, they all knew that bellboy at the Biltmore who had a thing like a horse, and he would get all excited when parties were going on and after everybody was gone he would swing the door open and with the horse-thing extended, run into the room.

"Oh no! You're not going to stick that thing in me!"

The poor guy simply had too much. He'd put 3 women in the hospital.

They went on talking and laughing about men, and I had to go to the john. I took a good one and when I came out it was over. May had passed out on the couch and Jerri was in one bed and Deedee was in the other. The lights were out.

I took off my clothes and sat in a chair. Now isn't this a shame? I thought. Three women with bodies like that, all passed out. What a hell of a party. Well, they'd been drinking all day.

I just sat there and kept drinking. I was mixing beer and wine. I smoked several cigarettes, and then I thought, what the hell?

I checked my woman May first to be sure she was out, then I walked over to Jerri's bed and got in. She was a tall woman, almost 6 feet, and with very fine breasts. I picked up one of her breasts and put the nipple in my mouth.

"Hey, Hank, what are you doing?"

I couldn't answer. I got to the other breast. Then I said, "I'm going to make love to you."

"Oh no, Hank, if May finds out she'll kill me!"

"May will never know, my darling!"

I was the greatest lover from Kiev to Pomona. I mounted. I knew that bed; the springs squeaked. May had a terrible temper and was perfectly capable of murder. I had never had such a strange copulation. In order to keep the springs from making a sound, I moved in the slowest slowest of all motions. Nature had never meant it to be that way. Nature didn't know what it was doing. I will never forget that bit of lovemaking. Moving so slowly, slowly, in order to keep the springs from tattling, I heated up beyond all comprehension. It was working on Jerri too.

"Oh, my god, I love you!" she said.

"Shhhhhhh, shhhhhhh," I whispered, "she'll kill us!"

Then I was doing it. "O, o, o, my god. . . ."

"Shhhhhh," whispered Jerri.

Then I made it, we made it.

I used the sheet and then got out of bed. I sat in the chair as Jerri went to the bathroom and came back. I sat in the chair for some time, drinking beer and wine and smoking. I was the 63-cent lover of the Suicide Hotel. Maybe it was better not being a duck. I thought again about that poor guy floating down past my window, then I had a drink to him and walked over to Deedee's bed. The springs on Deedee's bed were soundless. Deedee was short, but juicy, you might say. She was energetic, always walking about, laughing, cussing; she wasn't too brainy but she was honest and funny, and like I said, juicy. That's what you thought when you looked at Deedee: juicy, ripe, ripe, overripe. I simply got into bed with Deedee and plunged straight in. She didn't protest at all. She lifted her legs and reached up and kissed me, her tongue working in and out. She didn't let go. Her tongue worked in rhythm with my penis. It was a good one. I rolled off, used the sheet, then sat in the chair as Deedee went to the bathroom.

The 63-cent lover of the Suicide Hotel. Deedee walked on by going back to bed. I decided that it had been a fair night. I drank a half a bottle of wine, 3 cans of beer, and walked over to the couch and climbed in with May. I was ready to sleep it off.

May reached out and grabbed me. She had a good hold of me, and I mean me.

"Unhand me, woman," I said.

"I'm burning up," she said," "I've just got to have it."

"Not tonight."

"Why? Why?"

"I'm tired. I don't know, I'm just very tired."

"But it's getting bigger."

"Believe me, it doesn't mean a thing."

"But it must. Why does it do that?"

"No brains, I guess."

"I've got to have it! I'm burning up, I tell you!"

"I can't."

"Why not?"

"Damn it, I'm not a machine! Don't you understand?"

"No!"

May bent down and put her mouth upon me. I couldn't resist. It must have lasted 20 minutes, then she smoked it out of me. I was really finished.

I awakened the next morning, alone on the couch. The girls were in the kitchen, talking and laughing. I listened.

"Oh, Jerri, I just love that new hat! Doesn't she look sweet in that new hat? Put it on again, Jerri! Don't you like it, Deedee?"

"Yes, it brings everything out in her. It's darling, a darling little hat!"

I got into some clothes and walked into the kitchen.

"There he is!"

"Hi, Hank!"

"Hello, girls."

"How do you feel?"

"Oh, I don't know. A bit weary, I guess."

"Care for some coffee?"

"O.K."

"Breakfast?"

"Hell, no."

"How do you like Jerri's new hat? Put it on again, Jerri."

"It really makes her look sexy," I said.

"Oh, you men! I think it brings out the features of her face."

"I think it brings out the features of her ass."

"Hank, do you have to be nasty?"

"Sorry. Bad head. Yes, she looks nice in the hat. Green's her color. Her eyes are green, and with all that red hair, it works. O.K.?"

"That's more like my nice daddy," said May.

I got down a can of beer and then May made breakfast for us all. The girls just chatted back and forth. They each had on different dresses than the night before, and they looked scrubbed and untouched; they glowed.

"Why don't you girls stay another night?" I asked.

"What do you think, May?" asked Jerri.

"I'd love it. Why don't you?"

"O.K., then, we will."

I smiled and lit a cigarette. Then I leaned back and blew out a large and perfect smoke ring. It floated toward the ceiling.

The girls applauded and the world was good.

When you're starving, or drinking and starving, there's hardly anything to do but make love, if you have anybody to make love to. I had Claudia and Claudia never said no and we didn't have anything else to do. Besides, she was one of the best lays I'd ever had. We were on the wine, heavy. Up in a fourth floor apartment. My unemployment insurance had run out some time back and the rent was up; everything was ended. We took long walks at night, and stole cigarettes from cars with open windows. We read old newspapers we found in the trash (we were always particularly delighted to find the Sunday funnies) and also picked up empty bottles for deposit money. Everything had been hocked but somehow sometimes money showed. But we knew it would finally end and it was sad because our love was good and our sex was good.

Of course, somebody would take care of Claudia. I knew that. I was the one who was finished.

"Why don't you get the hell out now?" I asked her. "I'm a bum. I can't face life. I don't fit. Life scares me. I'm a coward, a misfit. Jesus Christ, *look* at me. Who would ever hire a guy who looks like me?"

"I can't leave you, Hank. I've been closer to you than any man I've ever known. You'll make it as a writer someday, you'll see."

"A writer? What'll I write on? Toilet paper? And we're almost out of that."

The hock ticket on the typewriter had long expired. We'd hocked it while I was on unemployment and couldn't even get it out then.

"Look, Hank, those people out there are just a bunch of damn fools, subnormals, and madmen. Don't get so down on yourself."

"But, baby, those damn fools and madmen control us."

"Yeah, I know. How about some more hotcakes?"

"Well, since that's all there is on the menu."

We were down to that. Flour and water. We didn't have any grease. And no grass. The flour and water burned a bit and it was like a tasteless cracker, but when you get hungry enough, even that filled some kind of hole. It made you think that you weren't right up against the wall, even if you were.

We ate and then had a couple of stolen cigarettes and started in on the wine. We heard footsteps and we were very still. We were afraid it was Mrs. Dennis, the manager. I'd told her that I was expecting my income tax refund any day. But the days had gone on and on, and of course I'd already gotten my check some time back.

I was getting good at stealing wine. I stole it from the bargain basket near the register when Dick turned his back. I just stood around in there conversing with him and waiting, until a customer came in.

"Somebody's stealing my wine," he'd tell me the next time he saw me.

"How?" I asked.

"That basket there."

"Why don't you wire the bottles in?"

"That's a good idea."

Dick wired the bottles in. When he turned his back I unwired the bottles and stole them anyhow.

So, that day, we started on the wine. We had nothing but time. Claudia had fine legs and a great ass; a bit of flab on the belly—in spite of our starvation diet—but when we got to working on the bed, it was hardly noticeable.

I got up and walked over to her chair, kissed her hard. She had to hold one hand out, the one with the wine glass in it, holding it out there so the wine wouldn't spill. It felt like rape. I worked her over good, mauling her breasts. Then I backed off, with something in front.

"You bastard, you almost made me spill my wine!"

"What?" I laughed.

"That's not funny," she said.

I got up and pulled her out of the chair, felt up her legs, pulled her skirt up around her waist, spun her so her back was facing the mirror, then I pawed her butt as I bent her backwards, kissing her.

I watched it in the mirror.

"Stop it!" she said.

"Why?"

"You're watching me in the mirror, that's why!"

"What's wrong with that?"

"I just don't think it's right."

"How you going to think? We're not married; is that supposed to be right? Right's no good. Right means doing dull things."

"I just don't like that mirror!"

I threw her on the bed, crawled on top of her.

"Damn bitch! I'll show you a salami like you never saw before!"

Then Claudia laughed. "I know all about your salami."

"Damn bitch!" I pulled her dress up, ripped her pants off. Her tongue entered my mouth and I sucked at it as I entered.

Each time was a new time; that's the way it was with a good woman. While we were eating and as much as we were drinking and as much as we were making love, we usually lasted quite some time. And when we made it, together, there was never anything quite like it.

We made it again. All the walls in that cheap apartment house shook with sound and passion. There had been some complaints from the other tenants. A guy I knew pretty good, down the hall, Lou, asked me one day, "What the hell's going on down there three or four times a day and night?"

"We're making love."

"Love? It sounds more like somebody getting murdered."

"I know. There have been complaints from the tenants. All the way down to the first floor."

(We were on the fourth, as I told you.)

"You guys must really get some positions."

"No, not really. Seven or eight different ways which we worked out, mostly by accident and luck."

"All right. It still sounds like two or three people getting murdered."

Those damned tenants were jealous, that's all.

It's difficult to explain, and love's a bad word but I do suppose that in the sense of the word, we were in love. There's little doubt in my mind that you can never really know a woman until you have sex with her, or she with you. And the more you have, the better you know each other. And if it keeps working, that's love. And if it stops working, then it's what most other people have. I'm not saying sex is love; it can possibly be hate. But when the sex is good, other things enter—the color of a dress, the freckle on an arm, various attachments and detachments; memories, the laughter of it, and the pain.

One can get fond of many things besides the sex but it's best if the sex is there somehow, and with Claudia and me, it damn well was.

And we knew damned well it would end and it did.

Mrs. Dennis knocked. I opened the door.

"Mr. Bukowski?"

"Yes."

"The owners have asked me to tell you and your—wife to move. I'm sorry."

"I'm sure the check will arrive any day now."

"The owners say they'd rather not wait for the check. They'd rather you move."

"When?"

"Six o'clock. Tonight."

"Six o'clock?"

"Yes."

I closed the door.

"You heard?"

"Yes," said Claudia.

It was 4:30.

"It's over," I said. "We're finished."

"Yes, I know."

"Damn it, why can't I be a tractor operator or a typesetter or an insurance salesman or a bus driver like other men? What's wrong with me? I'm crazy. Now it's over; the fools, the fools will own you, sticking their stupid cocks in you. I hate it! O, Jesus Jesus Jesus. . . ."

I threw myself on the bed.

"Hank?" I heard her.

"Yes?"

"I don't want to sound corny or cold, but I guess we won't be seeing each other for a while, and—"

"Yes?"

"We don't have much time." She laughed. "Well, I mean, how about one more time?"

I laughed too, and she got down on the bed with me. It was really funny—we were both crying like babies as we went at it. Call it love. Who knows?

When we made that last one, everybody in the apartment knew it and maybe some of the people in some of the other apartments too.

Claudia had a suitcase and I sat and watched her pack. I gave her my alarm clock. That's all I had left. I suppose I was in shock. Her body, her body and her mind and all of her were going someplace else, to somebody else. She wasn't crying but her face told it all. She was on the cross. I looked away.

Then we had to walk all the way because we didn't have bus fare.

"He's not too bad," Claudia said. "I don't like him but he's not too bad."

"At least he'll be able to feed you and buy you some clothes."

"What are you going to do?"

"Try to get straight. If I can just get a dishwasher's job, I'll be happy."

"I'm going to be worried about you, plenty," she said.

"And I'm going to be worried about you," I said.

"We'd make a great comedy team."

"Yeah," I said, "the laughs are killing me."

"He's a salesman," she said, "a big fat guy but not much up in front, thank god."

"How do you know he'll let you in? Maybe he has a woman."

"He'll let me in. He can't get a woman."

"And I can't keep one."

"Hank?"

"Yes?"

"When you get straight, let me know. I'll come running."

"Sure. Thank you."

"You won't forget me, will you Hank?"

I dropped the suitcase and grabbed her by both arms. "Goddamn you, you talk that way once more and I'll kill you right here on the street, you understand?"

"I understand, Hank."

We were on Hoover right at the corner of Olympic as we kissed. Two hundred people on their way to work saw us.

We found the apartment house.

"He's on the first floor front. Been there for years."

"I'll wait to see if he lets you in."

"He'll let me in."

"I'll wait."

I opened the apartment house door and put the suitcase in her hand. She sat it down outside the apartment door. I couldn't take another farewell kiss. I stood back by the edge of the closed entrance door.

She looked at me. "Hank," she said.

"No," I said, "I can't take any more. Ring the bell, please ring the bell."

She was going to say I love you, but I saw her tremble all over and then reach toward the bell. I was glad she didn't say I love you. Then she looked at me and gave me one of those little female smiles. She was crying.

"Get straight," she said. "Hurry, hurry, get straight!"

Then she turned and punched the bell. He opened the door.

"Claudia! Great to see you!"

His arms were around her and he was kissing her along the throat. I opened the door, walked out, heard it close. I walked up Hoover and the east along Olympic Boulevard. Skid row was a long walk. Everything was a long walk. I saw the people going by in their cars, headlights on, owning each other, owning what they owned. On that walk east, I don't think I ever hated the world so much. And I don't think I'll ever hate the world that much again, though it's possible.

# I JUST WRITE POETRY SO I CAN GO

# TO BED WITH GIRLS

I had forgotten the suitcase.

"Let's go get the suitcase," I told Jon.

"All right."

We walked back through the sun, which was still plenty warm. When we got to the train station it was closed. It was 5:45 P.M.

"What the hell kind of a town is this?" I asked Jon.

We walked around in back. There was an old Chicano walking around there behind a green wooden gate. Suitcases were everywhere.

"Sir," said Jon, "this man wants to get his suitcase."

The old guy walked up.

"Got your ticket?"

I handed him my baggage ticket with a dollar tucked underneath.

"What's this?" the old Chicano asked.

"For your trouble," I said.

He handed the dollar back.

"We don't take tips."

Then he came back with the suitcase and unlocked the gate and passed it through.

"Thank you," I said.

"It's all right," he said.

We walked back to the street. The suitcase was very heavy because it was filled mostly with my books, and, like a fool, I had brought the hardcover editions. I switched the suitcase from one hand to the other. It was a 7-block walk but I didn't like waiting on buses and if I got a taxi it was too much money for the short haul.

Well, after about 4 blocks, I was wishing I had a drink. Jon said there was a bar a block further down.

When we walked in the entrance way, a Chicano hit a little bell twice. Everybody in the bar stopped talking and looked around. We walked up to the end of the bar, the end away from the door, and I told Jon to order up, it was on me. I left a 5 for the drinks and walked back to the crapper.

I was pissing in the toilet when 2 Mexican-Americans came in and started pissing in the urinal. They were young guys, a little drunk, no, quite drunk. Yes. But I was tired. I looked ahead and pissed.

"HALLOE!"

(Pause.)

"I SAID, 'HALLOE!' WHATSTHEMATTA WITH YOU, YOU DON'T ANSWER!"

I turned.

"Shit, sorry man, I thought you were talking to your friend. Hello, there."

"BULLSHIT!"

"Peace, brothers," I said.

"SHIT!" screamed the little one in the t-shirt, "SHIT!"

They walked out, slamming the door.

I walked out, sat next to Jon, picked up my drink.

"Let's get out of here," I said.

"What's the matter?"

"I'm paying for the sins of my glorious forefathers in American history."

"What happened?"

"Nothing yet. Let's keep it that way."

"A white guy was knifed on the steps last Friday night. But that was late at night. It's only evening now."

"Let's make it," I said. "It's getting dark."

When we got back to the place, I started on the beer. They were used to my ways and knew that before I went to sleep, I would drink 10 beers, 12 beers, 14 beers. Half of their refrigerator was stacked with beer bottles. They even had cigars for me. I took off my shoes, lit up and relaxed for the first time in hours.

Jon looked at me. "You know, Buk, Gene Rumpkin—"

"That guy. Yeah. He put out a bad mag. *Just Lines*. A real atrocity. I wonder what ever happened to him?"

"He's in the English department at UNM."

"Well, that figures."

"What I mean is, I took some of his poems, kind of trying to be nice because he's in the same town, and the poems didn't look *too* bad at first, but now I know they're very bad and it bothers me."

"There, you see—never be kind. Always be a bastard and you'll stay out of such things. Kindness is a bad motive, especially when considering marriage or literature."

I was getting expansive. The beer was opening me up and I was beginning to feel like a depraved G.B. Shaw.

I played with the dogs. There were two of them—full of hair and friskiness. But they were all right: they didn't blame me for being white.

The phone rang. Jon got it. He handed it to me. It was Prof. Steve Rodefer, the guy who had arranged the reading.

"Bukowski?"

"Yeah?"

"The university has decided not to sponsor your reading."

"O.K., Steve, I know how it is. I'll lay around another day and take the train back in."

"No, wait! The reading's still on, same time, same place, but it's being student-sponsored."

"O.K., I'll be there."

"Give me Jon."

I handed the phone to Jon and they talked quite a while.

Jon hung up.

"Steve's a hell of a guy but it's probably going to cost him his job. He's responsible for you and Kandel being here. This town's red hot. The lid's off."

"Yeah," I said.

Lou Webb was already asleep. She was always up early and ran around doing things—hocking brooches and trinkets, calming the landlord, trying to fix meals out of nothing. By 10 P.M. she was done. I missed her company: she was one of the last truly honest and passionate people I knew. . . .

The phone rang again. Jon picked it up.

"Yeah? Yeah? Is that so? You really think so, eh? Well, well, well. Is that right? Oh, yeah? Well what the FUCK was wrong with it? So *you* say. What? All right. . . ."

He turned to me. "It's Rumpkin. He wants to talk with you."

I took the phone. "Hello, Gene."

"Bukowski, you remember me?"

"Yes, you helped edit that horrible magazine *Just Lines*."

"We published you."

"You weren't wrong all the time, just most of the time."

"I didn't think we were that bad."

"Of course you didn't."

"Did you see that poster Jon put out on you? Most of the people in the department felt it distorted your image. Did you see the poster?"

"Yes."

"What did you think of it?"

"I didn't pay it much attention."

"Put Jon back on."

I handed the phone back to Jon. They talked quite a while. I could hear Rumpkin's voice. Gene boy was quite upset. It finally ended. Jon put the phone down.

"He demands his poems back. He says he doesn't want to be in *Outsider 6*."

"Fine. That solves your problem."

"He says he's driving right over to get his poems. I wanted to tell him I'd mail them back but he hung up first."

"Jesus," I said, "it's a hell of a town. The bayonetings, Kandel, all that shit."

"They claim I'm trying to keep you from reading here. Rumpkin said, 'Now that wasn't very smart, mailing those posters to the mayor and the governor.'"

"Why don't they let me worry about that?"

Jon didn't answer. We were sitting there waiting for Mr. Rumpkin. Chicano teenagers walked by and drummed on the windows. The dogs ran up and barked.

"I think the kids rather like us," I said. "They just want us to know we're in their part of town."

"It's the only place we could afford to rent," said Jon.

"They should sense that."

"They do."

We sat up very late waiting for Mr. Rumpkin to come get his poems back. Jon gave up and went to the bedroom and slept. I stayed up another hour, drinking beer and waiting for Mr. Rumpkin. I finally gave up and went to sleep. . . .

It was sometime the next day when a very angry man knocked on the door. I couldn't make out the words. Lou Webb ran and got the poems. Impassionata, Italiano, innocent wonderful Lou.

"Here, here, here's your poems! Listen, Bukowski is in here! Don't you want to say hello to Bukowski?"

He took the poems and leaped into his car and drove swiftly off, away from the poison of us all. I laughed. It was kind of Charlie Chaplin madness without the grace of it.

"Jesus," said Lou, turning toward me, "he wouldn't even say hello to you!"

"Lou," I said, "Mr. Rumpkin and Mr. Bukowski have a perfect understanding of each other."

"To hell with it!" She threw out her arms, beautiful fingers tapering from hell to hell. "I'm going to the POST OFFICE!"

I thought that was an immense statement and applauded accordingly.

We walked across campus where some of the students waited outside *The Kiva*. We walked on in and they followed us in. The place was built like a bullring with the seats rising up around the speaker.

There were no troops. Just young quiet people. I found the crapper and went in and had a pull of scotch. Steve walked in and I gave him the bottle for a pull.

"We about ready?" I asked.

"We might as well start," he said.

We walked out and Steve stood in a thing that looked like a preacher's pulpit. He explained that the university had withdrawn support of the reading and that it was being sponsored by a student fund. He gave some initials which I couldn't make out.

Then a shrink took the pulpit and introduced me. That figures, I thought. I'd once stayed at a shrink's place in Santa Fe. It had been a bad stay. But the shrink spoke as if we were friends. The only thing the shrink had was money. And I mean that was all he had. The shrink talked on and on, trying to steal the show. But the young people were harder to fool than his patients. He was simply dull. Then, he finally stepped down.

"Well, after that," I said, "there's nothing to do but begin reading.

And I don't like that thing," I pointed to the pulpit, "I'm going to read right here."

I took out the pint, had a pull, and began:

*"I think of the little men*
*coming out of the north*
*with rags around their bodies*
*and wanting to kill*
*you.*
*you dead bastards,*
*you have death coming to you. . . ."*

It was, what the pros call, "a responsive audience."

*"I've known some crazy women*
*but the craziest was*
*Annette. . . ."*

I kept the pint out, threw away the bag, set the bottle down, and just drank from the table.

*"the fire engines swing out*
*and the clouds listen to*
*Shostakovich*
*as a woman dumps a bucket of piss*
*into a row of geranium pots. . . ."*

I gave them about 30 minutes, then called for a 5-minute break. I walked out and sat in the audience. There was a guy next to me with a cassette.

"How's it going?" I asked.

"Fine, you're coming through fine."

"Have a drink."

"Sure."

I bummed a cigarette, smoked most of it, and went back. The shrink had left and was not to return.

"All right, let's get it over with," I told the crowd.

*"the pig is fighting for the*
*size of the sun*
*as a thousand zeroes like bees*
*land on my skin and*
*the nomenclature of my screams*
*in a small room. . . ."*

I got away with each poem. The bottle was getting light. I needed more to drink. I cut several poems I had planned on reading and gave them "Something for the Touts," "The Nuns," "The Grocery Clerks and You," then ended up with "Fire Station."

The applause was good, quite.

Look, I thought, we have come through. On student funds.

Steve went to the board and wrote down the address of the Webbs' place.

"There will be a party here," he said.

The crowd worked their way out. A few of them came down and I signed a thing or two. "It's over," I said. "Let's get drunk. Steve, let's get out of here."

We packed into the car and made it back. There was a crowd there when we arrived. We went in. I had stopped off for replenishments but the crowd had brought stuff—there was tequila, wine, bourbon, scotch, beer, and vodka. I drank from all of them. We sat on the rug and drank and talked. I was fairly far out of it by then, but I noticed a well-developed girl sitting next to me. I put my hand around her hip and kissed her. She had this easy smile and one tooth missing, it was very endearing. I couldn't keep away from her. She had long black hair, very long, and was splendidly put together.

"I just write poetry so I can go to bed with girls," I told her. "I'm 50 but I just *love* young pussy!"

She gave me that tooth-missing smile and I kissed her again. . . .

I don't remember much else. I always blackout after I drink quite a bit.

When I awakened I was pressed against some rump and my cock was still in the vagina. (Portrait of the Artist as a Dog.) It was warm in there; it was hot in there. I pulled out.

She had long black hair and was splendidly put together.

I got out of bed and walked around. It was a fairly large house. I looked in one bedroom and there was a kid running around in a crib. Then a boy of about 3 ran up, dressed in pajamas. I patted his head, looked at the clock: 10:30. It was late morning. I walked over and saw a letter. It was addressed to a "Mrs. Kathy W." I walked into the bedroom.

"Hey, Kathy," I said, "do you know there are kids running around all over this place?"

"Oh, Hank, I want to sleep. Make yourself some coffee until I pull around."

I walked out, put on some coffee. Then I sterilized a bottle and put some milk in it and gave it to the kid in the crib. He went right to it. Then I got the other kid out of his pajamas, dressed him in an orange t-shirt with black stripes, light blue pants, and orange tennis shoes. He looked like a Van Gogh ready to chase ravens. But he liked me. He stood there smiling at me. I twisted his nose, pulled his ears, and drank the coffee. Went to the bedroom. Van Gogh followed me.

"Let me use your phone, Kathy."

"Sure."

I phoned a Yellow Cab, went back in, and held her hand, squeezed it. She squeezed back.

"Listen, I've got to leave. I'll see you later."

"Sure, Hank."

I took the cab back across town. . . .

I had to stay in town until Monday to get my check. For $225, it was worth the wait. I drank beer all day, then that night the phone rang. It was Steve. He was coming over with Gregory Corso.

Webb looked at me. "Man, he's a wild guy. Wait'll you see him."

"O.K.," I said.

"Ginsberg came by earlier this year, but you ought to meet Corso. Only thing is, he's stopped writing. You haven't."

"Not yet," I said.

We sat around waiting for Steve and Corso. I was a little nervous about meeting Corso. Although I was an older man, I had not begun writing until I was 35, and Corso's name had been household for some time—like Burroughs, Ginsberg, all that gang. Not that their writing overimpressed me; nobody's does. It was only that you got used to names and accepted them as part of something.

Corso and Steve showed. Corso was dressed in tight-fitting white pants with little rivulets running down the sides. He had an opaque hair-do, rather fluffy; a strange-looking nose jutted out, all this mixed with a fighting chin and eyes that looked, looked, looked and a mouth that was busy. His accent was English crossed with Brooklyn and he had a bottle of wine in his hand. He was high.

We shook hands.

"I am your peer," he said.

"I know, Greg."

"I am your peer, I want you to remember that."

"Yes, Gregory."

There was something likeable about him, something quite likeable about him, and I was glad it was there. We sat and Gregory talked and we listened. He was not as wild as advertised. High, of course, but in definite control . . . that night, anyway. He liked rings and trinkets and asked why I didn't wear any. He had something dangling from a thong about his throat, which he explained to us.

"Why don't you wear anything?" he asked.

"I don't know. I just don't think about it."

Then he got onto astrology, drawing things on pieces of paper. Then here came the tarot cards. He read Lou. Then he tried me. I pulled out the cards. As he turned them over, they all seemed to state power. Then, he said, before turning up the last card, "You see, it all leads up to this, which is the final force. . . ."

He turned up the card. It said: THE EMPEROR. Greg was a very likeable guy.

"But remember this, I am still your peer."

"O.K."

"I'm sorry I couldn't make your reading."

"It's O.K."

Not much happened the rest of the night. When they left, Jon said to me: "I never saw him so subdued."

"I liked him."

"Did you?"

"Yeah." . . . . .

I left town 2 days later. Jon and Lou, Steve and Greg sat in a skid row bar with me across from the Albuquerque train station. It was really a low-life place. I had sat in a bar like that in Philly for 5 years. Memories: I went into the crapper and heaved. Corso was wandering around looking at people. I bought the first round. Five drinks. A tequila, a scotch, a coke for Lou, a beer, and a mixed drink of some sort. The charge was a dollar thirty-five. You could drink in there for a week for ten dollars. If you didn't get killed first. Two women who had been around awhile waited on bar. They were big and expressionless. Put together they must have weighed 600 pounds. Steve got the next round. It was getting close to train time.

"I don't care for the fond farewell scene," I said. "Why don't you people just let me go across the street and into the train station? Let's say goodbye here."

I shook hands with Steve. Corso came up and kissed me on the cheek. That took some guts. Then he walked out.

Jon and Lou walked into the train station with me. I paid a couple of bucks extra to get on the Chief. The El Capitan was just too damned slow. The Chief was too slow. Next haul anywhere, I was flying, like anybody else. We found the train car. Lou kissed me goodbye. I told Jon good luck with Henry Miller. Then I climbed on in. After the conductor hung my ticket up over the seat I got up and asked the porter where the bar car was.

The train was moving. The train was moving toward Los Angeles. I found the bar car, sat down, and had a scotch and water. The windows were nice and there weren't people climbing around in front of you.

Then I noticed a young lady in a tight yellow dress staring at me from the next table. I wonder what she wants? I thought. I looked down into my drink. When I looked up she was still staring. She smiled.

"I was at your reading," she said.

"Oh?"

"I liked it very much. It's a long trip to Los Angeles. You mind if I come over?"

"I'd hardly mind at all."

She brought her drink over. I didn't know what it was. I'd find out when I ordered the next one. She was a juicy young thing. I imagined myself mounting her, legs up in the air.

"My name's Susie," she said.

"My name's. . . ."

"I know your name."

"Oh, yeah . . . sorry. . . ."

I reached out and patted her hand. I felt one of her knees against mine.

"I liked the poem about the beautiful actress who was decapitated in the car crash."

"Thank you, Susie."

"Life can end so suddenly. We never make the most of our moments. It's so sad."

I pressed harder against her knee.

"What're you drinking?" I asked her.

"I'll drink what you are."

"I'm drinking Life," I said, and then laughed: "That was corny, wasn't it?"

"No, it wasn't," she said.

We leaned close together. Her lips were a quarter inch from mine.

The University of New Mexico, I thought, has been honored by an old wolf.

I had 15 hours to score. There was no way I coud miss. We kissed and I ordered two more drinks.

# THE HOUSE OF HORRORS

Talking about writing is like talking about love or love-making or love-living: too much talk about it can kill it off. Without seeking them out, I have, unfortunately, met many writers, both successful and unsuccessful—I mean at their craft. As human beings they are a bad lot, a distasteful lot, bitchy, self-centered, vicious. One thing they almost all have in common: they each believe their work great, perhaps the greatest. If they become successful they accept it as their normal due. If they fail, they feel that the editors and the publishers and the gods are against them. And, it's true that many bad writers are pushed and manipulated to the top, whatever the reason may be. It's also true that many great writers have starved to death, or almost starved to death, or killed themselves or gone mad, and so forth, and were later discovered as fine (though dead) talents. This historical fact gives heart to the writer who is truly bad. He likes to imagine that his (her) failure is caused by any number of things besides simply being a poor talent. Well, so we have all that.

Also, when I think of the writers that I know, mostly poets, I notice that they are supported by others—wives, mostly mothers carry the economic load of those that I know. And they are quite comfortable with TV sets, loaded refrigerators, and apartments or houses by the sea—mostly at Venice and Santa Monica, and they sun themselves in the day, feeling tragic, these male friends (?) of mine and then at night, perhaps a bottle of wine and a watercress sandwich, followed by a wailing letter of their penury and greatness to somebody somewhere. Anything but writing, working, getting it *done*, getting the word down. Well, I guess it beats working a punch press. The wives and the mothers will work the punch press, don't worry about that. And the poets, having not lived in the outside world in reality, they will then really have nothing to write about, which they do with great ego and much dullness.

It is almost impossible to write about writing. I remember once after giving a poetry reading I asked the students, "Any questions?" One of them asked me, "Why do you write?" And I answered, "Why do you wear that red shirt?"

Being a writer is damning and difficult. If you have a talent it can leave you forever while you are sleeping one night. What keeps you going in the game is not easy to answer. Too much success is destructive; no success at all is destructive. A little rejection is good for the soul but total rejection creates cranks and madmen, rapists, sadists, drunkards, and wife-beaters. Just as too much success does.

I too have been misled by the Romantic concept of writing. As a youth I saw too many movies of the great Artist, and the writer was always some tragic and very interesting chap with a fine goatee, blazing eyes, and inner truths springing to his tongue continually. What a way to be, I thought, ah. But it isn't so. The best writers that I know talk very little, I mean those who are doing the good writing. In fact, there is nothing duller than a good writer. In a crowd or even with one other person, he is always busy (subconsciously) *recording* every goddamned thing. He is not interested in speechmaking or being the Life of the Party. He is greedy; he saves his juices for the typewriter. You can talk away inspiration, you can destroy god-given genius with your mouth. Energy will only spread so far. I too am greedy. One must be. The only juices that can be given up, the only time that can simply be given away is the time for Love. Love gives strength; it breaks down inbred hatreds and prejudices. It makes the writing more full. But all other things must be saved for the work. A writer should do most of his reading while he is young; as he starts to form, reading becomes destructive—it takes the needle off the record.

A writer must keep performing, hitting the high mark, or he

is down on skid row. And there's no way back up. For after some years of writing, the soul, the person, the creature becomes useless to operate in any other capacity. He is unemployable. He is a bird in a land of cats. I'd never advise anybody to become a writer, only if writing is the only thing which keeps you from going insane. Then, perhaps, it's worth it.

# UNTITLED ESSAY ON D.A. LEVY

Why does a man destroy himself or what destroys him? I would have to judge that suicide is mostly the tool of the thinking man. The right to suicide should be the same as the right to love. The former certainly has more lasting qualities, which, in a sense, gives it more nobility. One suicide, many loves. One levy, many levies. What destroyed him? I didn't know him that well. Many men are killed and still living. Only a living man can die. Most funerals are the dead burying the dead. levy buried himself. From scarce readings of his works I would have to guess that levy had yet to round out into a plausible talent. What killed him is the same thing which keeps us awake nights, is the same thing that grips our guts when we pass face after face upon the streets; what killed him is the same thing we love and hate, the same thing we eat, the same thing we fear. What killed him was life and lack of life; what killed him were cops, friends, poetry, Cleveland . . . belief and betrayal—this and that: a worm in an apple, a look in an eye . . . poetry, poetry, cops, and friends . . . maybe a woman, maybe a sonnet, maybe lack of proper diet.

A poet is simply too sharpened. The nature of his art makes survival almost impossible. levy printed some of my things in the *M. Quarterly* [*Marrahwannah Quarterly*], and his notes were always short but lively. The *M. Quarterly* was badly printed (mimeoed) and badly bound but still had the flavor of levy. Perhaps he was also badly printed and badly bound. They didn't give him much chance. Perhaps he didn't give himself much chance. Men have been killed for more and for less. levy also published a long poem of mine called *The Genius of the Crowd*, a nicely-done job using cut-up envelopes as pages. He wrote me, "You've said it here, you've said it almost all. And they'll read it and still not know." It was not long after, it seemed, that he was dead. I must guess that Kent State is certainly aware of death. Death keeps coming and running, one hell of a Sammy. It was last night that Louise Webb phoned me that Jon Webb had died. Jon Webb, editor of *The Outsider* and publisher of 2 of my books, and a friend and a beer-drinking companion. I was bombed when Lou phoned (other troubles), and here was death again and I walked about the room with a Coleman burner on and symphony music on the radio, and I thought, no, goddamn it, I was supposed to go first, I am always talking about suicide and death, and here I am, and hardly feeling fine, and today the letter came asking me to talk about levy. I can't say anymore except that I get angry and sad when a good man dies or is killed, and that isn't reasonable because we're born to die, and maybe that helps make poetry and anger and sadness. The music plays; I smoke half a cigar stub, there's a beer. . . . levy, levy, levy, you're gone. jon, jon, jon, you're gone too. My heart heaves out the belly of itself.

# HENRY MILLER LIVES IN PACIFIC PALISADES AND I LIVE ON SKID ROW, STILL WRITING ABOUT SEX

If you think getting off one of these stories once or twice a week is an easy way of paying the rent, you're insane. It worries me. "Listen," I asked this woman I used to sleep with, "what am I going to write about when sex dries up inside of me?" "You'll be a writer for the People, you'll be a writer for the betterment of the Masses, that's what you'll be."

"Listen," I said, "when are you going home? I knew there was some reason I stopped sleeping with you."

Right now as I sit here typing, my girlfriend sits behind me writing her mother: "Dear Mother: Bukowski wishes to thank you for borning me. He claims I am the best piece of ass he ever had. . . ." She laughs, types some more: "He says that he has given up on the landlady and even the landlady's daughter and sends you his fond regards. . . ."

We have just finished making love and it was plenty good, but we do have our problems—every time we get into 69, we are interrupted. Today we were working away when somebody knocked on the door. We had to stop. I got up and looked. It was the landlady with two dresses for my seven-year-old daughter who lives in Santa Monica. The time before that we were into 69 and the phone rang. It was somebody telling me that Tiny Tim's son was on TV right then. Another time we were into it, and the door was open, unlocked I mean, and this little black kid from the neighborhood walked in. "What the hell do you want, man?" I asked. "You got any empty bottles?" he asked me.

To me, sex is good and necessary—like food, sleep, music,

creation, things you need to live well with—but it can get humorous. In fact, I was just going to tell you how humorous it can get but the phone just rang, a collect call from Florida. I took it. A girl. She had just moved out there. "I'm pregnant," she said. "I don't want the baby." "Abort it, then," I said. "Abortion's only legal in California and New York; can you lend me some money?" "Hate to be a dog, kid, but I can't help you." As I said, sex is funny. I read in the paper today that a woman was convicted under a 1868 Florida law and faces twenty years for having an abortion.

Oh, ha ha ha.

I remember this one lady I shacked with for seven years. She had some very good qualities but she had one particularly bad one. I'd be asleep and this hand would come over and grab my penis and almost yank it from my body. Let me tell you, it is not a very good way to be awakened.

After I had finished screaming and pulling her hand off my penis I'd ask the lady, "Good Lord, woman, why did you do that?"

"You were playing with yourself, I caught you, I caught you!"

"You're crazy! It's soft. Listen, you almost ripped that thing from my body. I've only got one of them, you know. . . ."

She got on a streak and did it seven or eight times within two weeks. I learned to sleep on my belly. I was giving her more than enough sex; if I wanted to masturbate in between times, I considered it my right. This lady had another bad habit. She'd walk into the bathroom and scream.

"What's the matter, babe?" I'd ask.

"Look at that tub!" she'd say.

"What's wrong with it?"

"Just look, look, you beast!"

"I'm looking."

"Can't you see it? Stuck to the edges? You've been playing with yourself in the bathtub!"

"You're crazy."

"Just look at it! Can't you see it hanging there?"

"Where?" I'd ask.

"There! There!"

"Now look," I'd ask, "when I put my finger there you tell me if that's what you mean? Is it there?"

"No, further down. To the left."

"Here?"

"No, just a bit further down."

"Here?"

"Yes, there. You're touching it now."

"There's nothing there."

"Yes, there is. You're touching it, you're touching it!"

She had this bathtub complex. And here we were going through it five times a week. I will admit I am oversexed but I didn't use that bathtub as much as she claimed I did. Many of those little hangings were rough lumps in the enamel.

Then there's this lady I know. She lives in a new apartment with swimming pool. It's a nice swimming pool. But she can't use it now, she tells me. You see, there is this fourteen-year-old girl who is making love to these four or five guys ranging from thirteen to fifteen years old. They make love when her mother is at work. Then they all go out and swim in the pool; they wash off in the pool. "I can't swim in there," she tells me, "all that come floating around." The weather has been quite hot, too, going up to 115 degrees. There isn't any lifeguard there but outside of that, it's a very nice pool. I checked the water for sperm but I really couldn't see any. Of course this lady is very afraid of sperm and I suppose there might be some reality in her thinking. She said her best girlfriend once got pregnant by getting into a bathtub and bathing after a male had masturbated in the same tub. You see I am not the only one who uses a bathtub for more than bathing.

I get letters in the mail from people saying that I am surely one of the greatest writers around. I don't get too many of these letters because most people don't know where I live. But I wonder about these letters and these people and wonder if they ever read *all* the things I write, things like I am writing now, for instance. Surely I am vulgar, obscene, and write much too obviously. I would suppose that anybody could yammer on about sex and seem fairly interesting. If I tried to write on ecology or world affairs or the Meaning of Life, I would be a very dull fellow indeed. I am clever and just work in all this dirty stuff. Now, let's see, this piece isn't long enough, let's see if I can get more and more into my dirty mind.

You know, I wonder if Henry Miller is really all that good? I've tried to read his books on cross-country buses but when he gets into those long parts in between sex he is a very dull fellow indeed. On cross-country buses I usually have to put down my Henry Miller and try to find somebody's legs to look up, preferably female. I am a fine one for looking up legs of ladies on cross-country buses . . . city buses, bus stop benches. . . . I must thank myself for buses. I've gotten hotter on and around buses than anywhere else. I often get hotter looking up legs than I do making love to the average woman.

I think I got hotter on a bus than I ever did in my life. I was a young man, poor, and not getting much and I was on this cross-country bus one night alone in my seat and this young girl got on. Well, you know how it is, you pretend you are sleeping. They turn the lights out. I have never been a bold one but after a while I felt this girl's leg touching mine ever so slightly. She'll pull away, I thought, but she didn't pull away. She gradually put on more pressure, so slowly that it was hardly noticeable. I put on a little pressure myself. We were both sitting, seats back, and stretched facing upwards. Our flanks, our legs were pressed together from ankle to butt. There wasn't a sound. People snored. I got hotter and hotter. It was a hotness that flowed through my entire body, never had I been so heated. The pressure increased. Why doesn't she speak? I thought. Then we began moving our legs, rubbing them against each other in the silence and darkness. It was gross and mad, indecent. It went on and on and on, this rubbing and twisting . . . for hours. Then the bus would make a stop, the lights would go on and I would sit up and rub my eyes as if I had been asleep. I didn't look at the girl, she didn't look at me. She got up first and went in for her hamburger and coffee. I had to wait for my erection to go down. Then I got up and went in, sitting far away from the girl. After eating we re-entered the bus and sat there staring straight forward. As soon as the lights went out we began again. Pressing and rubbing. I tell you that it is hard to imagine the intense hotness I felt. It was all so deliciously rotten and stupid and fearful, riding along there rubbing together and not speaking. Then into another café, sitting apart, then getting back on that bus again. We never kissed, never spoke.

A more intelligent and less thwarted man than myself would have gotten acquainted, would have gotten addresses, phone numbers, names, perhaps would have gotten off with the girl and gone to a motel with her. But I was young and had lived a strange and bitter, involuted life. I couldn't break through. I would break through now because I've learned certain ways through the years. But you see, I had all the luck then. For instance, I remember that ride and that girl much better than many of the women I have had sexual intercourse with and have long since forgotten. I remember the intense heat and I remember her leaving, getting off at her stop somewhere in the early morning before the sun came up. I watched her outside as she got her suitcase. I saw her for the first time, really, and she was a handsome girl, nicely built, nicely dressed, and intelligent-looking.

I rode cross-country buses a great deal when I was young. There was something that I needed, *constant* movement, somehow I needed this constant movement to survive what was happening to me inside and what the world was doing to me. I even came up with the theory that I might live on buses forever. But, of course, there were hindrances—lack of income, and I couldn't sleep on buses, and they made me constipated, as well as hot.

I had a similar experience with another girl soon after but I began a conversation which led to kissing and an exchange of information. She said she wanted to study to be a dancer but her parents wouldn't let her. I said, "Ah, that's too bad." And we rode along, kissing and friendly in the dark, and we ate and talked together and some of the heat vanished. It was not nearly as sneaky and dirty and foolish as the other. The girl even asked me to get off with her at her stop, which was in the middle of a plain in nowhere. It was very dark and empty out there. "Get out here?" I asked.

"Yes, my parents live in a farmhouse here. I want to introduce you. You can live with us."

"What?" I asked. "Your father might beat me up."

I wasn't so much afraid of that as the fact that her father might put me to work on his farm and work all the soul out of me. Then I wouldn't be the great and dirty writer that I am now.

I watched her walk away in the moonlight. There was a certain amount of sadness on my part. But it did look lonely out there. It's good we did all that talking and kissing or I might have gotten off with her, and I'd be raising corn now and killing hogs. There you go. . . .

Writing stories about sex, humorously or otherwise, has had its effects upon my life. I suffer for my writing. Once in my early twenties, having come back home from the bum (and being charged room and board), I was coming down the hill, intoxicated, when my mother leaped out from behind a tree.

"What the hell's wrong, old woman?" I asked.

"It's your father, it's your father!"

"Yeah? Whatsamatta?"

"He found your stories, he read your stories!"

"He shouldn't have gone poking around my suitcase."

"He's in a rage, your stories infuriated him. Don't go back, he'll kill you, he'll kill you!"

"I'll kick his goddamned ass! I've done it before."

"Please don't go back. He's thrown all your stories and clothes out on the lawn. I've never seen him so angry!"

"I'm going back and bust him up. Anything I hate, it's these literary critics."

"No, no, my son! Here, I'll give you ten dollars not to go back. Please take this ten."

"Okay, I won't go back if you make it a twenty."

"All right, my son, here's a twenty."

I put the bill in my front pocket and walked on down the hill. My shirts, pants, stockings, shorts, comb and brush, all the pages of my writings were spread across the front lawn. I was writing about sex then too. The wind had blown the pages of my stories all across the lawn and into the street and across the neighbors' lawns. My suitcase was out there, too, thrown open. I walked about gathering my clothing and things, putting them into the suitcase. I picked up most of the pages of my writing except those in the street and on the neighbors' lawns. I knew that I had plenty more of those good stories in me. My father watched me from behind a drape. I took my suitcase up the hill and waited for a streetcar. I got a place at Third and Flower, a small dirty room full of roaches and life and romance and freedom, and I went outside and sat in a cheap bar and drank for a few hours, then I got a bottle of wine and went back to my room with it and sat in bed with it and drank it in the dark. My father was a fool; how had he ever bred such a brilliant son? . . .

This writing of sex, it has cost me women too. It cost me the mother of my only child. I went to New Orleans for four weeks at one time. It was a most pleasant stay with the great editor Jon Edgar Webb and his wife. We had some fine nights on the town but I didn't live with the Webbs. I had a place around the corner. Well, never mind. I got back to Los Angeles. The mother and baby were waiting for me as I came up in the taxicab. Everything was all right.

Then it was two weeks later. I came in one day. The lady was all packed. We hadn't had an argument. It appeared to be the end. Well, I thought (being a male ch.p.), that's women. But what it was, I didn't find out until three or four years later when the lady happened by for her child support.

"I read all those stories you wrote after you came back from New Orleans that time."

"Which time? I've been there three four or five times."

"That time you stayed four weeks, that time you went to see the Webbs."

"Oh, that time. . . ."

"Yes, that time."

"You read my stories? Did you like my stories?"

"It was about you climbing in and out of bed with those women."

"I write fiction, woman."

"They sounded real."

"That's my talent."

"Your talent is climbing into bed with women. How about that story about the fat woman who burned the pot of strawberry jam?"

"That was a good story. She burned that jam. Boy, what a stink that was!"

"I mean, you went to bed with her, didn't you?"

"Listen, my bed was right by the doorway where she went in and out. She had to go right past me when she went to bed. She cooked for me, she gave me a beer, we watched TV together. It was all free. She was a good woman."

"So you went to bed with her?"

"It's always best for a writer to really experience his material."

"You sonofabitch, and here I was sitting with a three-month-old baby of yours."

"Sure; I went to bed with *you*."

"That one with the harelip. The one where you both sat in the bathtub drunk and urinating together, laughing . . . I suppose that was fiction?"

"Is that why you left me all those years back? Reading those stories?"

"You'll never keep a woman, Bukowski."

All right, the moral is you've got to have morals. And write dull stories about the Betterment of Man. I'm for the Betterment of Man but I'll be damned if I'm going to sit around writing stories to aid the situation. When Man gets better there will still be sex around, humorous and the other kind. Besides, there's a certain freedom in being hated for your work. They'll never have me sitting in the May Company basement autographing my books for old ladies. In fact, I'll be lucky to be rid of this story. Because I don't always treat sex with its proper reverence.

Sherman said war was hell, but sex can be hell too. I suppose it's all the way you work with it or don't work with it. I've gotten into many beds and lived many years in order to do research for you people. Don't expect me to retreat now, lie down, and be quiet about it. There's such a thing as love, too. I love to write these dirty stories and you love to read them and hate me for it. Regard the ultimate, go fishing, attend party meetings, and don't burn the strawberry jam.

# A FOREWORD TO THESE POEMS

from *ANTHOLOGY OF L.A. POETS* (1972)
ed. by Charles Bukowski, Neeli Cherry, and Paul Vangelisti

I was born in 1920 and brought to this city (Los Angeles) at the age of 2 and have lived most of my life here. I feel that I am qualified enough to speak of this city and, perhaps, its poets, and, perhaps, upon poetry.

There have certainly been enough anthologies and there are too many poets and few enough readers—the fault, I believe, of the poets. Poetry has long been an in-game, a snob game, a game of puzzles and incantations. It still is, and most of its practitioners operate comfortably as professors in our safe and stale universities. We have a professor or 2 or 3 in this book—exceptions, believe us.

That poets can only live and produce in certain cities—New York, San Francisco, Paris, or that these cities have more ability to sustain, accent, and enliven poetry—is just another order of garbage to be fed to the hogs. It is time we brought poetry down to the ground and that the best of it might be given credit for existing wherever it exists—for instance, here in Los Angeles.

You know, I can't think of another city that takes more mockery than Los Angeles. It is the unloved city, it is the target. We contain Hollywood—and in a sense, Disneyland, Knott's Berry Farm. . . . We are corn. We are mistakes. We are tourists. We are the lonely drunks of a Saturday night sitting for hours over warming beer, watching nudie dancers we can never possess.

Los Angeles is also Main Street and E. 5th and East L.A. and Watts. Los Angeles has its poor and Los Angeles has its real, and Los Angeles has its poets, some of them pretty damned good. We'd like to think that we have gathered most of the pretty damned good ones here in this book. Of course, somebody is going to holler. That's one of the reasons we put this book together: to hear some hollering. Los Angeles is also Pasadena, Long Beach, Irvine—anyplace you get to within an hour drive or two. Technically, no; spiritually, yes. We have included 2 or 3 "spiritual yeses."

I think it's important to know that a writer can live and die anywhere. I think it's important to know that a writer can live in Los Angeles for a lifetime without ever having visited Grauman's Chinese or The Wax Museum or Barney's Beanery or Disneyland, or without ever having attended a Tournament of Roses Parade. I think that it is important to know that man or woman, writer or not, can find more isolation in Los Angeles than in Boise, Idaho. Or, all things being fair, he can with a telephone (if he has a telephone) have 19 people over drinking and talking with him within an hour and a half. I have bummed the cities and I know this—the great facility of Los Angeles is that one can be alone if he wishes or he can be in a crowd if he wishes. No other city seems to allow this easy double choice as well. This is a fairly wonderful miracle, especially if one is a writer.

Cities are no more than dwellings, places of business, streets, cars, people—people set down somewhere into all the agony and trouble and love and frustration and death and dullness and treachery and hope that they can get into. I must admit that I have gained a love for Los Angeles that forces me again and again to return to it once I have left. Someday there will even be songs about Los Angeles if the smog doesn't get us first.

The true Angelo also has a certain sophistication—he minds his own damned business. This is often mistaken for coldness but if you have ever lived in New York City or Chicago, you know what coldness is.

It's hard to find good poets anywhere. Our search here hasn't been easy. Very little good poetry is being written anywhere. Yet there are people, old and young, male and female, who have been doing it quietly—if a bit desperately—here in L.A. We'd like to think that we have chosen the best. But mistakes are made; omissions are easy. This isn't a bible, it's a tentative gathering. It's a city of poets and here are some of them. I think you'll find power here, and clarity and humor, and feeling enough.

Now let the hollerers holler.

See you at ZODY'S.

# THE OUTSIDER

As I sit here to write this, I have these things in front of me: *The Outsider* magazine 1, 2, 3, issue 4-5, and two books: *It Catches My Heart in Its Hands* and *Crucifix in a Deathhand*. It is a cold Los Angeles afternoon; I sit among these high-rise apts., wondering when they will raze this last skidrow court on DeLongpre Ave. The books and magazines sit to my right and I have just washed my shorts and stockings and they sit on a rope over the gas heater. So? I would have to say, that in the short time that it existed, *The Outsider* made more of a landing upon our literature than any other magazine. Perhaps because Jon and Louise selected and then *printed* their own selections; perhaps it did add a dimension. Of course, selectivity had much to do with it, and their poverty had something to do with it, and their hard luck and their eccentricity, their genius. . . . I, perhaps, knew them better than anybody, and I would like to tell you a bit about them, how they lived, how I lived with them, how I saw it work.

Let's look at *The Outsider* #1. Gypsy Lou is on the cover. There are names here—Sinclair Beiles, Corso, Di Prima, Snyder, Charles Olson, Ginsberg, Langston Hughes, Sorrentino, Lowenfels, Ferlinghetti, Creeley, McClure, Henry Miller, LeRoi Jones, Burroughs, Kay Boyle, Paul Blackburn, so forth. . . . Jon told me later that the known writers had tried to place rejected and stale work upon him and that he had to keep insisting to get a vigorous and fresh work. Too many magazines simply print names without content. In *The Outsider* the work is good, plenty, and there are photos of the writers, and in the back, advertisements for the now defunct littles: *statements, Chicago Choice, Between Worlds, Kulchur, Nomad, Agenda, outburst, Yugen, Two Cities, Satis, Big Table.* . . .

*Outsider* #2 has Gypsy Lou again on the cover. There are also a couple of jazz men working out. As with the first issue, this issue again came out in New Orleans. Both of these numbers were run off by a small hand-operated press at the expense of much labor and agony. There is less emphasis on names in this issue, although there is Genet, Burroughs, Nemerov, Corso, Kerouac, Henry Miller. Some of this issue is taken up by a jazz documentary with photos and comments. Also there are some black and write reprints of Patchen drawings. Since much of Patchen's warmth is in his child's use of color, it does seem a shame, but even in black and white the drawings are warm and Patchen. On the first page is a reproduction of a New Orleans building. And there just aren't any buildings like those old French Quarter rusty iron railing, swaying, rat- and roach-infested buildings. Underneath is this interesting note: "In the building on the left above the renowned *Double Dealer*, which helped introduce Hemingway, Faulkner & Sherwood Anderson to a world unlike today's, was first published in 1921. In building on r . . . in a room Whitman wrote in, *The Outsider* was born in 1961." There are some Henry Miller, W. Lowenfels letters perhaps not as interesting as they should be. *The Outsider* made some mistakes. The jazz section, too, seemed more milk than gold. But in the selection of prose and poetry the genius of editorship was evident. If you think there are few good writers around, then, my friend, try to find yourself a good editor. Good editors are rarer than good writers, and when you consider that the editors are responsible for what we read, then you must realize the type of literary hell we are forced to live in.

*The Outsider* #3 has a photo of the mad poet Charles Bukowski on the cover, and in the upper right-hand corner, Gypsy framed in a painting. Bukowski is not very pretty. One well-known literary figure in England wrote Jon a long letter of outrage, one of the lines being: "How *dare* you run a face like that on your cover?" Well, Jon liked dares. He dared attack the untouchable Robert Creeley in one of those early issues.

There are some personal notes from Jon and Louise in this issue I have, and an ad for Bukowski's *It Catches My Heart in Its Hands*. But there's more than a Bukowski section of poetry in issue #3. Oh yes, I see, they have reprinted a NOTICE TO QUIT that slid under my door one night . . . in part, and in handwriting: ". . . Aragon Apts., 334 S. Westlake Ave., Los Angeles, California. Apartment occupied by Mr. and Mrs. Buckowski. Said apt. to be Vacated, for Reasons: Excessive Drinking, Fighting, and Foul Language. Disturbing other tenants." I thought this was the funniest thing in the mag but there was also Patchen, Snyder, Creeley, McClure, Burroughs, Irving Layton, Genet, Diane Wakoski, Norse, Miller, Anselm Hollo. . . . The selection of printed works again is forceful and evident of balls and flame. Good writing immediately catches the eye. But the thousands of manuscripts to be read in order to achieve this, and the way you must blister "names" in order to make them roar the eternal and immortal roar, it just ain't easy. The Webbs achieved it.

*The Outsider* 4-5 was a double issue. On his deathbed, Jon was saying something about a "triple issue. . . ." Which showed that old Jon was always one jump ahead of the literary gang. Anyhow, 4-5 is in book form with a photo of Patchen on the cover, dark shades, in cast, that famous back in cast, and he's smoking what appears to be a Lucky Strike, with medicine bottle and lamp in the background. This photo catches the dissolute agony of the situation. This issue left New Orleans for the graces of Tucson. Lou's emphysema was getting worse. This is an homage to K. Patchen section from the boys who knew him then. . . . There are many non-names in this huge issue and they stay right in there with the names, slugging and interesting. Some of the names that remain: Elizabeth Bartlett, Di Prima, Levertov, Lawrence Durrell, Robert Kelly, Thomas Merton, Lenore Kandel, Jackson MacLow, Jean Cocteau . . . also,

Edson, William Wantling, Eigner, Howard McCord, David Meltzer, Margaret Randall, Brown Miller, Gene Fowler, d.a. levy, Robert Bly, Norse, Dick Higgins, David Antin, Anselm Hollo, T.L. Kryss, George Dowden, Simon Perchik, Emmet Williams, Kay Johnson (kaja). . . . Jon didn't mind mixing schools. And if you are a student of snob literary America, you know how little this is done. All Jon demanded was the best from each and I believe he got it. On the homage to Patchen, which I found more lively and interesting and earthy than expected were some of the following: Norman Thomas, Bro. Antoninus, Ginsberg, J.B. May, Norse, Millen Brand, K. Rexroth, Bern Porter, David Meltzer, Ferlinghetti, Jack Conroy, Fred Eckman, and Henry Miller.

If this seems like a name-dropping contest, it isn't. It was simply that the *flame* bent toward *The Outsider*. It was the gathering place, the tavern, the cave of the gods and the cave of the devils . . . it was the place, it was *in* . . . it was literature jumping and screaming, it was a record of voices and it was a record of the time, it was *The Outsider*, it was Jon and Louise Webb, and now Jon Webb . . . has vanished.

Two books. *It Catches My Heart in Its Hands*. Charles Bukowski. "Small birds who go the way of cats sing on inside my head." New and selected poems 1955–1963. It is not a bad book, but it is not immortal except for one or two poems. Cork cover, almost violently-colored pages, a photo of Bukowski, a half of a Bukowski, long cigarette, Bogartish, worn, simple. O.K. It is a work of love, a work of love that the poet may not have returned.

*Crucifix in a Deathhand*, new poems 1963–1965, with the exception of one poem, was written right into the face of a waiting press and does not represent Bukowski's best work, but it is a work of heat and it is lyrical (for a change) and it flows and sings sad songs & it is printed on paper that is supposed to last 2,000 years, and you know that anything that lasts 2,000 years—like Christ—can become tiresome. The book is decorated by Noel Rockmore, and it is rumored that 1,800 copies of this book lie boxed and rotting in a damp Lyle Stuart cellar in New York City. . . .

All right, that's the record of the works on hand. I had the Henry Miller book about, the one about his letters to a French painter, but I sent it up to Elizabeth Bartlett, who auctioned it off with other items, not so long ago, in an effort to get the Webbs out of the red or to keep them alive. The recent Henry Miller book was being issued (I believe) about the time of Jon's death and I never received a copy.

So, now, if you'll allow (and you must since I am writing this), I'll go into more personal things about these strange people behind the Work. . . .

After coming out of the L.A. County General Hospital around 1955, still alive, having been told it would be my sure death if I did so, I began to drink again. I am still drinking. In fact, the phone just rang and Jon's son, Jon Webb Jr. just phoned. "What you doing?" "I'm writing about your old man and his wife." "Well," he said, "It might be a good time for a few beers. Should I come over?" "All right," I said.

So there'll be a slight interruption here, but I'm going to write this thing yet. . . .

All right, I came out of the hospital around 1955 and got a job—shipping clerk for a light-fixture plant in east L.A.—got an apartment, a typewriter, opened the beer, and began writing after a 10-year layoff. Only now I was writing poetry instead of prose. I mailed the first 40 or 50 poems to a mag in Texas, then somehow I heard of *The Outsider* at the beginning of it. I smelled good action. I sat in that kitchen on Kingsley Drive and later in that kitchen on Mariposa Street, symphony music on, smoking, alone, the sound of the typer, the words banging and wailing . . . those 10 years and the near-death and my bad health all helped make it go. The next batch went to *The Outsider*. I got an immediate response. It seemed that no sooner were the poems in the mailbox, I got the answer. Jon had a way of saying it that urged one on. It was Romantic, if you'll forgive me; it was also important enough and real enough. I wrote letters with the poems. I believe I was about half-mad, which is as good a state as a man could ask to get into. I missed most of *The Outsider* #1 but by #2 things were really working between us all. The poems began to build and then, suddenly, Jon said, how about a book? Here he was in contact with the greatest writers of our time and he wanted to do a book by an unknown. I mean, fuck, man, I said, why not?

Jon and Lou asked me to come down and see them in New Orleans. All right, I thought. Let them see the flesh of the words and then if they don't like the flesh, they can tear the book.

The place dipped down below the sidewalk in that rotting French Quarter building. Jon seemed to accept me as if he had known me a lifetime. "Buke," he said. "Hello Buke . . . want a beer?" We talked a while and then he said, "Why don't you walk down and see Lou? She's down a couple of corners selling paintings." "How'll she know me?" "She'll know you," he said. "You'll know her."

It was true. We knew each other. It was cold that day. The paintings were not moving. A buck apiece, two bucks apiece . . . they weren't moving. Gypsy was wrapped in an old shawl. The paintings were hardly immortal, but the people were less so. We walked across the street and got a coffee in the tourist place. It was a deathly place full of deathly people.

"So you're the poet, eh?" she asked.

"This place makes me sick," I said.

"Well, we might as well drink our coffee," she said.

Louise was tougher than I, more real, and more forgiving. I would never forgive Humanity for what they had become. She could. She felt they couldn't help it. I wasn't yet ready to accept that. In a sense, I had met a better person.

We drank our coffees, picked up our paintings, and went back to the sunken room. Jon was feeding pages delicately into the P & Chandler and I sat in a chair, half-asleep, while Louise put dinner on. Then I got up and went out and bought 4 or 5 six packs of beer. I got back and opened a few. Then I looked around the room. Here were these trunks all about, stacked up against the walls. Bukowski, they said, page one. Bukowski, page two. Bukowski, page three. Their bed was up on stilts so that pages could be stacked underneath. Bukowski was everywhere. Bukowski was stacked in the bathtub. They couldn't even bathe.

"Bukowski, Bukowski, Bukowski EVERYWHERE!" screamed Louise, "I hate the son of a bitch! And now he's here in our place drinking beer with his big belly and looking wise!"

Lou was *Italiano*. Fiery *Italiano*. She said what was on her mind. Jon was more introvert. He said clever little delicate and subtle things, rather rolling the last word off the lips, giving the clever smile and checking your eye for reaction. They were the perfect pair; they may have lived in hell but they were married in heaven. It was the mating of the sun and the moon, the sea and the land, the horse and the bird. What one didn't have, the other gave.

Anyhow, I felt I owed them something so I drank and I drank and I told these stories, one after the other, about women and life, and the death-jobs and the crazy things that happen to a man who moves from woman to woman, from place to place while being half crazy in the head; the miracles and the luck and the horror. I could see that they were enjoying the stories so I told some more. It was a fine night, the roaches crawling the walls, so many roaches that they seemed to be a wall, wavering of black hard backs and feelers and unfeelingness. Here were a people trying to improve the literature and poetry of the world and living with bugs and drunks and madness, and hardly a chance at all.

Well, they went to sleep and I went to sleep somewhere and the days went on. We made the bars at night and I met Jon's fiction editor, a mute, and we wrote on paper napkins all night and got drunker than what? We got drunker than James Joyce.

Anyhow, it was that. Paintings on the corner. The press. The bars. The drunken stories. *The Outsider*. All the people. And there is a streetcar named *Desire*. I left town. The book came out. . . .

I don't know. Jon and Lou lived in many cities. I remember another book—*Crucifix*. But there were cities in between and after. It was simply a love affair without saying it. They enjoyed me; I enjoyed them. I met Corso. Corso and I raged around a bit, but for all our flair and wordage, there was always a gentleness underneath it all. Corso was one of the most gentle, and Jon and Louise. I played the hard guy because somebody has to or you don't have a backdrop.

All right, with *Crucifix* it was strange. I'd come by (they had me living with a fat and nice lady around the corner) with a hangover every morning and Jon would let me in and he'd say, "Bukowski! More Poems!" And I'd sit down to the typer and write one and he'd immediately set it up for printing. Well, the book came out. I left town. . . .

They were always on the move, dragging that press behind them, and 2 dogs, and manuscripts and books and and . . . "Come see us, Bukowski. . . ." And out I'd go. This time Santa Fe in the rain. A rich psychiatrist's place. 2 or 3 wives. I'm drunk. I'm in bed with one of the wives. 6 bathrooms within 10 feet. Across the way, a tower of a house. You've got to climb 100 feet to get into a doorway. The psychiatrist rents these places. I meet the psychiatrist. He is like any other p. I ever met—emptier than any insanity.

"Bukowski," Jon asked me, "should we stay here?"

"Stay here for what?"

"*The Outsider*."

"What's he want?"

"We gotta break down one wall to get the press in. Then he cements the wall back up. We'll be locked in here, you know. It's difficult. But he says rent free. I can stay here forever. But he rather hints that I should print a book of his poems. . . ."

So, Jon and Lou moved from there to elsewhere and from elsewhere to someplace else. . . . Once again, back in N.O., I'd walk up to Lou on the corner where she was selling paintings. She'd have a large map on her lap. The map of the U.S. She'd crossed out, with pencil, all the places that it is impossible to live in. The whole map was blacked out.

"Look at me," she'd say, laughing, "it took me 5 goddamned hours to go over this map and I find out what?—there's no place to live."

"I meant to tell you," I'd say. . . .

Jon always meant to get at a man. He was under one of the false misconceptions that is so popular nowadays—get a man angry and he'll really tell you what he is and what he has to say. Jon was always trying me but it led to nowhere. Jon was as lonely and mixed up and crazy as the rest of us, yet he was one of the 2 or 3 great editors of the 20th century. Along with Whit Burnett of *Story* and Mencken of the old *Mercury*. . . .

I tell you that those people lived in so many places that I can't keep them in order. Right now, I remember 3 different storefronts in Arizona, or maybe one of them was in New Mexico. Jon was a good carpenter and he'd fix up these storefronts and really make them livable. Although all the livability circled around the printing press. They never found their place, though; they always had to move again, and again. They became disgusted with the people. Once in New Orleans, they hired a crew to move their printing press and undo the electric hook-up (the press needed a special power line). Then they changed their minds, had the crew move the press back, hook it up, then they changed their minds again and the press was unhooked and pulled through the window. Their funds were fucked by this constant moving, looking for the place. Paying freight for that press and paper stock, belongings, 2 dogs. I tried to tell them, I tried to tell them that the people all over America were rotten and decayed and false and unreal.

Jon died in the State of Tennessee. It was a simple and routine operation that failed.

Jon's son was with me at my place while his father was in the hospital. We phoned Louise first. "What you guys doing? Drinking while Jon is in the hospital?"

Jon's son was in contact with the doctors. He was a med student about to graduate. I heard him discuss the entire operation with them. It was not be a dangerous one. They hadn't operated yet. His son talked to Jon. "You heard anything from Bukowski?" he asked him. "No, Bukowski doesn't write anymore. Henry Miller still writes me though, Henry Miller just wrote me the other day. . . ."

"Have you given up on Bukowski?"

"Oh, no, I haven't given up on Buke. . . ."

The operation didn't work. It was a matter of correcting something along the neck, one side of the neck. The part on the other side of the neck was gone. One part left to fix up. They operated. Jon went into a coma afterwards. Lou was there. She was religious. I'm not too religious but her business is hers. She stayed at the bed and prayed. The doctor came in and asked her what she was doing. "I'm praying that my man lives," she told him. "Well, I'm praying that he dies," said the doctor.

Lou leaped up: "You're praying that he *dies*? What the hell kind of doctor are you? What the hell kind of a human being are you?"

"If he lives he'll be like an idiot. He'll be like a child, he'll be useless. . . ."

"What do I care? What do I care if he's like an idiot? I'll take care of him. He's my man!"

Women like Louise Webb come along about one in two million. Jon died.

"Everything seemed all right with the operation. He seemed to come through it and then . . . BINGO! . . . something wrong. . . ."

That's the way the doctor described it. One of the best surgeons in the state.

*The Outsider* of the decade was through. The greatest editor since Mencken and Burnett was finished. Our great nights of beer and talk were finished. Visits from Corso and Ginsberg were finished. Pulling that press all about the country looking for Nirvana, that was finished. I doubt that *The Outsider* will continue. There has been some talk by Louise and Jon's son of continuing the magazine, the press, but I feel that it is over. I wish now that I had told some of the funnier stories about Jon and Louise and myself, but I've written too long now.

The miracle of Jon Edgar Webb, ex-con, ex-writer, ex-editor. . . . It would seem that now the skies would come down a bit or that the streets would crack and open up, or the mountains waver. But they don't. It's history, history, and the game goes on. A new deck. Another drink. And the sadness. That they built us not to last, and that we waste so much, make so many mistakes. Look, Jon, I see you grinning. . . . You knew Buke would write it for you. It's cold now and a white Corvette pulls up outside and a beautiful girl gets out. I don't understand it.

—Charles Bukowski 11/25/71

# VERN'S WIFE

Vern was a photographer and he had this young wife, Claudia. They had just moved to Florida and then discovered that Claudia was pregnant. They didn't want the baby and knew that abortion was illegal in Florida, so he wrote me, Vern did, saying they were broke and could I lend them the money to come to California and have the thing taken care of?

Having just had one of those unusual good weeks at the track, I sent the money out and there I was at the airport to pick up Claudia.

Now Claudia was one of the finest looking women I had ever seen. Her hair was long, red blonde, and the face and body exuded sex—plenty of sex. The blue eyes were large, and had a way of looking into you, looking quite into you. And her lips seemed the hottest part of her; so suggestive, ripe, always a little bit open.

She had on one of the shortest mini-skirts I had ever seen and every male eye was on her as she walked up to me with her little suitcase. She looked anything but the pregnant woman. I kissed her on the cheek and took her out to my car.

Claudia and I were not complete strangers. We had done some necking at times when her husband wasn't about, when they first got married here in Los Angeles.

"Am I going to stay at your place?" she asked.

"I guess you'll have to," I said. "It's the tight money situation. I've got stories on the stands and I haven't been paid for them yet. To top that, I've been drinking too much and not writing enough."

"Well, O.K. then."

When we got to my place, I put on some hamburger and Claudia went in the other room and took a bath. I could hear her singing in there.

When dinner was ready, she came out in this red silk gown,

nothing underneath. Dinner was quiet. Then she said she was tired and wanted to go to bed. I said I was tired too.

She got into bed and I stood there undressing. Her red gown was at the foot of the bed.

"Look at that thing sticking out there!" she whispered. "Listen, we can't do anything. Vern trusts us."

"How can you make a *pregnant* woman pregnant?"

"I don't know. But let's not try."

"Yeah," I said. "Vern trusts us."

I got on in. Her lips were still open. I got mine against them, pushing the insides of mine against the insides of hers. It was a hot kiss. I could feel my prong jamming against her. She broke off.

"Let's not," she said, suddenly looking very small, very hurt.

I pulled the cover back and got my head down there. I just touched it with the tip of my tongue, ever so lightly. Moved it off and on, ever so lightly. She began to slowly move her legs and body. I heard her breathing and groaning up there. I didn't relent.

"Oh, you son of a bitch! You son of a bitch!"

I continued for a few minutes more.

Then she screamed:

"STICK THAT GODDAMNED THING IN ME!"

As I rose to mount her, she grabbed my head and kissed me wildly. I put it in. She was wet. I went slow and easy. Her eyes rolled to the back of her head. I gave it a long slow ride then near the end I rammed and roared and thumped, my lips smashing down on hers. It was a good climax. I stayed there a minute, then rolled off.

"Vern trusts us," I said.

"He's a damn fool," Claudia replied.

A couple of hours later, I gave it to her in the anus. Then near midnight she gave me a bit of oral copulation.

"Vern's one helluva nice guy," I said.

We slept good. When I awakened she had breakfast on. I grabbed her from behind. The thing was up.

"God, you're the horniest old man I've ever seen," she said.

"It's all those dirty stories I write. They excite me."

"Can I read some of those stories?"

"Sure." I gave her one of my books. She took it with her in my car when she went out to make the abortion arrangements. When she got back she waved the book at me.

"You're right. These are horny stories. I'm hotter than hell."

Claudia took off her clothes and went to bed. I did likewise. I got down there and teased her a bit. She heated right up. Then I put her on top of me and let her do all the work. I just laid back. It was like being raped.

"I love you, son of a bitch," she snarled at me.

"You're losing your mind, Claudia," I told her.

We climaxed together and I almost lost mine. Then we got up and ate lunch.

"You guys who lay around all the time have all this energy," she said.

"Yeah," I agreed, "but a writer's life is difficult. Once you get used to writing, you're no good for anything else. Everything has to hang to that and if you don't make it, you're dead."

Claudia didn't seem very sympathetic.

I got on the phone and got May, who had a screening desk at the local chain of sex mags in town.

"May, baby," I said.

"Oh, Bukowski," she said.

"Listen, May, things are tough. I've got to get the rent up. How about some action on purchase order #1600? The thing's been on the stands for a month."

"I'll see what I can do, Charley. You know the old man's hooked on the market and the market's been bad."

"Hell, it went up 18 points the other day."

"Yeah, everything went up but his holdings. He even took minus five on one issue. I don't know if it's his broker or if it's the old man. They keep making wrong moves. . . ."

"Alright, May, get that 1600 in front of him anyhow. I don't write good on an empty stomach. . . ."

"Charley, you know you're my favorite writer. . . ."

"Really? What's the old man think of me?"

"The old man? Hell, he never reads his magazines. . . ."

I drove Claudia down for her abortion the next day. I sat around reading *Life* and *Time*. When Claudia came out an hour or so later, she acted as if nothing had happened.

"It's like a vacuum cleaner," she said. "They suck everything out. . . ."

I drove her back. She undressed and went to bed.

"I lost my baby," she said, "I'm kind of sad."

"Cheer up," I said. "We can start another one."

"Doctor says no intercourse for six weeks."

"Six weeks?"

"That's what he said."

"God. . . ."

The next afternoon I took her down to the airport. All the male eyes were on her. She had on a shorter mini than the one she arrived in the first day.

"Well, thanks for everything," she said, "and good luck with your writing."

"Maybe I'll write about us. We had some good sex there."

"How can you make a story out of it?"

"Maybe. That's my problem."

I put her on the plane and as I got to my car, I saw the bird rise into the air. Vern's wife was on her way back to Florida.

I got on the freeway and drove back to my typewriter. I was in love with Claudia and needed a new ribbon.

# NOTES OF A DIRTY OLD MAN

*NOLA EXPRESS*, APRIL 14–27, 1972

Sitting with a bottle at the typewriter is not the easiest way to cut through terror. I dreamed a lifetime of being a writer and now the demons are upon me. Writing heightens the feelings to such an extent that we are at the mercy of all happenings. A blade of grass becomes a sword; an affair of love claws the guts out. With the few people I know, I pretend to be the tough guy but I don't fool anybody. One of the saving graces (there's a platitude) is the ability to laugh now and then. Without that, going on might be impossible. The average man puts in his 8 hours, comes home beaten and satisfied. With the writer there is never satisfaction; there is always the next piece of work to be done. We are honed by our words. My gal friend says to me, "My god, you're touchy. You remind me of one of those fish down at Marineland. They've got these points sticking out all over them. Touch one and that fish goes crazy. I'm going to take you down there and show you one of those fish."

"O.K., take me down there. I want to see one of those fish."

We have our own little show going on. Once I stood in front of the bathroom mirror with a razor to my throat. I looked at myself—dim little serious eyes—and I had to laugh. Another time I tried gas. It didn't work. I was awakened by a most terrible headache. John Berryman, the poet, did it recently by jumping off a bridge into a river. Now that's style. I have a friend who writes. He has razor scars on both wrists.

Writing means creating and waiting. The mail is slow and the pay is low. I manage to give readings at some of the universities. It is an odd feeling to be flown off somewhere and to be paid for reading your poetry. And to have some of the ladies want to go to bed with you, and there are also the free drinks. I don't go to bed with the ladies because I'm in love with my gal friend, but I have accepted some drinks.

I don't like to read but it is survival and most audiences are surprisingly live and understanding. And amusing things do happen. Once in Michigan I laid my poems down and arm-wrestled with some student. Now, that's something—I got paid $400 to arm-wrestle. I won but the kid said I cheated. Hell, when you get as old as I am, you've got to cheat.

Another time in Kansas City, my ride arrived drunk at the airport. And it was *snowing*, in late March.

"Welcome to Kansas Shitty, Bukowski," my ride shoved a bottle of tequila at me. I accepted and we got into the car. The expressway was icy and slippery. There were ditches on the side and every now and then you'd see a car in one of the ditches.

"Those people can't drive on these roads," said my ride.

"Listen, Andre," I said, "let me read you this poem."

My gal friend had written it and I mean it was SEXY. I reached a certain line and Andre said, "Jesus Christ!" and he lost control of the car. We spun around and around in these circles and I lifted the bottle and said, "Andre, we're not going to make it. . . ."

We spun off into a ditch but remained right side up. It was cold and there wasn't any car heater. Being the sensitive poet I stayed in the car and drank while Andre stuck out the thumb.

And who stopped for us? Another drunk. He had bottles of beer all over the floor and a fifth of whiskey. We made the reading.

Another time I was given a room in the *women's* dorm. Now if you don't think that's a situation to test your love. . . .

At a Patchen benefit in the Hollywood Hills I was pouring a couple of drinks behind the bar after the reading when this young girl walked up to me. She was a handsome creature—body, face, eyes, hair, all that was needed.

"Bukowski," she said, "your poems are the only ones. You really make the other poets look bad."

"Well, thanks. I may not be immortal but at least I'm understandable."

"I want to fuck you."

"What?"

"I want to fuck you."

"Pardon me, I'm taking this drink to my girl."

Fringe benefits? It killed Dylan Thomas and it has sucked many other poets into a grand imbecility. The poetry audiences must be respected, and, denied. . . .

Céline, after *Journey*, went into a rant about how publishers were taking him. A writer is made to be taken. All a writer can ask for is a bare survival (another platitude) so that he can go on writing until he dies. Céline lost his humor after *Journey*. Of course, he got roughed up by the war, ran out of town, and his patients didn't pay their bills. But at least he was a doctor, he had something to go on beside a typewriter ribbon. Writers are nothing but beggars with a good line. Freelancing is slow; God is the mailman and God often doesn't seem to care.

Luckily for most of us we don't have the habits of the masses. New cars bore us; television is inane; clothes don't matter. Our biggest worry is that drunken phone call to East Kansas City. And we often have a good woman about to hold us together. We are faithful to our women because we give over our total feelings, but in other areas we treat them badly. We are not good listeners. Her friends appear to be stupid. Dull. We can't understand how anybody else could be interesting at all. . . . Writers are a bad breed. The ladies have been good to us. . . . I'd say that almost always, behind each good writer stood a damned good woman. Take away love and half an artist's work fails. . . .

All right, it's better than the punch press. No layoffs. Of course, a man can go to bed at night being a writer and wake up in the morning and be nothing. Talent can vanish in one tick of the clock. Yet it's a good fight. It's good to die on your own battleground. How many men and women are actually doing what they can do best? That 7:30 A.M. freeway on weekdays is the sight of horror of the century. One of them, anyhow. We've each given the hours of our lives in dull rote jobs for other men's profit, and have been asked to be grateful for doing that. Surely, for all the weeping we do about writing, we are the blessed. The price is almost beyond reason but the fight is good.

There are moments and moments of glowing: you are wary of it but you allow yourself to be happy at times & stupid. Why not? Most of the others are. What cause is so holy that a man can't be happy at moments? Why not? We've gone through the other . . . the gas jets hissing, or standing in front of that mirror with the rusty razor blade. Child stuff. Shit, you can feel like a Hemingway sometimes. Say going to a bullfight, cigarette dangling (I'm one-half Hem, one-half Bogart), pint of good whiskey in coat, and on your arm, a woman 20 years younger and spirited, a woman who knows you are making the good fight, the words running around inside of you and waiting to form, you walk in with her and the flame is good, the fire is good, the coals are glowing, sure, walk like you have it, this hour this moment this time, she loves you, Bukowski, and you've got a Royal Standard and enough ribbon to strangle in, she walks beside you, proud and good, and the first bull is already out, they are sticking it, weakening it, all those summers gone by, all those other women, the jails, the suicide mirrors, the funerals, the nights in the bedroom alone, torn by the wolves of rotten salami: Jane, Gertrude, Barbara, Frances, even Frances, and Linda, Linda, Linda. I can't hold all my insides together. I am stuck underneath the bottom of the sky.

You're writing these columns now, Bukowski. How long are you going to be able to go on writing these columns?

I don't know. Dostoyevsky did it. I guess I can do it.

What's the best thing you've done lately?

Well, I picked up a girl with the clap on Hollywood Boulevard.

You mean you caught it?

I mean, I didn't catch it.

Meanwhile, I'll see you guys and gals at the Olympic some Thursday night, my Bogart cigarette dangling, beer in hand, and if I'm lucky, my love near me. If I'm unlucky I'll be alone. Wish me luck. The Jap and Mexican fighters have the guts. The black man and the white man are the sulkers. They go on inbred talent but they are no longer angry enough. I am still angry and amused. It is only by looking at other things that I can tell you who I am. If I buy you a beer, you ought to buy me a beer. Not that you have to. The bulls and the fighters and the word. Suddenly I feel good. It's not going to last but I'll accept it. You tell me something now.

# NOTES OF A DIRTY OLD MAN

*L.A. FREE PRESS*, JUNE 1, 1973

He phones from a bar; I can hear the juke music. He's in town from San Francisco, been hustling the Ferlinghetti strand, gave a reading for Bob Kaufman. Duke's in town, wants to know if he can come on up. "Come on up," I say. I tell Karen that Duke Santeen's in town and on the way over.

Duke's a street poet. Duke's been hustling the Muse since the early '50s. He can write good poetry *when* he writes it. But Duke carries his own energy, he's no dead hustle. I get into the '62 Comet and go get the beer. Then I get back and get a few down and wait for Duke's arrival.

He arrives. His hair is getting a little more silver, the shoulders are slumped, but he's still the boxer, he can duke it, and he can laugh and he's been burned and he's been north and he's been south, and he knows the way—*All American Poets Are in Prison* is the title of one of his books.

Duke can write, there's no doubt about it, he can write the ass out of nine out of ten, no 95 out of 100. He should be published more than he is; I know that and he knows that. Meanwhile, I introduce him to Karen. Karen sculpts, is working on a play soon to be produced in a little theatre in Hollywood, has a book of poems out via underground press, and has a novel knocking on doors. I am surrounded by talent.

Duke sees the heads all about. "Beautiful, beautiful! You got a real talent," he tells Karen.

"That head there," I tell Duke, "that's Jeffers."

"Jeffers, eh? How about the other head? That Jeffers too?"

"No, that's her father."

"I knew I was back in Los Angeles. First thing I see when I hit the streets is this woman walking by, her skirt's so short so I can see her pussy."

"It's a great town, Duke."

"I saw the Foot up in Frisco. Great cat, beautiful cat."

"The Foot?"

"Allen Ginsberg. He broke his foot."

We suck at our beers. Duke takes out a square record from his valise. "This guy's good. I'm gonna be his agent. Listen to this. He's great."

We listen. Cowboy songs. Most of them are derivative and not too unique. One of them is pretty damned good, though, so his man stands a chance. We suck at our beers.

"I was crossing Sunset, we'd just come from Barney's, this babe and me, and this cop stops us. We're drunk, I reach out to touch him, I reach out to touch him and tell him he needs a friend and the mother draws a *gun* on me!"

I get Duke for some cigarettes. I always forget to buy cigarettes.

"Once I was back east, I hadda shit real bad, you know, no place to go. I really had the runs so I just squatted in the street and this cop came by and said, 'What're you doin' there?' I said, 'Officer, what does it look like I'm doin'? You wouldn't want me to shit my pants, would you?' And the cop says, 'Yes, I want you to shit your pants!'"

We laugh and then Duke says, "I just made that one up."

"Come on, Duke," I say. "You're burning my dream."

Duke gets up. He has a way of carrying a beer bottle on his hip. Elan. He stands looking out the window. It's dark out there, and cold. We're up over the reservoir.

"I suppose they'll print me when I'm dead. They'll discover me after I'm dead."

It's difficult to respond to a statement like that. We don't say anything. Duke keeps looking out the window. The beer bottle is still on his hip.

"I got a whole trunk full of stuff buried under a tree."

"Where's it at, Duke?"

He names some Midwestern state. Then he comes back and sits in a chair, lifts his bottle. "Death," he says. "Then there's death." He laughs. "Why don't they kill us all at once and get it over with?"

Duke's silver hair hangs down on both sides of his head. He has the handsomeness of a man who still has all the burners going, all the burners going all the time. I bring out more beer. Duke has his line of shit but much of it isn't shit; he's indulged himself but you don't pass a better human being on the street once a month, or maybe once a year. Or maybe. . . . Anyhow.

"I came down to get my typer out of hock," he says.

"Listen, Duke," I say, "why don't you get a part-time job, anything, get into a small room and get the writing down? Stop hanging around the bars and the poetry holes, forget the ladies and get it down?"

"I've written my last poem. I'm through with that. I'm writing songs now. I'm into songs."

There are holes in the bottom of his shoes yet I get him for another cigarette.

"Ginny, you met her last time I was here?"

"Yeah."

"Well, Ginny, she dropped me over at this other gal's place and she was gone a half and hour and she had to come back for something and I'm already under the sheets with this other gal, but Ginny's cool, she understands."

The beer seems to go very fast, three six-packs is nothing, nothing at all for the Duke and the Buk. We go out for more. In the car he tells me about Karen. "She's all right, man. She looks like she can ride a horse. She's a real woman."

"Yeah, she's all right."

Duke and I go in and converse with the liquor man. He hasn't seen two nuts like us in 20 or 30 years. I remember to get cigarettes. Back at the place we talk some more.

Duke states once more that they will print him after he is dead. He puts on the cowboy record again. I tell him I like the one song real well.

"Yeah, man, he's raw," says Duke. "He's got up there on the stage and in between songs he yells out, '*I wanna suck some pussy!*'"

Karen talks a bit about her sculpting and then I tell Duke I'm not doing too bad at the track; after 30 years' play I am only $10,000 in the hole. Duke drops some names: Kerouac, Ginsberg, Lamantia, Ferlinghetti, and others. He has known or knows them all. Neal Cassady and all.

"I hear names dropping all over the room, Duke," I tell him.

"So what? They're beautiful people, all beautiful people."

"Sure, Duke."

I bring out more beer. Things are reaching the sad, quiet stage. A few more strong swallows and we're all feeling better. "It's some game," says Duke. "It's some hell of a game."

I say, "Leo Durocher said it. 'I'd rather be lucky than good.'"

Duke doesn't answer. He looks down into his bottle.

"I'd rather be lucky and good," I say.

I guess we're not feeling better. I'm trying to make conversation when Duke is the conversation man. We speak small bits and then guide Duke to the extra bedroom. It's nice to have an extra bedroom even if the house isn't mine.

In the morning Karen fries us up some scrambled eggs and weenies. The Duke has been up for hours, prowling. His face is scrubbed and there's no sign of a hangover. He's eager to move on, to get back on the hustle. Soon we're in the car.

"I gotta get back to Frisco."

"Sure, kid."

"Drop me at Hollywood and Vine."

"O.K."

Duke has his valise of songs and poems with him plus one of his rolled-up paintings. We drive down Hollywood Bl. and it's my time to feel down. The beer and talk is done. The sun is up and the sun is hard and Hollywood Boulevard on a Sunday morning is hard. Hard? It's impossible. But Duke wants Hollywood and Vine. Duke is a romanticist. We drive on down and we pull over. I look into my wallet, and there's a dollar bill and a ten. "Duke," I say, "I can either give you a dollar or a ten and I won't give you a ten."

Duke takes the dollar. A dollar from a writer with a place to sleep to a writer without a place to sleep. I let him out there and he stood there facing me with his valise and his silver hair. "Well," he says, "if they find me at the bottom of the drink, remember me."

"Sure, kid."

I drive off leaving him there in the hard Hollywood sun. The ghosts of Garbo and Grable and Harlow and W.C. Fields wander about. I U-turn back and driving back I'm thinking, well, he's gone, he's gone, he's gone, he's gone, and I'm glad he's gone and I miss him at the same time. When I get back to the place I tell Karen, "I dropped him at Hollywood and Vine."

"I don't think he had any money," she said.

"Oh hell, he's an old-time hustler. You ought to see his little black book, all the names. He'll make it."

"It must be hard, doing that."

"He loves it. He wouldn't want it any other way."

I go into the kitchen and find a 7-Up. I drink half of it in one swallow. It tastes good. I have a very bad hangover.

You know, writers will arrive and knock on the door, mostly the bad writers, and I remember one particularly bad writer who after drinking a great number of beers seemed to become angry and he said, "Come on, Bukowski, you don't expect us to believe all that shit!" "What shit?" I asked. "All that shit about you bumming around on all the jobs, and all those women, and that shit about you not writing for ten years and drinking yourself into the hospital with the blood rushing out of your ass and your mouth?" This boy was really angry. Not much had happened in his life so he couldn't believe other men's lives could be different. That most men don't gamble with their lives or their creativity is not my fault. And it makes for dull writing and dull writers.

The factories, the slaughterhouses, the warehouses were not exactly a choice and then they were a choice, and so were the women and so was the drinking. Yes and no. It was movement and it was restricted movement. And so was sitting in the same bar day and night, running errands for sandwiches and fighting the bartender in the alley. This was my literary training, and so was living in tiny rooms with roaches, or with mice or with rats, and so was starving and so was self-pity and so was disgust. But stories came out of it and poems and some luck; not an immense luck but some luck, and if the luck came late, say at the age of 50, then so much the better for me. You know Huxley's saying in *Point Counter-Point*: "Any man can be a genius at 25, at 50 it takes some doing." Many *are* geniuses at 25, and recognized and destroyed. Not many writers go the route; the bad ones keep writing and the good ones are destroyed early. They are destroyed the same way rock stars are destroyed: by over-production, over-praise, over-push, and the good old fat head.

The gods were good to me. They kept me under. They made me

live the life. It was very difficult for me to walk out of a slaughter-house or a factory and come home and write a poem I didn't quite mean. And many people write poems they don't quite mean. I do too, sometimes. The hard life created the hard line and by the hard line I mean the true line devoid of ornament.

The gods are still good to me. I am still underground but not underground enough to be completely buried. The only time I read in San Francisco, 800 people arrived and 100 of those arrived with buckets of garbage to throw at me. At 2 bucks a head, that garbage didn't smell too bad. The gods are good to me in that I cause extreme reactions—the crowd either seems to go for me totally or hate me totally. That's luck; and at readings when somebody shouts an obscenity at me, I enjoy that almost as much as when somebody hands me up a bottle from the audience. I have been there and the crowd knows that I have been there. I am no tidy professor with a home in the hills and a piano-playing wife.

One will always have detractors and most of your detractors will be other writers who are in a hurry to bury you. "Oh, he's slipped." "Oh, he's an awful drunk!" "He beats his women." "He knifed me." "He got a grant without filling out an application." "He sucks." "He hates fags." "He lies." "He's jealous." "He's vengeful." "He's sick."

Most of these detractors almost directly copy my style or they are influenced by it. My contribution was to loosen and simplify poetry, to make it more humane. I made it easy for them to follow. I taught them that you can write a poem the same way you can write a letter, that a poem can even be entertaining, and that there need not be anything necessarily holy about it. I am much afraid now that there are too many people writing like Charles Bukowski, or I should say attempting to write like Charles Bukowski. But I am still the best Charles Bukowski around and my style keeps adjusting and changing as my life does, so they just aren't going to catch me. Only Papa Death will catch me, and I have cut my drinking in half so that those who hate me will just have to suffer a bit longer. While my copiers are dying of alcoholism, I will be slipping out to health spas at midnight. Ah, I am the clever one.

It is hard for me to find heroes anymore so I must create my own hero: myself. This makes for some hard nights. And days. One must remain pliable, open to changes, but one can't simply change on a whim. The moves must be natural and come out of the living. I am sorry if *this* sounds holy but I think you know what I mean. I think much of the works of Knut Hamsun as a man who grew and widened, even though his first book *Hunger* was the most interesting, you mostly admired his later work because you could feel the growth, the white air, the valleys, the women, the pain and the humor and the lack of bullshit. I doubt that I will ever be another Knut Hamsun; I am too lazy a man; I like to lay around afternoons and stare at the ceiling or rub my scrubby beard; I lack ambition and perhaps I wait too long on the word, but for either my admirers or my detractors, I am not boxed into a certain area, so when you speak of Charles Bukowski, you can only speak of the Charles Bukowski of yesterday. I will throw one right past you tomorrow and you won't know what it is for a while.

To the accusers I say, go ahead and accuse; to the praisers I say, go ahead and praise; to the woman who loves me, I say go ahead and love me; to Marina I say, go ahead and become a wonderful woman; to my car I say, go ahead and keep running so I won't have to buy another one; and to my typewriter I say, go ahead and tell me more things, more and more things, different things; go ahead, go ahead, go ahead. . . .

Holy or unholy, this is about it, and about all I can tell you right now. Now I'm hungry and going to eat a sandwich. I like lots of hot mustard, don't you?

# NOTES OF A DIRTY OLD MAN

*L.A. FREE PRESS*, JUNE 28, 1974

To find the proper place to write, that's most important; the rent should be reasonable, the walls thick, the landlord indifferent, and the tenants depraved, penurious, alcoholic, and lower-middle-class. With the advent of the high-rise apartments, small courts, with their own private entranceways, have more and more vanished, and the wonderful characters that once infested these places have vanished along with them.

I lived for eight years on a front court on DeLongpre Avenue, and the poetry and the stories flourished. I'd sit at the front window typing, peering through excessive brush onto the street; I'd be surrounded by beer bottles and listening to classical music on the radio, sitting in my shorts, barefooted, my fat beer belly dangling. I was surrounded by rays and shadows and sounds, and *I* made sounds.

My landlord was a drunk, my landlady was a drunk, they'd come down and get me at night. . . . "Stop that silly typing, you son of a bitch, come on down and get drunk." And I'd go. The beer was free, the cigarettes were free, they fed me; they liked me, we talked until 3 or 4 in the morning. The next day they'd knock on the door and leave a bag of something: tomatoes or pears or apples or oranges, mostly it was tomatoes. Or often she'd come with a warm meal—beef stew with biscuits and green onions; fried chicken with gravy and mashed potatoes and bean salad with cornbread. They'd knock, listen for my voice, then run off. He was 60, she was 58. I put out their garbage cans every Wednesday, eight or 10 cans gathered from the courts and the apartments in back. The alcoholic next to me fell out of bed at 4 each morning; there was an ATD case in one of the apartments in back; 14 Puerto Ricans lived in one of the center courts, men, women, and children; they never made a sound and slept on the rug next to each other.

Mad people came to visit me—Nazis, anarchists, painters, musicians, fools, geniuses, and bad writers. They all imparted their ideas to me thinking that I would understand. Some nights I would look around and there would be from eight to 14 people sitting about the rug, and I only knew two or three of them. Sometimes I would go into a rage and throw them all out; other times I just forgot it all. Nobody ever stole from me except one who professed to be my friend and was always fingering my bookcase, slipping first editions and rare items under his shirt. The police raided continually but only took me in once or twice, yes, it was twice. Once they came bearing a shotgun, but I told them I was a writer and they left. Yes, it was a good place to live and to write.

Then love came and I moved out and into this house with this lady. She was good to me and it worked well, I liked her two children; there was space and shadow, a crazy dog, and a large backyard, a jungle of a backyard with bamboo and squirrels and walnut trees, wild rosebushes, fig trees, lush plants. I wrote well there—many love poems and love stories; I had not written too many of those. I walked about and it felt as if the sun were inside of me; I was finally *warm*, and things seemed humorous, gleeful, easy; I felt no guilt about my feelings. Yet, that finally went bad as those things do go bad. One or both begin to build resentments; things that once seemed so marvelous no longer seem that way. Each blames the other—it's *you* . . . you did this, you said that, you shouldn't have acted that way, *you*. . . .

I had to move quickly. I searched the streets for a plausible place, somewhere a man might possibly get off a short poem. The afternoons and mornings mingled: First and last month's rent, $200 security, $75 cleaning, references. None of the places even seemed livable, and the landlords and managers gave off the worst of vibes:

greedy, suspicious, dead-meat creatures. One of them wouldn't even look at me; he just kept staring at his TV set and tolling off the charges. I began to feel dirtied, like an imbecile, a man without a right to hot and cold water and a toilet to rent as his own. There was actually no place to be found. In weariness I simply paid somebody and began moving in.

It was a modern apartment, a place in the back, up one flight, apartment 24. There was a garden in the center and two managers, man and wife, who lived downstairs and they *never* left the premises; one of them was *always* there, especially the lady, who dressed in white and walked around with a little brown bag and often caught the leaves as they fell from the bushes; she got them before they hit the ground. She was immaculate, face heavy with white powder; she wore much lipstick and had a rasping voice, a voice that always gave the sound of somebody lying. Her husband had the booming voice, and he boomed about the Dodgers and about God and about the prices in the supermarket. My first night there the phone rang and he told me that my radio was on too loud; they could hear me all over the court. "We can hear you all over the court, Hank," he said. He insisted that we call each other by our first names. My radio had not been on loud. I turned it off. Then somebody started playing an accordion. "Oh, that's beautiful!" I heard a voice. The guy ran through all the Lawrence Welk tunes.

*She* was always there, ubiquitous, most ubiquitous, and I'd have a hangover, be coming down the stairs, listening, thinking, she's not around, I've gotten by her this time. And I'd have my bag of empties full of ashes and crap, the bottom wet and wanting to rip open, myself feeling like vomiting, I'd get down on the ground and then go through an opening in the back garage in between the cars, trying to get to the trash container, and *out* she'd pop with her broom: "It's a nice day, isn't it?" "Oh yes," I'd say, "it's a nice day."

And she was always at the mailboxes when the mail came, she

was out there with her broom; you couldn't get your mail. Or if somebody unknown came to the court she'd ask: "What do you want?" On warm days she placed herself in one of the deck chairs and reclined, and it seemed as if all the days I lived there were warm. And others came out and joined her and one was allowed to listen to their voices and their ideas.

The modern apartment-dwellers are all the same; they spend much time scrubbing and waxing and dusting and vacuuming; everything glistens—stoves, refrigerators, tables; the dishes are washed immediately after eating; the water in the toilet is blue; towels are used only once; doors are left open, blinds parted, and under the lamps you can see them sitting quietly reading a safe paperback or watching a laugh-track family-affair comedy on a huge TV screen. They buy knickknacks and ferns, things to hang about, fill the spaces; a Sunday afternoon at *Akron* is their Nirvana. They have no children, no pets, and they get intoxicated twice a year, at Christmas and at New Year's.

There were two small couches in my place about a foot and a half wide. Upon one of these I was supposed to sleep. It was impossible to make love to a woman on either one of them. I discovered 18 roaches behind the refrigerator, and whenever I typed the woman below me beat up on her ceiling with a broom handle. And there was always somebody knocking on my door saying that I was disturbing them. Then one day all the tenants were given forms saying that there would be an automatic $5-a-month boost for each apartment. The roach spray I used almost cost me that. The writing had dwindled, almost stopped. My editor phoned me and assured me that every writer had his slumps. He said that I had five years left; that I needn't write anything for five years and that I still could make it. I thanked him. . . .

And I lucked it. I found this court just off of Hollywood and Western; I found it by getting the inside that somebody was moving out before that somebody moved out. It is my kind of neighborhood—massage parlors and love parlors are everywhere; taco stands, pizza parlors, sandwich shops; cut-rate drugstores full of wigs and old combs, rotting soap, hairpins, and lotions; whores night and day; black pimps in broad hats with their razor-sharp noses; plainclothes cops shaking down people at high noon, checking their arms for needle marks; dirty bookstores, murder, shakedowns, dope. I walk up Western Avenue toward Hollywood Boulevard and the sun shines inside of me again. I almost feel in love again. My people, my time, the taste of it. . . .

I've only been here a week and just last night I looked around, beer bottles were everywhere, the radio was on, and in my place there were some people who live in this court: a guy who runs one of the love parlors, two guys who work in a dirty bookstore, and a dancer from one of the bars. We talked about dildoes, shakedowns, some of the ladies of the boulevard and the avenue; we talked about the freaks and the good people and the hard-hearted; we talked all through the night, the smoke curling, the laughter O.K. We ran out of beer and the delivery boy came in high and screwed-up and stayed an hour. We sent out for chicken and potatoes and coleslaw and buns. The night rolled easy. Finally I called an end: I'd been drinking beer since 11 A.M. They left in good form. I went to the bathroom, pissed, and then went to bed. Hemingway couldn't ask for better. The light was coming through; I was in love with the world again. Ah.

# NOTES OF A DIRTY OLD MAN

*L.A. FREE PRESS*, AUGUST 22, 1975

Down around Sunset, about Sunset and Wilton, near the freeway exit and by the gas station, you'll see them sometimes in their uniforms with swastika. They wear pleasant looks on very white faces and hand out literature. They also wear helmets and some of the boys are big enough to play for the L.A. Rams. They are ready: members of the American Nazi Party. Well, it's Hollywood and one thinks of it more like part of a grade B movie, but then there are those who will tell you that it began that way over there, too—just a few guys standing around who should have been fingering girls in the back seat of the movie house. Next thing you knew they were sitting at the sidewalk cafés of Paris, getting it off. But then if you're going to allow the Communist Party and the Socialist Party and the Gay Party and the Demos and Repubs, you can't very well say, well, the Nazi Party has no right to exist. So there they are but they intend to get the average person more wrought up—memories of ovens and *Pathé* Newsreels of Hitler screaming, and then they *are* wearing uniforms that don't exactly remind some of Jack Oakie in bell-bottoms.

Sometimes the police arrive in three or four squad cars. I was gassing up at the station one day when it got very goosey around there. There were seven or eight cops looking very nervous, unsure, grim. The Nazis were gathered in squad formation, standing at attention except for the leader who was speaking to one of the cops. Then back toward Wilton was gathered a group of New York Marxist intellectual types, thin, some Jewish, black-bearded; most were around 5′6″, wore old black coats—even in the heat of day—with white wrinkled shirts open at the collar, and they were screaming: "Hey, go back to Glendale, you bastards! Go back to Munich!"

One could sense conflagration, moil, and murder just a tick away. One curious wrong word and they would all be together, upon each other: cops, Marxists, and Nazis.

Sitting there in my car the old thought came back to me: How was it possible for people to believe in such opposite things with such rigor, such energy, such righteousness? How could some people be so sure there was a God and others so sure there was not? How were people unlucky enough to believe in anything? And then if you didn't believe in anything wasn't that a belief? Tra lala.

I got out of my car and walked toward the Nazi leader and the cop he was talking to. The cop saw me approaching first and stopped talking to the Nazi. He watched me. He had red eyebrows and looked as if he were wearing suntan lotion. I stopped three feet away.

"What do you want, buddy?" the cop asked me.

"I want a pamphlet. I want to know what this man's ideology is."

"You can't have one."

"Why not?"

"Because I have given an order to disperse and anybody within this area in five minutes will be under arrest."

"But I'm getting gas."

"That your car at the pump?"

"Yes."

"All right. Fill up and get out."

Cops can kill you and I've been jailed often enough but I can't help getting a sense of the comical out of them. I do suppose that the very fact of their ultimate and unmolested power is what makes them ludicrous. One realizes that power when given even to one man is a very dangerous thing and that man must be of very good soul and mind not to misuse it, and to use it judiciously. Yet in a city like Los Angeles thousands of men are given this power and sent among us with guns, clubs, handcuffs, two-way radios, and high-powered cars; and helicopters, disguises, green-beret training, plus gas, dogs, and even more dangerous: women.

Yet the sense of the comic remains. Once I gave a party at my place and drank too much. I passed out on the rug and the party went on. Then somebody pulled at me and I regained consciousness. "Bukowski, somebody's at the door and wants to talk to you." Still stretched on the rug I looked up. It was a policeman with cap tilted rakishly and smoking a cigar. "You own this place, pal?"

"No, officer, but I pay the rent."

"Well, look, pal, I know this place. I've been here before." He inhaled on his cigar and took it out of his mouth and looked at the red and glowing end of it. Then he put it back in his mouth. "I've been here before, pal, and I've got to tell you this: one more call and I'm throwing you in the slammer!"

"All right, officer, I understand. . . ."

Back to the Nazis. I sat in my car and got gassed-up. As I did I saw the leader of the Nazis leave the cop and then stand in front of his troops. Then he gave some commands and they marched off down the street. The New York Marxists followed somewhat behind, still cursing but feeling some minor victory. The whole moil of them turned north up Wilton and I paid for my gas and followed slowly in my car. I couldn't understand what attracted me. I suppose it was only the action, like horses breaking out of the starting gate.

One block up Wilton the troops crossed the street and marched toward a large van. The doors opened in back and the Nazis entered in orderly fashion, sitting down and facing each other, very straight, on long ledges on each side of the van. The doors closed and the leader and one other Nazi got into the front seat. One of the Marxists threw a rock which hit against the rear of the van and fell into the street.

The van full of Nazis moved off. I followed them and behind me were two carloads of Marxists and a police car. I looked back and one of the Marxists hollered at me: "Let's get those sons of bitches!" I nodded and looked forward again. When we reached Franklin I made a sudden right. The disparate fellows continued north. Like fights with women, history never ended. The history of politics, that is. Maybe the balance of everything was the secret: all lawn and no weeds or all weeds and no lawn, and we're really doomed: all spiders, no flies; all lambs, no lions; all me and no you and we were doomed.

I turned south down Western and drove into the liquor store. Two six-packs. All you and no me.

# NOTES OF A DIRTY OLD MAN

## NOTES OF A DIRTY OLD DRIVER OF A LIGHT BLUE 1967 VOLKSWAGEN TRV 491

*L.A. FREE PRESS*, NOVEMBER 11, 1975

Many of the irritable things about life and in people come about when I am driving the boulevards and streets of Los Angeles. Allow me to begin right away: one of the most obnoxious things that many drivers do is to turn out part of their left front wheel (and often a portion of their car) just a shade into your lane as you approach them. They are getting ready to make a left turn and they block part of your lane either out of greed or stupidity or anxiety or bluster. I do suppose they want you to stop so they can make their left turn in front of you. I've never seen it done. All drivers take a quick scan of their rearview and side mirrors and float out into the lane to their right, just a bit.

Another obnoxious type is the one who has such a great difficulty in simply making a right turn. They slow and grip the wheel; they slow to 5 mph and then drift way out left in order to make the right turn, twisting the wheel as if they were steering a great ship through a storm. And you make your right turn, following them, and you have too much time to study their ears and their necks and their bumper stickers which usually say something like: "Christians aren't perfect. They are only forgiven."

Obnoxious type K-5b is the one in the left lane ahead of you. He is going at a good speed toward the corner while the right lane is cluttered with sun-dreamers. You follow him along figuring that you will finally cut to the right lane and get clearance so you won't have to look at his bumper sticker which usually says something like: "Honk if you're horny." My bumper sticker would like to say:

"Honk if you can't come." Anyway, type K-5b will apply his brakes and his brake lights won't work and either his left blinker won't work or he doesn't use it and he walls you in there as the sun-dreamers in the right lane pass by. Then he makes his left turn and leaves you at the red light.

Type K-5c will be sitting in the left lane and the sun-dreamers again will have the right lane blocked for one-half the distance to the goal line, and you will pull up behind type K-5c, believing that you will pull out behind him as the signal changes. But no. *As* the signal changes he'll hit his left-turn blinker and you'll sit there behind him, locked, and his bumper sticker will say: "God is Love."

Types 45 KLx will not even know each other but their psyches will hang from the same stem. They will each possess one lane apiece in a two-lane street (I mean going in the same direction) (which ought to get us into Driver Examination Tests soon). And they will each be driving at 18 mph in a 35 mph zone. And behind each of them will be rows of automobiles. It *would* seem a conspiracy, and one wonders. I find myself usually directly behind one of the two leading cars. Finally after much patience and some luck, I am able to break through and pass one of the cars. What happens then? One of the slow cars that has been blocking traffic *suddenly accelerates* with me trying to keep even.

The total ugliness and indifference of the worst features of the human race come out in their driving habits. To those who believe that the assassination of world leaders might move us forward into some direction—perhaps the removal of small non-world leaders and asshole drivers, golfers and Safeway bag-boys might bring better results, although I am for neither method. But if we have to have one or the other I'd suggest the latter, Fyodor Dostoyevsky and *Crime and P.* and the Christ-structure of morals and non-movement be frigged.

Oh, yes. And well. Then there is type 62 4fa. He or she will take the one lane going in the same direction at 18 mph. They deserve to read the collected works of Edgar Guest and probably have, but you can't honk—that makes them happy. I use various in-tricks like falling back and then roaring up to their bumper. Another device is to put it in neutral and glide along behind them and rev your engine up to top roar. Of course, you're reacting and that's what they want. Type 62 4fa is clever. Their quite flaunting and vicious move—after holding you back for five miles—is to run a red light at the last moment, leaving you there staring at their vanishing bumper sticker which says something like: "If Nixon makes a comeback I'll let you clean the rings out of my grandmother's bathtub."

I did mention (earlier?) the Driver's Examinations. I mean the ones on paper. They are easy enough. One simply uses the old common sense. One is asked a question and is told to mark one of three choices. But on each examination I have ever taken, there is always one question where two answers are *correct* and one is false. Not that it matters. But it is an irritant, and if you believe it is a deliberate foil, of course, there's something wrong with you. But there *is* always one. Example:

> *If you are approaching the crest of a hill, you must not change*
> *lanes in a divided highway with a lane going in each direction:*
>    *a) If you've just had a fight with your girlfriend*
>    *b) If your dog has just shit on the backseat*
>    *c) If you've just picked up a Communist hitchhiker*

Now it's obvious that either a) or b) is the correct answer, either or both, but no matter which one you mark, the other will be correct. . . .

One can talk (or write) almost as long about the oddities of driving as one can talk about the oddities of sex and all the braggadocio that goes along with it. It's bad enough just driving along the streets of anywhere with other people, but along with that cars do develop characters and characteristics of their own. Strange things happen among all that tin. That tin ingests things. Car junkyards are much sadder and more real to me than human graveyards. The human graveyard lacks definition—it doesn't hum and clash, throw back the sun; it quits. Old cars, old junkyards fight on like punch-drunk fighters. I'm not a car freak but one finally falls in love with what one lives with. I doubt that any man can walk into Pep Boys without at least getting a spiritual hard-on. I can't speak for the ladies.

I had one car that would refuse to start again if I parked it on the parking lot of this liquor store at Hollywood and Normandie. The car would be running quite well, but each time I came out with my liquor and got in the car to drive off, it would not start. I would have to push it off of the parking area outside the liquor store and then onto the street and then it would start. After three or four repeats of this, I would just leave the car in the street. I suppose it was a technical matter, something about an unworkable carburetor level or some such but, then, you really didn't know.

Or maybe the car just didn't like certain things I did. I remember once I had a fight with my girlfriend, and I ran out of her house to leap into my car and drive off and the forward gears wouldn't work. I'd never had that trouble before. The car would only run in reverse. It refused to run forward. I checked the transmission level. It was all right. For a moment I considered driving the car backwards all the way to my room. But convenience can sometimes overtake madness. So I swallowed my bile and went back: "Look, baby, hahaha," I said, "I want to tell you something funny. My car only runs backwards." "Only runs backwards?" "Yeah, I can't leave. I don't know what the hell." "Come on, show me."

I walked her out to my car and got in. "Now look," I said, "it will only drive backwards. I'll put it in forward and it won't move."

I put it in forward and she yelled after me, "Hey! Where the hell you going?"

I did my U-turn and parked on the other side of the street. Then I got out. "I don't understand it."

So that's how we got back together—that time. . . .

And there are the car geniuses, too. I bought this car off this man one time and he told me all about it. "Now this car is going to give you trouble now and then. Now when it does, there are two buttons over on the left side of your dashboard. Now if the car runs rough or won't start, just push this No. 1 button. That will cure your trouble. If it doesn't, still try to keep using it. If that doesn't cure it, then finally go to your No. 2 button. That will automatically get it going." I sometimes did have to go to button No. 2, but it never failed and when I resold the car, I passed the message on. . . .

Automobile mechanics, body-shop men, brake-shop men, transmission repairmen have a special swagger and aplomb that far out-hotdogs our M.D.s and lawyers. And don't forget that red light in your rearview mirror. As he walks toward you, it is almost like the approach of a god. You've done something with your car that *shouldn't* be done, you know. But it's almost worth it—he'll seem kindly, judicious, won't fart or tell a bad joke. He'll just hand you a piece of paper and then tool his bike off and you can do it all over again. Like sex.

Endurance is important in our society, and some luck, but show me a man with a good car and a good woman and most surely a special light will fall upon him: the love of dependency and the dependency of love. You will be moved if you chose what moves wisely. And next week we'll get back to dirty stories. I haven't lost my mind. And as I drove this copy down to the *Free Press*, a small metal Maltese cross leaped about as it hung from a shoestring from the rearview mirror. And my automobile insurance is paid up for a year in advance.

# THE BIG DOPE READING

They had mailed the tickets, and I came flying into this little town off the east coast of Florida. I waited for the passengers to climb out, and then I got up and walked down the ramp and saw the two poetry-hound types waiting, so I walked up to them: "I'm Chinaski," I said, and they grinned and grinned. We walked over and waited for the bags, and then I said, "Shit, let's not wait here; let's make the bar." So we went into the bar—Clyde and Tommy and me—and there were *more* poetry hounds: "They all want to meet you, daddy." I looked them over. Lots of women, eyes hot with reading my erotic shit. I glanced at them, shifted from face to face, from body to body. One of the bodies looked really heavy, but she looked ready. I was introduced around. "Oh, Mr. Chinaski," one of them said, "I really *liked* your story *My X-pert Hock*!"

(I write stories, poems, and novels. I usually write my stuff along the sex trail to keep them awake, and while they're awake I give them the rest of it. I sneak it to them. I give them morphine and then pull out their slim souls.)

It was near midnight, and the airport bar closed at midnight, so we drank up. Tommy got the tab for the drinks, and we left for Clyde's place, after picking up my baggage. At Clyde's, a lot of beer and grass—Colombian—went around while flat, loud music blasted on the stereo. I drifted around and checked out the female bodies. "Oh, Mr. Chinaski, I really *loved* your poem about the man who cut off his balls and flushed them away like apricots!" I kissed that one, and a flashbulb popped somewhere in the room.

I was rotten: I sucked upon their adulation like virgin pussy. We smoked and smoked and drank and drank, and soon people began leaving. The first poetry reading was 9 P.M. at the Jiz-Wiz Club, the next night. Then I had to stroke it up again the next night. Two readings for $500 plus airfare, lodging, maybe some food, and prob-ably some ass. Ginsberg got a thousand for a reading, but then he sat on a rug and did mantras and hollered out pretty damned good. I just get drunk and fucked up.

Anyhow, people kept leaving and leaving, and it was about 4 A.M., so Clyde left for his bedroom and said the couch was mine. I was left with a lady of about 22 with this rag tied around her head. She had a fairly good body, wild eyes, and kept talking about retarded children. She taught retarded children, so she talked a lot about them. I was next to her on the couch. Every now and then I would interrupt her conversation about the children with a long kiss. She knew how to kiss. Or I knew how to kiss. Anyway, the kisses were furiously warming. Oh, hell, they were divinely ecstatic. You fur-nish the words; it's my genuine bullshit that keeps me going. Well, after each kiss, she got back to the retarded children as if the kiss hadn't even happened, and this heated me more. She had a good trick going, with that rag around her head and those wild, glowing eyes. Schoolteachers always make everybody hot; they even make you hotter than nuns do.

Her name was Holly, and when she left, I left. I got into the car with her, and when she started the engine, we embraced.

It was a long drive, and Holly kept talking about the retarded children, their problems, how to help them, how to approach them, and my cock got harder and harder. We stopped at a signal, and I reached up and undid the rag from her head and all this long blonde hair spilled out. "Christ," I said, "why do you *hide* that? I'm going to yank on it."

"It gets filled with cigarette ashes at parties," she said.

She had a fairly private apartment on the bottom floor. She parked, and we went to her place. Holly opened the door, and I fol-lowed her in. "My husband's out of town for a week. Business. He introduced me to your writing; he really worships you."

"Yeah?"

Holly went into the bathroom, and I walked to the bedroom and undressed and then got into bed. "How far away is your husband?" I asked.

"Forty miles."

"Is he jealous?"

"I don't know. I've never been unfaithful."

I heard the toilet flush. In the dark, I could see my cock pushing up the covers. Holly was going to have another retarded child to fathom. When she came out of the bathroom, she was naked; so she climbed under the blanket. I thought, well, now I'll have something to write about. I pressed into her, and her teacher's tongue flicked in and out of my mouth. I caught it in the center with my teeth and sucked on it. She gagged, had trouble breathing. I played with her pussy; it gradually opened, getting wetter. I could feel the clit, and I circled it with my finger. Did Céline ever do this? I thought. Or Hemingway? Hemingway probably didn't do it enough to as many. Hemingway lacked humor and vitamin E. That's why he blew his brains away and then fell into the orange juice. Also, he got up too early in the morning. The world always looks worse before noon because too many ambitious people still have energy to burn.

I ducked my head down to eat her pussy, and she pushed me away, saying "No, no!" Most like it; some don't. I never forced that part. I got back up and grabbed her hair and yanked her head back until her mouth fell open, and then I drove my lips inside of her lips. It was like entering the guts of a flower. She was nailed to the sun and I was the sun. Then I fell from her mouth, sucked her left breast, then the right. Then I turned her, my right arm underneath her body and my left arm coming over the top, and I took both of her hands and held them from the outside. I just let my cock poke and slide its way; it knew, and I waited on it. It found the open-ing and the head entered. Then gradually the cunt opened, and the remainder of my cock entered. It was tight and wet in there, and I let my cock lay on in, not moving. She began wiggling, and I still held my cock motionless. Then I let it jump without moving my body. It was one of my tricks. Then I slowly pulled my cock out and just entered the head and a tiny portion of the cock back into the cunt, making slow movements. "Jesus!" she said, "do it!" I kept on teasing the rim and the inside of her cunt. Hemingway just didn't know, I thought, and Céline never wrote about it, and Henry Miller never really knew how to fuck.

I finally gave her half of my cock, feeling her grip me. Then I worked it in gradually, barely increasing the speed. Then I lost my technique and just started ripping. I stopped just before climaxing and held it still. I allowed myself to cool and then began again. I repeated the process four or five times, and then I lost control and let her have it. Holly came first, and as she did I followed. We both hollered like juveniles, and as I came I kept looking at all that hair on her head, thinking, Christ, Christ, I've got the luck, the luck and the way. Nobody can beat me now.

Holly got up and went to the bathroom. I reached down and got one of my stockings from under the bed and wiped myself off with it. I didn't want her husband coming home to hard spots on the sheets. A pro always made little clever moves like that. Yeats or Dante would never have known how to do that.

When Holly came back, she fell asleep with her backside to me. She had a gentle little snore, very sexy, and my cock half-hardened and I let it slide into her ass. It was warm and comfortable there, and I thought, well, look, Chinaski, once again you're in bed with a woman 30 years younger than you, and you can't dance, shoot pool, or bowl. They all want to fuck immortality, and as long as they think you're immortal, you can go ahead and fuck them, and when they find out that you're not, well, you've got all that young ass stored up, and you can go back to your one-thumb, four-finger love.

My problem is that I fall in love with every woman I fuck. I fuck good, but I am overemotional. To me, when a woman gives me her body, I feel as if she is giving me her soul; that's part of what makes me hot. And then the whole act has overtones of death and murder and conquest. But mostly I just feel a rush of fondness and love, and I can't overcome it.

I throbbed throughout for the woman I had just fucked. I wasn't worldly that way, and it cost me, but I couldn't correct it. Most people shrug off a fuck like they shrug off a picnic. I don't understand that attitude.

The alarm awakened us, and Holly shut it off. "Look," I said, "take a day off. Let's sleep. Maybe later we'll do it again."

"No," said Holly, "I'm out of sick leave, and besides, the children need me."

I pulled the covers up and stretched out.

When I awakened, Holly was gone. I got up and walked around her apartment. Hangovers always make me horny. Drinking makes me horny. *Not* drinking makes me horny. But hangovers make me horniest of all. I found two of her shoes in the front room, standing side by side near a chair. There was a strange loneliness and warmth there—like buttered toast or cries from people shoved over cliffs.

The heels and the base of the shoes were made of wood, and the heels (although sadly thick) were high. The shoes heated me. I am a leg and shoe man. Breasts mean little to me, although I suck on them because women like it. But legs and shoes set me off, and I don't fight it.

I had a hard-on, and I picked one of the shoes and ran my cock in and out of it. The bottom of my cock ran along the wood, and the top was held by the soft fabric that ran up from the toe.

Maybe, I thought, someday I'll marry a shoe.

"Do you, Henry, take this shoe as your. . . ."

I ran my cock in and out, then withheld the impulse. I had to preserve my sperm. I went back into the bedroom and looked in the closet. I found a pair of blue panties—no shit stains—and I rubbed them back and forth over my cock. It was good. I almost gave way.

Some people, I thought, think that I am America's greatest poet. Suppose this shit got out? I'd be doomed. I threw the panties back into the closet. Then I saw a shoe. Just one shoe, alone, with a high spiked heel. That shoe was a *hot* shoe. I picked it up and started fucking it. I walked around the room, giving it to that shoe. I even made a few swift runs in circles, giving it to that shoe. Then, at the last moment, I ripped it away and threw it back into the closet.

Then I had to take a shit, bad. I went and did it. All that beer. I'd never die of constipation. There's no doubt that when a man sees his shit the first thing he thinks of is, I have a chance to live, *ah!* At least, that is what I think of. And then if you have hemorrhoids, you get a double break. I had hemorrhoids. And I looked over at the toilet paper holder, and there wasn't any paper. I ran into the kitchen and found a box of tissues, and I took eight or ten tissues and started getting off wiping my ass and making sounds. Then I was rubbed bare and raw, and the turds and the paper stuffed the bowl as I flushed. Some of it went down, then the water rose and the tissues and turds started rising. They came up to the level of the lid and held. I knew better, but I flushed again, and then it came: turds, tissues, water, all over the floor in front of the toilet. I took the back lid off and started playing with the big ball, the chain, the black rubber stopper.

I flushed again. More of the same—turds, tissue, water, defeat. I took away the floor mat and started wiping up the business. I got most of it. I took newspapers and picked up turd parts and carried them to a paper bag I found on the sink in the kitchen, and I put them into the paper bag. When I came back, I saw that the floor mat had shit stains on it. I turned it over. It looked better. Like an Indian weaving.

I had Clyde's phone number. He was home. "Listen, Clyde, I've fucked up Holly's plumbing. I've got beer turds floating about like the ultimate defeat of everything. Oh, my God, these brown sycophants."

"Doesn't she have a plunger?"

"Neither green nor black nor blue nor red."

"I'll send help."

Clyde didn't show. Tommy did. Tommy said that Clyde sent him. He had a red plunger. We sat down and smoked some more of his Colombian.

"I'm honored, Tommy. This, I think, is the first poetry reading sponsored by the dope dealers of America."

"Feels good," said Tommy.

I took the plunger and worked the bowl. Then the suction took effect. I flushed the bowl several times, and it worked. We sat and talked for a while, then Tommy drove me back to Clyde's, where six or seven people were spread out on the floor, smoking, drinking, maybe smacking.

The first reading wasn't bad because I wasn't too drunk, and nobody likes to gyp an audience—entirely. But there was a party afterward at the house of another teacher of retarded children. It was the fat one I had seen at the airport, but she had a very nice sense of gamble about her. Her name was Kali, and she had tremendous thighs. She could take three horses. I wasn't a horse, but I sure as hell bet on them. What's a man to do in his spare time, chew on old burned-out light bulbs? So I began kissing her and running my hand up her dress. There were 35 people in that house, but the sign was in: America's greatest poet wanted to be Kali's horse fuck. It was accepted, and Holly sat there pissed, looking at me. But I was angry at her for not having any paper on that roll.

So they left, and it was Kali and me. I climbed into bed and watched her undress.

"That was a great reading," she said. "You make poetry sound so simple and real and easy."

"Genius," I said, "could mean the ability to say a profound thing in a simple way."

"Tell me more," she said.

"Endurance is more important than truth," I replied.

"But tell me what's really happening."

"I'm riding a winning streak all to hell, that's all. It's going to vanish, but I'm taking it for whatever ride it can get me. I've got some soul, but basically my luck is better than my psyche."

Then Kali stood there naked. She had plenty—in places of plenty. She got into bed. I grabbed and grabbed. But it was solid. She was built the way Norwegians like women; the same way Icelanders like them; women, women, women, the kind of women who built the few real men, the kind of flesh, the real mold, the kiln, the vagina to bear the miracle and the big ass and the tight cunt to cause it and accept it.

Kali kept laughing and saying, "No, no, I can't *do* it until I feel the passion, I can't do it. . . ."

I tried most of my tricks. She liked the kissing best, which was all right with me. Although I'm not sure whether eating pussy or kissing sets me off most. But the kissing was good, and then suddenly my teeth were clamped around one of her ears, and I held that ear while almost ripping the hair out of her head, and she gave way.

I mounted her—on top—and there was trouble at first. I slipped over or under, and then she took her hand and guided me in. I was too drunk to be totally hard, but once I got it in I lucked it—the steel came along. It was a good ride, but I fell back once, quit, and then she started playing with me. She had a way of jog-gling my balls. She slid her tongue up and down the backside of my cock, then she took it all in—suddenly—and I ripped it out of her mouth, mounted her and came within 15 strokes—which wasn't too kind—but I didn't care—readings wore me out, and I still loved Holly better.

Kali didn't make it to work, and the phone rang about 8:45 A.M. Kali brought it to me.

"What?" I asked.

"This is Zana," she said.

Zana was my girlfriend from Texas. She probably cared for me a lot more than any woman cared for me. She was fine, not a bitch (except on certain off days), and she had the most beautiful eyes I have ever seen in any living skull. She was good but damned, mostly because she knew me. However, she carried it well, and I thought I loved her. But I wasn't sure.

"Hey, baby, I'm sick, but it's sure good to hear from you."

"I'm flying out to see you."

"Good, good," I said, "that's great. And I've been a good boy."

Zana gave me her arrival time, which was to be in a couple of days—after the second reading. I still had a chance to build up my sperm count. She had gotten the telephone number from Clyde, that ass. She didn't ask about the woman who had answered the phone. That was style. Zana had style. Also she was capable of kill-ing me. What more could a man ask of life?

I don't remember the second reading because I began drinking too early in the day. I did come out of the blackout in the middle of the last poem. I read it on out and told them that was it. They kept hollering, "MORE! MORE! MORE!" so I must have fooled them again. I walked offstage and went out back to Clyde's place, and there was another party. We smoked Colombian and drank beer.

People kept walking in, but none of them bothered me. Then a guy walked in, and by the look of him I knew he was a suck. His beard was perfectly trimmed and he wore a beret, an orange beret. His face had an essential and unforgiving emptiness. He gave off not only rays but waves of rays—muddied, stinking rays that made you look away from him.

He sat at my feet and introduced himself.

"I'm a poet," he said. "Just like you."

"You may be a poet," I said, "but you're not a poet just like me."

"Anyhow, I'd like to ask you a question."

"All right."

"Well, Mr. Chinaski, I've read about you. You wrote for a long time without success. What did you do during this period when you weren't getting published?"

"I drank and I didn't bother anybody."

"Well, I'm a printer and also an actor. I feel that I'm ready for publication, so I'm going to publish my own book. Then I'm going to go about reading my poems, and I'll sell my books at the readings. I'm an actor, so I'll read my poems very well."

"O.K.," I said.

"The only trouble is that when I give readings nobody shows up," he said.

"Excuse me," I said. I got up and went to the bathroom. When I came out, I sat elsewhere. The party went on and on, and gradually the people gave way and vanished. I found myself sitting with a young girl, Alacia, about 18. She rented a bedroom from Clyde, and she lived there with another guy, although *he* probably paid the rent; but I didn't know where the guy was. Anyhow, Alacia and I sat there talking, and I kept rubbing one of my feet along the top of one of hers and said, "Let's make it."

She said, "No."

"Shit, let's do something," I said.

Alacia said, "Like what?"

"Well, give me a hand job."

"Hell, I don't know."

"There's no way it can hurt you, Alacia."

"I don't know. It just seems kind of dumb."

"So does talking about poetry and life."

"Well, I don't know," she said.

I took off my pants and stretched out on the couch. I pulled it out of my shorts. Alacia just sat in her chair, staring at it. She kept looking, and it excited me. It was dumb; the dumbness of it excited me. The thing began to grow and rise. It reflected in her eyes.

"Is this all it comes to?" she asked.

"What comes to?"

"Your novels, your stories, your poems, is this all it comes to?"

"Yes, a hard cock. Touch it, baby, rub it, kiss it. I'm going crazy! Watch it grow and spurt under your eyes! Forget about writing and art. Almost all male writers have cocks, remember that. Whack me off, you blue-eyed witch!"

Alacia reached over and grabbed it.

"Oooh," she said.

"Spit on your palm. Rub me."

She put her hand up to her mouth.

"Spit on it good," I said. My cock was throbbing like a cello in an earthquake, a major earthquake that would rattle the strings and kill 800 people. Her hand came down and closed around my cock. I had drunk a great deal of beer, but I had the faith. For a 55-year-old guy, I was as horny as a Catholic altar boy.

"Oooh," she said.

"It's getting bigger," I said. "Look."

"Yes."

"It's purple. See all those veins? That's from strain and trying to stick my dick in my ass. I've got hemorrhoids. And rub harder.

Get it up near the head, mostly, and now and then give it a long, hard stroke. See how it's bending back? Shit, that son of a bitch is *ugly*!

Alacia stopped talking. She just looked and rubbed. Her eyes were transfixed like a creature looking at a rattlesnake. Her lips began to open, and I could see her teeth. I could see Alacia's white, even teeth as her lips pulled back. I watched her lips and her eyes, and I began to get very excited. She beat harder and bent closer. I could feel the climax rushing up. I took both of my hands and reached up and got her behind the neck and pulled her head down over the head of my cock. She fought, pulled away. It angered me, so I pulled her back with one hand and opened her mouth with the other as I jammed my cock toward her mouth. I missed and came all over her cheeks.

Alacia jumped up. I could see the sperm rolling down the left side of her face. Not much of it, but I could see it. She felt it, and with the back of one of her wrists she brushed it away. Then she ran into the bathroom. I found my pants, pulled them back on, waited, then got up and went to the refrigerator and unscrewed another beer.

It was some time before she came out, so I stretched out and thought, conquest, conquest, conquest.

Alacia came out of the bathroom looking younger and more beautiful than ever. She looked *untouched*, strangely untouched, virginal, and yet it was just as it should be because I had hardly *penetrated* her except in the worst way—spiritually. It's always better for a woman to get simply fucked than played with.

Looking at her, it almost made me hot again, yet I knew I had lucked it as far as my luck would go.

She stood over me and said, "America's greatest poet. You want to know what you are? You want to know what you really are?"

"What?"

"You're a shithead, you're a shithead, a SHITHEAD!"

"Now wait a minute, baby. The food goes in the mouth and comes out the ass."

"Shithead, I gotta tell you something. I'm going to tell Marty what you did to me! Shithead, shithead, *shithead*!"

"Who's Marty?"

"The man who loves me."

"Really?"

"He'll kill you!"

"O.K."

"You're a smart fuck, aren't you?"

"Yeah."

Alacia abruptly walked out of the room. I rolled from my side to my back, thinking, ah, boy, you see, you've gotten most of it back. You've fucked and sucked and reamed and rammed. You've got to be king.

Alacia came in; I could hear her walking slowly. "Here's a memory from me to you."

"Thanks, baby."

It fell all over me. A dishpan of cold water. It was a *large* dishpan. It was cold, and there was plenty of it.

Alacia laughed wildly, and I stretched out there, soaked.

"Bitch," I told her, "if I had any sperm, I'd rape you for that!"

She kept laughing as she walked into her bedroom. She closed the door, still laughing. Now and then she would stop, then begin again. I took off my wet clothes, turned the couch pillows over and was soon asleep.

I met Zana at the airport the next day. She looked good and healthy, the way Texas women looked. Tommy had the car, so he drove us to Holly's place. Holly had agreed to let Zana and me have her place for the weekend. She was going off somewhere. We stopped for beer and smokes. Tommy gave us a bit of Colombian, and we also bought some toilet paper. Tommy had a smoke with us, and then he left. I saw one of Holly's shoes that I had tried to fuck, and I thought, Jesus, how am I going to fuck Zana? I think I'm out of sperm, and I love her more than any of them. She's got soul and class, and she cares for me—maybe even loves me. Goddamn, why couldn't I have waited? Well, there was one thing left, and something I hardly minded doing. We sat around drinking and talking.

"I've been a good boy," I told her.

"I'm sure as shit glad to hear about that. There are a lot of star fuckers in this world. Just think how much Elvis must get? He must get so much that he's lucky to get it up anymore," she said.

"Is that all it comes to?" I asked.

"What?"

"My novels, my stories, my poems—is that all they come to: a hard cock?"

"Baby," she said, "I don't know which I like better, your writing or your cock. And when either of them stops working, I'll be the first to let you know."

We went to bed three or four hours later. She had flown thousands of miles to see me. That was flattering, and frightening. I held her close and began playing with her hair. Strangely, my cock hardened, but I still felt spermless. I gave her my one-tenth kisses, just brushing or leaping at the mouth quickly, then pulling away. I yanked at her hair, sucked her ears, bit her on the neck.

Then I moved to her breasts, then her bellybutton, then I was down there where the hairs started over the cunt. I pulled at a few strands of them with my teeth. Then suddenly I gave it the nose run, starting down at the ass and running it up and through. She groaned, and I gave her yet another nose run. Then I let loose the tongue, but quite subtly. I began far away, circling the whole area and approaching closer and closer. Then I ran it up and down, ever so lightly, and I could feel the tip of my tongue brush her clit. I shoved my tongue, once, into the cunt proper, then I worked it on the clit, lightly and continuously. I imagined her to be a strange woman in the back seat of my car who was powerless to resist me; she wanted to but didn't know how. I increased the pressure and began rhythms against the clit with my tongue—one, two, three, quick, then stop, then one, two, three, quick, then stop. "YES, YES, YES, YES, YES!" she said. Then she farted. "I'm sorry," she said. I hit it again. She farted again. Then I sucked the clit into my mouth, and she really began to roll and react. I worked it up and down, now and then getting the flick of the tongue behind it, and I almost let it go out of my mouth several times, then sucked it back in. Her legs closed about my head, and we bounced about. I still tried to work the magic, but it was more difficult. She unwrapped me, and I fell back.

"Listen, baby," I said, "I don't think I can fuck tonight. The readings, all that drinking. I'm burned out."

"Hey, daddy," said Zana, "it's all right. I'll be fine."

We fell asleep after that, and when we awakened we decided to leave that day, Saturday, instead of Sunday. We lucked it with the airport reservations, and we left a note for Holly: "Thanks for letting us use your tub, basin, springs, garbage disposal, and potty. We leave you a touch of Colombian, one mescaline capsule, and our love. Zana and Chinaski." We also left behind a couple of steaks and four rolls of toilet paper.

Clyde drove us to the airport, gave me the $500 in cash, mostly 20s and 50s, and I knew what Whitman meant when he said, "To have great poets we must have great audiences." Although I think it worked better the other way around. I bought a couple of rounds at the airport bar, and then we got on the jet. It stopped off at Houston, and they discovered motor trouble. All the passengers waggled around the counter clerk as if he were some inside God of information. It was flight number 72.

Zana and I walked down to the bar, which was eons away. We sat at a corner table, alone, and started on the vodka: vodka and 7-Up for me, vodka tonic for her. I remembered being locked in at O'Hare during a tornado warning. All of us were in the airport six and one-half hours. You've never seen so many drunks, except on a New Year's Eve night. One poor fellow stepped out of the bar and started rocking back and forth, teetering. All eyes were watching him. When he fell, he hit in the worst way possible—backward, his head hitting the cement, bobbing up and down a few times, then settling. I was one of the first to run toward him, but others were swifter. The first to get to him was a kindly old man with a long white beard, which was stained with some yellow substance, and he wore a Chicago White Sox baseball cap. He said, "Hey, buddy, you all right? I'm gonna get you some help!" He found the guy's wallet in his jacket pocket, slipped it down the front of his own shirt and ran off hollering, "Help, help, there's a man hurt back there!" Then he was around a corner and gone.

Zana and I sat there drinking and waiting for them to fix the engine. We got into some kind of argument, although what it was about I wasn't sure. Zana was more sure of what it was about, and finally I just got quiet. She kept talking and we both kept drinking. I'm not sure just how much time went by, but these two people, a man and a woman, came into the bar and walked right up to our table and said, "Are you the two people missing from flight 72?"

"Yes," I said, "we are."

"Well, the flight is ready. Please *hurry*!"

I left the money for the drinks, and we ran after the two people. "Oh," said Zana, "don't run so fast. They're not *really* ready; they just act that way."

"No, no," I said, "they're ready, they're ready!"

I pulled her along by the hand. "HURRY! HURRY!" the two in front of us yelled back. We were drunk; it's harder to run in that condition. We ran out onto the airport ramp. All the passengers were waiting. Through their windows, they looked at us with something less than looks of love. The pilot stood at the cabin entrance. "HURRY! HURRY!" he yelled, and we ran up the steps and into the plane. There were two seats in back. We strapped ourselves in, and they pulled away the loading steps and the plane began moving. Soon we were in the air. We got free drinks, and Zana began crying, the tears rolled and rolled. And that was about all there was to the poetry reading sponsored by the dope dealers. Zana finally stopped crying, and when we landed at her hometown airport we were the last off the plane. As I passed by with Zana, one of the stewardesses asked me: "Do you folks have your problems solved now?" And I told her, "Not by *any* means. We're a *long* way from that."

Which has since proven to be truer and truer, though we are still friends.

# EAST HOLLYWOOD: THE NEW PARIS

East Hollywood sits in the smog in front of the purple mountains. It begins at Hollywood Boulevard and runs east of Western Avenue down to Alvarado Street, bordered by Santa Monica Boulevard on the south. Here you will find the greatest contagion of bums, drunks, pillheads, prostitutes per square foot, in Southern California.

I lived there. I sat at my typewriter in my underwear drinking beer at high noon, looking out the window and masturbating as the young girls walked by. At the age of 50 I was finished with the ordinary life. I quit my job and decided to become a professional writer. I wanted to make money writing because I liked to drink at night and I didn't like to get up in the morning. I could write a good dirty story, a rape, a murder, something that many of them wanted to do but didn't have the guts to do, so I wrote it down for them in a believable way and they creamed the white slime down their legs and I got paid. I liked words. I could make them dance like chorus girls or I could use them like machinegun bullets. So I was hustling, a lot of people hustle, like your mother probably got paid for letting dogs screw her in the ass in dirty alleys, only she didn't tell you about it.

The problem with my writing was that my drinking got in the way. I'd whack-off once or twice, get down 5 or 6 cans of beer, open a pint of scotch and sit at the machine. After typing an hour or 2 I'd just sit at the machine and drink. I'd get scared. Suppose the editors were too fucking dumb to tell good writing from bad? What was an editor anyhow? Just a guy whose mother had taken it in some dirty alley, had gotten creamed in the mouth, ass, and cunt simultaneously by 3 unwashed Arabs. Look at what happened to Céline. They stole his bicycle and spit on his shoes, hung cans of goat piss outside his window.

Well, you drink every day and the nuts come around, the crazies. The first was Rolph, the German. He just knocked. He had this black girl with him, Bonnie. He said, "Hey, what are you doing?" and I said, "I wait upon Christ to return as a Chinaman with a wooden leg." They came in. She was all right, I could tell by looking. But there was something very odd about him. I took a pull at my beer.

"You've been to the madhouse twice," I told him.

He laughed and jumped up and down on the floor. Then he stopped. They both sat down. Then Rolph said, "Hey, go get us some beer."

I got up and walked toward the kitchen. I'd walked maybe 5 or 6 steps when he leaped on my back, grabbed my throat with his left arm, and began beating me with his right fist. He was laughing. He was screaming something that I couldn't make out. His fist bounced off of me as he continued to strike. There was nothing gentle about his attack.

"Rolph," I said, "your mother is a stinking whore!"

He kept beating me.

"Rolph," I said, "stop that. I am beginning to get irritated. Here I am going to get you and your girlfriend a beer and you are hanging from me like some dumb prick!"

He kept beating at me. I reached over, got the back of his neck, turned, faced toward the couch, and hurled him through the air. Bonnie leaped aside and Rolph landed on the couch, then fell to the floor. He sat up and looked at me. His eyes became misty.

"You are unfair," he said, "I was only joking. We came by in good faith."

I looked at Bonnie. "What are you doing with this dufflebag of a man?"

"I love him," said Bonnie.

"You love dead shit in a hotdog roll," I said.

Then I looked at Rolph. "Get up, man, I'm going to finish you off!"

"Wait a minute," he said. "We know about you."

"Yeah?"

"Yeah. I run a bookstore on Kingsley Drive, *The Marmalade Switch*. We want you to do a poetry reading."

"How much?"

"Half the take."

"Half the take and all I can drink."

"You're on. . . ."


That Friday night at 8 P.M. I drove up. The place was packed. I had never read before but I was known in town because of my dirty stories and poems, and some rumors that I did wild and astonishing things. Some of the rumors were true; the most interesting ones weren't. The truth was that I was simply a desperate and unhappy man. I was confused, sick, and lonely, yet at the same time I had a very hard head. I was disgusted with continuing situations that only left me the choices to run, fight, or suicide. And the beautiful women only ran with the rich and the famous and soon the beautiful women were no longer beautiful. Everything was some big sack of turkeyshit.

There was no place to park so I parked in the supermarket parking lot across the way. There was no need to lock the car, a 1962 Comet. I was the only one who could start it.

I got out with my sheath of poems on a clipboard. Then I heard screams:

"THERE'S THAT SON OF A BITCH! LET'S TAKE HIS ASS!"

I could make out Rolph and some big fat guy running across the dark street toward me. The miserable fart-suckers were always thinking about me in terms of Ernest Hemingway: war. They were upon me. They grabbed me and tried to wrestle me to the ground. The fat guy was already sweating. He gave me an elbow into the gut.

"YOUR FATHER WAS A FAG!" he screamed.

I threw my poems down. The fat guy had on glasses and I didn't want to blind him so I cracked him one behind the ear. He blinked, farted, then ran off. I decided to finish Rolph off. I got him over the hood of one of the cars in the parking lot and I squeezed his throat good. His eyes bulged out real nice. Even in the dark I could see his face turning purple. Then some people pulled me off, some of the people who had come for the reading. I picked up my poems and went in to read. It was a nice crowd; they liked dirty poems. After it was over I said, "Thank you. Party at my place now."

Well, parties, they happened almost every night. Just when I wrote I don't know but I wrote a great deal, most of it not too bad. So this one night I was sitting there in the center of the rug and there were people all about. I didn't know who most of them were but they were everywhere—in the bedroom, in the crapper, in the bathtub, in the kitchen, puking, crapping, eating, drinking, talking, fighting, fucking. I just sat there and drank. The women were horrible, showing their stained and unwashed panties, their tits sagging to their bellybuttons. The men were no better: hyenas, coyotes, suckerfish, bird dogs, would-be writers. I passed away from drink and their dullness. . . .

Then I was awakened. Some guy was shaking me.

"Hank! Hank! It's the cops!"

I looked up. There were 2 cops standing in the doorway. There was also a citizen standing there with a shotgun. I was flat on my stomach in the middle of the rug. I raised my head.

"Yes, gentlemen?"

There was one small cop with a mustache. He was smoking a cigar. He had his cap tilted rakishly on his head.

"You own this joint?"

"No, I rent this joint."

He looked around the room. He peered at stained and unwashed panties. Then he looked back at me.

"Listen, buddy, I've been here before! I know you! And I'm tired of coming here! I want a modicum of silence around here! And if I have to come back here again tonight I'm gonna run your ass in!"

Then the citizen with the shotgun spoke. He was an elderly fellow with something like a small tomato growing out of the left side of his throat. The tomato dripped down over his collar.

"This guy," he said, looking at me, "is the cause of everything. Since he moved into this neighborhood two months ago, the decent citizens of this community have not had one full night's sleep! Nothing but partying and cursing and broken glass and music, women of shame! I need my sleep! I DEMAND MY SLEEP!"

Then he took his shotgun and pointed it right at me. The cops just stood there. I couldn't believe it. I heard the safety click off.

I raised my right hand, formulated it into a gun, pointed at the citizen, and went:

"Pop."

A whore laughed. The citizen lowered his gun. The cop with the tilted cap said, "Remember, one more complaint and I'm running your ass in!"

"And any more," said the citizen with the tomato on his neck, "and I'm coming over without calling anybody and I'm going to settle this thing myself. . . ."

They left and I made minor attempts to keep the noise down. They didn't return that night, the cops or the citizen. There were other parties after that but I never saw any of them again. It was like a little one-night play they had put on for our benefit and then they had moved on elsewhere. . . .

My 2nd reading was down at Venice, which isn't East Hollywood but it might as well be. It was a bar right down by the ocean. I drove down alone, early, took a half-pint of whiskey, and sat down by the water drinking it.

I finished the bottle and then walked up the sand and into the bar. They were waiting. There was a little elevated table with a mike and there were 2 six-packs of beer waiting for me. I walked on through the crowd. . . .

"Bukowski!"

"Hey, Bukowski, baby!"

Then a young man, sweating, in a blue workingman's shirt ran up to me, shook my hand, "Remember me, man? I'm Ronnie. . . . Remember me, man?"

"Ronnie," I told him, "eat a basketful of dried turds."

I climbed up there and cracked a can of beer. They cheered as I drained the can. They were assholes, readers of my works. I had created for myself. Now I was a victim. I looked down and noticed all the young girls. Many of them hissed and yelled at me, they called me a male chauvinist pig, but all most of them wanted to do was to fuck me. They wanted to fuck me; they wanted to find the seed of my wizened soul, as if it came out of the end of my cock. What the young girls wanted was to will me into their kind of death, which meant another kind of game: getting in and out of bed with them and seeing who came out with the most.

. . . I read to them and I got away with it and I grabbed the money and announced that there would be a party at a poet's place, nearby. I ran to my car, got in, roared off as well as a 1962 Comet can roar off. Drunk, radio on, I had it down to the floorboards. I drove up and down the dark streets of Venice and they followed, the rat pack. Then I took the Comet, ran it up a driveway, and got the car up on the sidewalk, and it felt good driving on the sidewalk. I got it up to 60 mph. and they followed in the street. Suddenly there seemed to be a house in the way. I sheered hard to the left but hit a fence, taking out part of it. I got back into the street, some of the white sticks of fence riding upon the hood like dead bones out of nowhere. Then they clattered off. I drove to the poet's house, climbed out, and they followed me in. . . .

At my place I had a way of discouraging people from visiting me too often but new people always managed to arrive. Robbie seemed a nice enough fellow, gentle eyes, a beard; he was intense but he knew how to laugh. He published a chapbook of my poems, *I Don't Feel Good Unless I Am Being Evil.* It sold some copies and we bought drinks with it. Robbie wrote poems too, not very good ones, and then he started bringing his friends around—all males. We drank wine and beer and talked. But they were political. I'm not sure what they were. They were anarchists or revolutionaries or something of that order.

I had no politics. I told them to go ahead and do whatever they wanted to do. They were organized, though, and dedicated. They had food and weapons and women stored in the Oregon hills.

Edward, one of the members, said to me, "Look, either you are a part of history or you are a useless segment of society. You are allowing yourself to be used and when you allow yourself to be used you are making it more difficult for the remainder of us who are trying to enact a change for the better."

"All I want to do," I said, "is to type things down on a piece of paper."

"You are being selfish," said a young man with red hair. "You must join the Brotherhood of Man."

"I don't like brotherhoods," I answered. "I feel good when I am alone."

"But you're drinking with us now."

"I'd as soon drink with anarchists as anybody else."

"We are not anarchists," said a brother called Jack. "Anarchy means political and social confusion, and also the will to destruct everything. We only wish to destroy the evil and the decayed."

"Stop looking at me," I told him.

"FUCK YOU!" brother Jack screamed at me.

We drank on into the night and the brothers discussed their plans in front of me. I was honored by their trust. And they were right to trust me because, although I didn't believe in them, there was no place I could go to that I did believe in. They were nice young boys and they drank right along with me, and they had brought their own drinks with them which was more than could be said for most of my visitors.

Suddenly, about 2 A.M. brother Jack focused upon me. He was then very drunk, bits of spittle running and hanging from his chin. "Then you don't believe in us?" he asked me.

"Not really."

"Well," said brother Jack, "fuck you! FUCK YOU, FUCK YOU, FUCK YOU!"

There was some silence, then the other brothers went on talking. Brother Jack just stared at me. I was the Enemy. I was either in or I was out. Join or jerk-off into that dark night.

"FUCK YOU!" he screamed again.

He slumped a bit forward on the couch, leaned a bit to the right, and then spilled over onto the rug. He was out.

"Where's your car?" I asked Robbie.

I walked over and picked up brother Jack. I followed Robbie out the door and into the night. The car wasn't far down. Robbie opened the back door and I dropped brother Jack on the rear seat. As he landed, his eyes opened and he looked at me.

"FUCK YOU!" he screamed.

I went back in with Robbie and the brothers and we drank a little more and then they left. . . .

Two or 3 nights later Robbie knocked on the door. I let him in and cracked 2 beers. Robbie took a hit.

"Well," he said, "the brothers took a vote on whether to kill you or not. . . ."

"They did?"

"Yes, and you won by one vote. It was 4 to 3 against killing you."

"Great. Which way did you vote?"

"I voted against killing you."

"Have another beer."

"Thanks, I will. But I'm here to tell you it's all set."

"What's all set?"

"The distribution of literature."

"What literature?"

"Hank, I told you all about it."

"I was probably drunk. Tell me again."

"All right," said Robbie, "I've written up the Ultimatum. I've got 40 copies in the truck right now. You've got to help me deliver them. You promised."

"What Ultimatum?"

"To Richard Nixon, to *Time* magazine, to the TV stations, to several governors, members of the Senate and the House of Representatives, to the *New York Times*, to the *Christian Science Monitor*, to all the people who should know."

"Know what?"

"That unless air pollution is stopped we are going to blow up the cities one by one. We are going to blow up the dams and we are going to blow up the sewers, we are going to destroy each city, one by one, until air pollution is stopped."

"Listen, when you get ready to blow up East Hollywood can you give me a couple of days warning? Last thing I want to do is drown in shit."

"We'll warn you. We are gong to get the air cleaned up."

"And you're going to put shit in the streets?"

"A few must be sacrificed for the good of the many."

"And I promised you that I would help distribute these pamphlets?"

"Yes, one night you did. And now the Ultimatums are all packed in large envelopes, stamped special delivery, first class. It really cost the brothers some money. Each pamphlet is 26 pages long, detailing our demands. What you and I are going to do is distribute one Ultimatum to each of 40 mailboxes throughout town. If we put them all in one mailbox we might be in danger of being detected."

"Jesus Christ, Robbie, I can't do that! I don't believe in your program! It's crack-pot, it's ignorant, you'll drown more people in water and shit in a year than bad air can kill in a decade!"

"One night you promised me, Hank."

"What's wrong with all the other brothers?"

"I admire you, Hank. This is a big thing to me. I want to be with you when we do it."

"Nothing doing, Jerko. . . ."

The poor freak sat there staring at his shoes. I walked out and got a fifth of vodka and two glasses.

"Look," I said, "let's drink this. You can sleep on the couch tonight and in the morning we'll take your truck down to the city dump and put those Ultimatums where they belong."

I poured us two full glassfuls.

"You came from the factories and the streets," he said. "When I first read your writing I knew that you were an exceptional man, that you were one of us."

"Don't butter my ass, Jerko. I like shit where it belongs. I consider the sewage system one of man's greatest inventions."

"We voted against killing you, Hank."

"That's no gift. I have a suicide complex. . . ."

. . . Well, we drank the fifth, we finished the fifth, and I stood up and said, "Well, let's go."

"You mean you're going to help me do it?" asked Robbie.

"It'll be a cheap thrill. . . ."

"I knew you'd do it!"

We walked outside and got into the truck. It had a flatbed in back but the brothers had built some kind of structure upon it, a round whorl of tin with another hunk of tin soldered to the back. And there behind our seats were stacked the 40 Ultimatums.

Robbie drove. We stopped at the first liquor store and got a gallon jug of cheap wine. We drove off.

"Now," said Robbie, "here's our first mailbox!"

It was at Hollywood and Vine. Robbie pulled up and I reached back, got an Ultimatum, got out, and dropped it in the mailbox. I leaped back in and we gunned off.

I felt something. I felt like a child rapist. We passed the bottle.

"A beautiful night," said Robbie. "Did you read the address label?"

"Yes."

"Who got mailed the first Ultimatum?"

"Richard Nixon."

From then on it was mailbox after mailbox. Robbie had a map, the mailbox distribution was carefully planned. Then we were in Watts, in honor of our black brothers. I dumped an Ultimatum into a Watts mailbox and leaped back in.

"Here I am," I said, "leaping in and out of this truck dumping literature into mailboxes and I don't even *believe* in what the literature says. I am more insane than you are."

After the last Ultimatum had been mailed Robbie drove me back to my place. We went in and finished the jug of wine. I offered him the couch for the night. He thanked me but said that he had to leave; he had to tell the brothers about the glorious night of the deliverance of the Ultimatums. He left and I locked the door and sat on the couch in the dark and drank a can of beer. I got up, walked to the bedroom, got my shoes off, fell on the bed and slept, fully clothed. . . .

It must have been 2 months later, about one o'clock in the afternoon, when Robbie knocked. He looked very sad.

"Sit down," I said, "I'll get you a beer."

"You go ahead," he said. "Nothing for me."

I came out with the beer and sat across from him.

"It didn't work," he said.

"What?"

"All those Ultimatums, to the president, to the press, the TV, the magazines, the governors, it didn't work. Nothing was ever published, nothing was ever said, nothing was ever heard."

"Did you really have the dynamite, the know-how to carry it through?"

"Yeah, we had it, we knew what to do. Then something else happened."

"What?"

"Women. Up in the Oregon hills where we were hiding out with all our foodstuffs, our guns, the dynamite, it didn't work. Some of the brothers had women with them, and then some of the brothers started cheating on the other brothers and fucking their women. And the other brothers started fucking the other women. All the trust left, everybody started hating and fighting each other. It just broke up, the whole thing just broke up."

"Robbie, that kind of thing happens everywhere, it's only normal."

"Maybe so, but it broke us up."

"You need a drink."

"I'm not like you. Drink doesn't solve my pain."

"No, it doesn't solve it, it just takes it into a different strato-sphere."

"I'll face it head on."

"Good luck."

Robbie stood there and we shook hands. He left then. I sat there. I heard an engine start. Then he was gone. . . .

Three or four weeks later I came home one night and there stacked high on my porch and against the door were the Oregon food-stuffs: sacks of flour and sugar, sacks of beans, hundreds of cans of soups; salt, coffee, dried beef, canned tomatoes, canned milk and cream, pouches of tobacco, cigarette papers. No note, just that, and air pollution. . . .

The next strange one who came by was a fellow about 10 years younger than I, one Martin Johnson, who claimed he was going to be the next Maxwell Perkins. He was almost bald and had little tufts of red hair about each ear. He was extremely clean, scrubbed, and carried what I thought to be a kindly and dangerous smile.

"You are one of the better writers around," he said. "It's good to meet you."

"Sit down," I told him. "Care for a beer?"

He sat down. "No, thanks. I don't drink much. I just bought Robert Creeley 18 cocktails."

"We can find a bar somewhere if you wish."

He ignored that. "I'm starting a press, the *Red Vulture Press*, and I'm going to start out with a broadside. Do you have a poem I might look over?" he asked.

"Open that door over there," I pointed to the closet.

Martin Johnson got up, walked over, and pulled the door open. A mountainful of poems wavered a moment, then spilled forward onto the rug.

"You wrote all those poems?" he asked.

"Yeah."

"What were they doing in the closet?"

"Well, when I finish 3 or 4 poems, I open the door a tiny notch and jam them in."

"Why don't you send them out?" he asked.

"No money in that. I write dirty stories."

"Mind if I look some of these over?"

"Go ahead."

I went into the kitchen for another beer. I stood at the kitchen window watching a young girl on the steps next door putting on a pair of roller skates. She was facing me and wearing a tiny skirt. She was about 8 years old. Quite a little lady. I watched her get up and skate off. Then I walked back into the other room. Martin Johnson was sitting on the floor reading the poems. After he finished each poem he made a comment:

"This one's good. . . ."

"This one's great. . . ."

"This one's not so good. . . ."

"This one's immortal. . . ."

"This one's good. . . ."

He kept reading. Then he stopped. "I really don't have time to read all these but I'd like to come back . . ."

"O.K."

"Meanwhile, I'd like to take this one to publish as a broadside," he said. It was called "An Afternoon Stroll Down the Avenue of Death."

"Help yourself," I said.


The next strange one who came by called himself Red Hand. He was 22, a kid off the road, slight, wiry, talkative.

"I ran across your stuff, man. Straight language like I've never seen before. I just had to come see you."

"It's O.K. Care for a beer?"

"Sure."

I went out and got him one. When I came back in he was doing the old cigarette roll with one hand act. He took the beer with his other hand.

"See this coat I got on?"

"Yeah."

"Looks like a new coat, don't it? Know where I got it? City dump! You'd be surprised what people throw away! There's nothing wrong with this coat. Just a slight rip in the shoulder. There's that rip, so the buyer threw it away. I got it, I put it on. Nothing wrong, a few bugs in it, that's all. Lots of good stuff in the dump. People throw away perfectly good things. I find oranges, nothing wrong with them. . . ."

"Sit down, drink your beer."

"Your stuff is straight, man. There are so many phonies. You know Bob Dylan? That Oakie wail he puts on? That's not him, man. That's a fake. Come on, I'll buy you a drink at a bar."

"O.K., Red."

We walked out on the street with our beercans. We walked down to *The Gored Matador* around the corner. It was about two-thirty in the afternoon and not very crowded. We sat down.

"Vodka 7," I told the barkeep.

"Whiskey and soda," said Red.

The barkeep brought our drinks and Red paid up. He said, "I first read your stuff in the *L.A. Free Press.* Only good thing in there, that column. . . ."

"'Notes of a Dirty Old Man.'"

"Those stories true?"

"95%."

"I thought so."

Just then a fat drunk who was fairly intoxicated came out of the men's room. As he walked close to Red he lurched and fell against Red's back. Then he straightened and lurched on.

Red leaped from his stool. "Hey, fellow!"

The drunk turned. "What is it?"

"Come here."

"Fuck off!"

"I said, 'Come here!'"

The drunk walked close to Red, then stopped.

"Now," said Red, "I want you to apologize."

"For what?"

"Don't *ask* me for what! I said, 'Apologize!'"

"No," said the drunk.

Red's hands flashed toward his pocket and the switchblade was out. One finger ran along the edge of the blade and the tip of his finger and the tip of the blade were at the man's stomach.

"Now," said Red, "apologize! Or you're gonna have a gash in front of you as big and as deep as that thing in back they call your ass!"

"I apologize," said the drunk. Then he walked back to his seat. It was very quiet in there. Then Red and I finished our drinks and walked out.

On the way back there was a big guy in boots walking about 45 feet ahead of us.

"See that damned fool?" said Red. "You never wear boots like that. Those big leather heels, they make too much noise! He can't hear anything behind him. He's as good as dead! Watch this!"

Red started running quietly and then he was behind the big guy. He walked directly behind him, making motions as if to strangle him. It went on a good 20 or 30 seconds. Then Red stopped and dropped back.

"You see? I had him. The son of bitch had no chance!"

"You're right, Red."

We went back to my place and had a few more beers. Red told me more tales of the road. He was a good storyteller. I would later use two or three of his stories.

"Well," he said, "I've got to go. I'm living with this Mexican woman and she's giving me a hard time! She wants to get fucked all the time and it's a job. She sits around and says, 'You don't fuck me anymore, what are you, a goddamned fag?' I met her coming through the 3rd Street tunnel one time and she looked very beautiful. We got together, we started living together. I give her a good sweaty horsefuck now and then but it's never enough; she's always bitching. I'm going back on the road soon, I can't stand it. . . ."

"Come around any time, Red."

"I wanna give you this," he said, and pulled out the switchblade.

"It's glorious, Red, thank you very much."

He left then, walking past the front of my window, west along the sidewalk. You couldn't hear his footsteps. . . .

One night Martin Johnson was back. He had an armful of broadsides with my poem printed on them.

"Is there any place you can sign these?" he asked.

"The kitchen table. . . ."

We walked in.

"It's full of beercans," he said.

"Just a moment." I ran the beercans out to the back garbage cans. Then I took a wet rag and tried to get up the ash stains, the beer stains, the puke stains. It took some time. It was almost impossible.

"Do you have to drink so much?" he asked. "It's bad for your health."

"It's bad for my mind if I don't. I write when I'm drunk."

Martin put the broadsides down and I started signing.

"I'd like to look at more of your poems while you do this," he said.

"Go ahead. . . ."

As I was just about finished he brought in another poem, said he'd like to broadside it, and I said he could. He wrote me out a $50 check. "For this broadside you've just signed."

"Thanks, Martin."

"Those 3 paintings out there. Did you do them?" he asked.

"Yes."

"I like them. Do you think you can do some more?"

"Yeah."

"I think I know an art gallery who can put on a show for you."

"Painting is not my big hard-on."

"I'd like to see you try it. Here, get some paints and paper."

He wrote me out another 50-buck check.

"Sure you don't want a drink?" I asked.

"No, thank you. . . ."

Then he was gone with his broadsides. . . .

One good thing about painting. You can do it anytime. I mean, I can. To write you must feel very good or very bad but to paint you can feel good, bad, or in between. Of course, everything is better for me when I am drunk, and this includes sex, writing, painting, or watching a bullfight. For others it is what it is. But painting, drinking, fucking, writing, they aren't one but almost one. So I painted and drank, the action was there, the dancing girls; the radio banging and the cheap cigars, paint on your fingers, paint on the cigars, smoking the cigars, swallowing the paint on the cigars, too interested in the show to care and awakening sick in the morning from the poison of swallowing drink and paint, you walk first to the bathroom and vomit and then to the kitchen where you've done it and there are 8 or 9 paintings on the floor and 4 or 5 on the table and sink. It's one bad-ass circus.

So I painted. And I remembered my 2 sessions in art class, the lack of fire everywhere; it were as if the whole mass of them, teacher and pupils, were giving way to some unmentionable law that everybody must get along together and really not do anything at all. I mean, they were all very gentle with each other, very chummy; it was more like a picnic, a social gathering than it was a striking out into the madness and the hopelessness.

So I drank and I painted, I painted and I drank. I painted right out of the tube, the brush was too slow for the melody. And since I painted out of the tube, spreading it on thick and rolling, it took the paintings several days to dry. The paintings were everywhere: kitchen, bedroom, bathroom, front room floors.

The party people came by and I ran them off:

"You'll step on my paintings. . . ."

I took the telephone apart and stuffed toilet paper between the bell and the hammer. I stuffed toilet paper into the doorbell trip above the kitchen door.

I got some masking tape and started taping the paintings to the walls, everywhere, and then I ran out of wall space and I started taping paintings to the ceiling. Most of my paintings were of animals and people and they hung all about me and over me. There was one night of drinking where I went out to a bar on Sunset Boulevard and I picked up a fairly classy number and I brought her to my place and she said, "God oh mighty, what is this? You're crazy, aren't you?"

"Sometimes I feel crazy and sometimes I don't," I told her.

"I'm leaving," she said, and she did. . . .

Martin and his wife Clara came over. I heard the knocking, recognized him through the door blinds, and let them in. Martin and Clara walked about looking at the paintings.

"You've been working," said Martin.

"Sure," I said.

"Can I have this one?" Martin asked me of one of the paintings.

"Sure," I said.

"Can I have this one?" asked Clara.

"Sure."

"Can I have this one?" asked Martin.

"No, that one is for me."

They each had a beer with me. "Keep going," said Martin, "I'm going to get a show going for you."

"O.K.," I said. Martin wrote me out a check for $150 for the paintings and then another check for another $50 worth of supplies. They left. . . .

The next day I sat around looking at the paintings. I began to dislike them. They weren't subtle enough; raw was good but when raw got blaring it got too much like Las Vegas neon. I remembered what the art teacher had said to the class, holding up my work:

"Now here is a man who isn't afraid of color."

But color alone wasn't enough. I kept looking at the paintings and I disliked them more and more. I began drinking and I began taking down the paintings I didn't like. I went from room to room taking down paintings. Soon there were only 5 or 6 paintings hanging. Then I took those down. I had nothing. It got into evening. I kept drinking.

Then I got an idea. By soaking the paintings in hot water in the bathtub I could diminish the overcoloring. I filled the bathtub and got a large painting. I pushed the painting in. Fine, it was working. I pulled the painting out and carried it to the breakfastnook table. I opened some paint tubes and just gave it a touch of color here and there. Fine.

I began marching my paintings to the bathtub and dumping them in. I pulled them out, touching some up with color, leaving the others as they were. Soon all my paintings had had a bath.

They'd never know my technique. I went to bed feeling much better. . . .

In the morning I got up and looked at my work and I was sickened. I vomited. Then I began crumbling up the paintings and jamming them into my two garbage cans out back. Soon the garbage cans were full but I crumpled up the remainder of the paintings and jammed them into all the empty garbage cans I could find along the row of courts.

Then I took the telephone apart and took the toilet paper away from the bell and I also re-engaged the front door bell.

I'd never be a Van Gogh, not even a Dali. It was back to the typewriter by the window while watching the girls go by. I drove to the racetrack that day and lost $80. I slept that night without drinking, and usually any first night without drinking was a wide-awake night but that night I slept on through. I was worn with disgust. When I awakened I just stayed in bed. I stayed there and stared at the ceiling. About 3 P.M. the phone rang. It was Martin Johnson.

"Hey, your phone is working again."

"Yes."

"How's the painting coming?"

"It's finished."

"What do you mean?"

"I gave them all a bath in hot water."

"Really? Then what did you do with them?"

"I threw them into the garbage."

"What? You're joking."

"No, they are in with the beercans and old *Racing Forms*."

"You've just thrown away $2,000!"

"I didn't like the paintings."

"Most of them were very good. Listen, when does your trashman come around?"

"Wednesday morning, about 9 A.M. This is Wednesday afternoon."

"Listen, will you do me a favor? Go look in those garbage cans. See if they are still full."

I got up and walked out back. The garbage cans were empty. I came back to the phone.

"The man's been here. Everything is gone."

"I'm sick," said Martin, "and I've got to tell you I'm angry with you for doing such a thing."

"O.K., baby," I said and hung up. . . .

Martin got over it and came for more poems. Red Hand came back and told me more stories of the road. Others came back, men and women, and we drank.

It was a stark time, and a grand time of gamble, and those who came to that East Hollywood front court were mostly those who were supposed to come, and I was weak and strong and alcoholic, and they wasted many of my hours but they also brought me material and light; voices, faces; their fears and their evil stupidities, and sometimes the amazing inventiveness. They brought me more than I could ever have had alone, even though I felt best alone. . . .

I left East Hollywood soon after that. What happened to me was that I simply got gathered in. One loses hold, the senses waver, and one is lost. I was with a handsome woman 20 years younger than I. She was a woman that all men looked at as she walked the streets or sat in cafés or was seen anywhere at all. "Beauty and the Beast," she described us. She had a few detracting factors: she was insane and had thick ankles which she hid in boots, and she was continually conscious of what the world considered to be her beauty. I hung around; she was trying me and I was trying her. But she was more the hunter. The dear child saw possibilities in me. She thought I had a soul of some sort and that her soul might capture mine, captivate it and slug the shit out of it. Meanwhile, while waiting for that to happen, I could entertain her and hers.

So look, what they don't understand is that those who work within the art form usually save their best juices for that. So then, I didn't particularly radiate for her mother or her stepfather or her sisters or her friends. "He can be charming when he wants to," she said. "It's just that usually he doesn't want to."

She had a large house and her two children slept upstairs. I liked the children better than I liked her. There was a large backyard full of bamboo stalks, thousands and thousands of them rising to the sky, spears poking out into nowhere. "We've got to clear those fucking things out of there," she said. It was my private jungle. I sat in there often like some kind of asshole. I sat there the last time I can think of at 3 A.M. in the morning, naked and shivering, I sat there sucking at yet another can of beer. She came out in her nightgown, looking heavy, thick-ankled, she walked with loud feet, crashing through the small brush and brambles, frightening the small night creatures.

She stood in front of me, swaying, some of the moon showing through her gown, exposing that body that so many men wanted. What a doll of flesh, what a girl, what a thing. I could hear her breathing as she said:

"What the hell's the matter with you?"

I answered, "I don't know."

And I still don't!

It was 4:30 A.M. when the phone rang and I picked it up and it was Stultz and he said, "It happened, they took my money."

"Who took your money?"

"They did."

"You mean you were robbed."

"No, I went back to the wheel."

"You lost it all?"

"Yes, fifteen thousand—"

"Jesus Christ, I told you to stay in bed!"

"They sent a woman up to my room!"

"So what?"

"They planned it, they do it—"

"Who?"

"Management."

"What are you talking about?"

"Well, I fucked her and then I couldn't sleep so I went downstairs."

"All right, you can sleep *now*—"

"No, I can't because I don't have any money."

I didn't answer. I just sat there on the edge of the bed, the neon lights flashing on my fat ugly belly.

"You got any money?" he asked.

"I'm sitting on eight grand."

"I'll sell you my car. I need the action."

"You don't have a car."

"I've got a wristwatch."

"Listen, I'm going back to sleep; I'll see you about ten or eleven."

I hung up. I had a headache. I hated Vegas. Stultz had talked me into it. I had only come up with $200. I played the wheel, a simple system just using the red and the black. It seemed to be working.

I stretched out on the bed. There was a knock on the door. I was in my shorts. I walked to the door, opened it, keeping the chain on.

It was a girl.

"Honey," she said, "I give the best head on the Strip—"

"Go suck a porcupine," I said and closed the door.

"Pops," she hissed through the door, "you're a piece of living shit."

About 5:30 A.M. the phone rang again. It was Stultz.

"Hey, a girl came by and gave me some head! It was absolutely great! Even better than that job I got in Tangiers once."

"How'd you pay her?"

"I gave her a check."

"Go to sleep."

"That black-red system isn't going to work. Each time the wheel turns it's a fifty-fifty shot, less the house-take."

"My system is based upon fluctuations."

"Okay, let's go downstairs *now*. I won't even gamble. I'll just watch *you*."

"Pretend you're watching me sleep," I said and hung up.

In six or seven minutes the phone rang again.

"I can't sleep," he said.

"Get a newspaper," I told him, "then take a shower, get in bed, and read the newspaper. Read the Help Wanted section, that will knock you out."

"I got a better idea."

"Yeah? What?"

"I'll jack-off."

"But I thought you already fucked and had head?"

"Yeah, but only jacking-off makes me sleep."

"Well, for Christ's sake," I said, "get pumping!"

It was around 9:30 A.M. when there was some heavy pounding on my door. I thought it might be a fire. I ran to the door and opened it. I forgot that I was nude.

"Well, well," said the big guy, "if it ain't Conan the Barbarian!"

There was another big guy next to him. Looking at those guys I got the idea that they just *enjoyed* being big.

No, it was more than enjoyment—they were sick with it.

"Whatever you got," I told them, "I don't want it."

I started to close the door but one of the big guys gave the door a tap and it flashed across my face and knocked me across the room. I got up with a bloody nose. I figured I was being busted for eight grand and that was too much money to lay down for. So I walked over, sat on the edge of the bed, wiped my nose with the sheet, reached into my shoe, came out with the blade, unsheathed it, and stood up.

"Easy, Conan," said the biggest guy, "we're hotel security."

"Yeah?" I asked. "Well, you don't make *me* feel too secure."

The biggest guy flashed some I.D. and the next biggest guy did too, both them smiling because they were both so big.

"You can get that stuff printed anywhere," I said. "How do I know that you guys don't go around boosting rooms?"

"No," said the biggest, "we don't. But we want you out of here!"

"Why? Because I'm winning?"

"No, because you and Stultz are buddies."

"Meaning what?"

"Meaning about an hour ago we caught him trying to steal some chips."

"And that complicates me?"

"By proxy."

"Where is he? In jail?"

"Oh, no," said the biggest guy, "we don't waste jail on him."

"Oh, no," said the next biggest guy.

"What'd you do?"

"We had a little talk with him."

"Oh?"

"Yeah. And we want you out of this hotel in thirty minutes or we're going to have a little talk with *you!*"

"I understand."

"It's best that you do."

They both turned and walked out.

I got packed and went down to my car. I threw my bag into the truck, unlocked the door, and there was Stultz sitting there reading the racing results in the newspaper. I sat down next to him.

"How'd you get in?" I asked him.

"Guess you were drunk. You forgot to lock the door on the passenger side."

"You look awful."

"I feel worse than awful."

Stultz had a hard time speaking through his puffed lips. He had one black eye.

"Any broken bones?"

"I don't think so. But they said if I ever came back, they'd break both my legs. All that for three blue chips."

"Why'd you do it?"

"I needed the action and I couldn't get you out of bed."

"Well," I told him, "you got the action."

I started the car and pointed it toward L.A.

This was some drive back and it got hot and Stultz kept reading the newspaper but just the race results and that day's entries. There really wasn't that much to read about.

"The harness is running right now," he said.

I didn't answer.

"I hit some good exactas the last meet," Stultz said.

I wanted to get him off the subject.

"Listen, Stultz, you ever think of women?"

"Women? What do I need with a woman?"

"Something to take your mind off gambling."

"I like to gamble. I don't care if I win or lose, I just want to gamble."

"It's all so *wearing* and it's really kind of dull."

"What else is there? Everything's dull."

"How about the great works of art?"

"Ah, that's just bullshit."

"I think you're right."

"I'm sometimes right," Stultz said.

"About how often?"

"About forty-two percent of the time on a fifty-fifty shot."

"You're an eight percent loser."

"When I lose I feel the pain. When I win I'm no good."

I just kept on driving. Stultz said he didn't need women but he always seemed to have one around. And each looked a bit like the other. All young bright pretty girls. But they soon were gone. He borrowed money from them which he couldn't pay back.

"You won eight grand, huh?" he asked me.

"Just about. It's in my bag in the trunk."

"Lend me five hundred."

"Go fuck yourself."

"You've lost your humanity."

"Had to."

I mean it was a *long* drive. . . . I almost fell asleep at the wheel a couple of times. After almost running it off the road one time, I raised my head from the steering wheel and asked Stultz, "Listen, man, you think you can tool this thing awhile?"

"I can try, good buddy."

We stopped, changed seats, and then started up again with Stultz at the wheel.

"Oh shit," he said, "oh shit."

"What is it?"

"I think my ribs are busted! I can't *steer* this thing!"

The car started to dart off the road. I grabbed the wheel and righted it. I reached my foot over and jammed on the brake. The car bucked and stalled in the road.

Stultz just sat there holding his sides.

"I just can't drive, man."

"It's okay, Stultz, I think I can make it back in. Let's change seats again."

"I really appreciate this, buddy," he said, "and sometime you'll know how much."

I got out to go around to the other side of the car and take the wheel, and as I did so he took off. In a straight line.

I stood there in the road in the middle of the desert and watched Stultz and my car vanish, plus my eight grand in my bag in the trunk.

I had no idea if there was a town within a hundred miles.

I just started walking. Then I heard a car approaching. I stood in the road and tired to wave it down. It went right on past. All I saw was a fat man smoking a cigar.

I walked along some more.

As the next car approached I turned and stuck out my thumb. Same result. Only this time it was a midget eating a Sno-Kone.

I walked along thinking, I might die out here in this desert.

I didn't particularly mind that—dying didn't matter much. What bothered was getting there.

As I walked along I thought of the things I was going to miss, and they were very odd. Like taking a crap in a cool bathroom at 10 A.M. in the morning, or opening a can of cat food for my cat or watching a good boxing match on TV while drinking beer. Or moving deftly through traffic on the freeway, gauging speeds and distances, threading through the drivers and at the same time checking the rearview mirror for the police. Or buying a case of good wine and carrying it to my car, always remembering the days when there was nothing to drink, or to eat, for that matter.

A car pulled up. I couldn't believe it.

Here was this cute little girl wearing a green hat over her blue eyes and smiling. . . .

"Ya out in the desert prospecting, old-timer?"

"Not really. Just kind of dehydrating and moving toward L.A. an inch at a time."

"Climb in, pops, your problem is solved. I'm driving straight to L.A."

I got in and the car rolled off smoothly. It was cool in there, the air conditioner worked fine, and the girl was in a neat little green dress and showing some leg.

"I can't believe this," I said to the girl. "Life isn't so bad after all—"

Then I heard it from behind me. From the rear seat:

"*Life is still bad, motherfucker!*"

I started to turn.

"Don't *turn*! Don't *look* at me! You look at me and you're *dead*, motherfucker!"

I looked straight forward.

"Okay," I said, "what's next, motherfucker?"

"Don't go callin' *me* no *motherfucker*! *I'm* holdin' the callin' card here!"

"I pass," I told him.

The cute little girl just kept on driving.

Then I heard him: "Okay now, just reach *nice* and *easy* into your back pocket, no fast moves, and lift your wallet out, hold it up in the air, and I'll take it from there!"

I did as I was told. I held the wallet up and he snatched it while almost breaking my wrist. I pulled my hand down.

"Look," I said, "I just got my car stolen and I was ripped off for eight grand—"

"I don't wanna hear that shit!"

He was back there, ripping through my wallet, taking my bills and my credit cards. Now he knew my address. If I ever got back there'd be nothing in my place but a roll of toilet paper.

Then I heard him laugh. "According to this here driver's license, you're sixty-three years old. Man, you look closer to *seventy-three!*"

"I've aged rapidly because of the kind of people I keep meeting. And besides, I've been told I've lost my humanity."

"*Humanity?* What's *that* shit?"

"Nothing."

The cute little girl looked over at me. "Guess you thought you were going to fuck me?" she asked sarcastically.

"Fuck you? No, I was going to squirt some Elmer's Glue-All up your pussy."

"*Hey, man! Watch your mouth!*" the guy yelled.

The cute little girl jammed a cigarette she had been smoking into the car ashtray in a vicious manner.

"Why don't we *waste* this old fuck, Hayward?"

"Don't *say* my *name*, you *whore!* Don't *say* my *name!* You dumb bitch whore!"

I said, "I didn't *hear* your *name! Honest,* Hayward!"

We drove along as Hayward's curses shook the automobile. Then he quieted down.

Then he said, "Okay, *chump!*"

And my wallet came flying. It landed on the floorboard. I picked it up, looked through it. Nothing. Just the leather.

Life began over and over again. Sometimes.

"Okay, bitch," Hayward said, "stop the machine!"

She stopped the machine. We sat there.

"Okay, bitch, get out and do your thing."

She opened the door and got out. As she did I reached out my left hand for the keys in the ignition.

I felt the gun at the back of my neck, stopped.

"Don't *think* too much," said Hayward, "because you don't know *how* or else your ass wouldn't be where it's at *now*!"

Then she got back in.

"Okay," said Hayward, "get this thing rolling!"

She dug it out and soon we were moving along nicely.

"Okay, *chump*," Hayward said, "*out*!"

"I think I'll stay—"

"I told you *thinking* wasn't your thing! Now, pops, I'm going to count to five!"

I felt the gun at the back of my neck.

"If you ain't bailed out by five, you got no more worries in *this* world!"

He started counting.

"One!"

"Two!"

"Three!"

When he got to "four," I kicked the door open and leaned out and just as I left I kicked out and caught her in the head with my foot. Then I was out into space and rolling. I heard the car skidding as she hit the brakes. Then I stopped rolling and felt myself face down eating sand.

I looked up and the car was slowly moving toward me. Hayward had his head out the window and I saw the gun.

"*Motherfucker*!"

The shots blasted at me. Geysers of dirty sand shot up around me like little atomic mushroom clouds. Then the car spun back. It passed me again in full roar. I forced my eyes open through the whirl of Nevada sand, determined to see the license plate.

The license plate was covered with a pair of red panties.

Hayward's bullets had missed me. I got up, dusted myself off halfheartedly, and began walking toward L.A. again.

# THE LADIES MAN OF EAST

# HOLLYWOOD

That's what he was. Tod Hudson scored continually, with an almost bored regularity. I believe I first met him at a party at my court down on DeLongpre. "Party" isn't the word. I just had an open door at my place. People just came in every night and sat about drinking. I didn't know most of them. My reason for all those, I told myself, was that I was gathering material. That was shit, of course, I just wanted an excuse to get drunk as often as possible.

Tod walked in this night and sat down with his lady friend. I noticed, because they looked different. They were dressed in clean, well-fitted clothing and Tod had his own bottle, a pint of *Old Grand-Dad*. His lady had on high-heeled shoes and hose. A trim blonde. Most of the other women were in stained slacks, several sizes too large. They had round mad faces with short-cropped hair. Most claimed to be Female Libbers. They blamed their failure on men. They were very depressed, angry, and dull. Each had some de-balled man with them and each of those men claimed to be a poet, a revolutionary of some sort, or a painter or a songwriter or a singer or something of that disorder. They all looked about the same: thin, with diseased goatees and long stringy hair, they seemed all elbows and shiny sweaty foreheads, and they smiled much and pissed continually and listened to their ladies.

I walked up to Tod.

"What are you, the fucking heat?"

"Oh, no," he said, "how about a drink?"

I slugged down my mix of port and beer, put my glass down. I hadn't had any *Grand-Dad* in a decade. Tod gave me a fill.

"This is Rissy," he nodded toward his lady.

"Hello," she said crossing her legs with that flash of magic.

"Look out!" I yelled.

I sensed something coming. You get that sense when you're a low-life hanging around other low-lifes. It's like having a rearview mirror in bad traffic.

I was right. It was a slime. Stumbling backwards, dumbly, gracelessly, flapping ignorant arms, a mass of dark and grievous zero. I blocked him off with a shoulder in order to save the drinks and he flopped back over the coffee-table and into a dung-like pile of cheap drunkenness.

I knew him. He ran a poetry workshop and lived with his mother.

I walked over, picked him up by the ass of his pants and his shirt collar, carried him out to the porch and threw him into the night. I usually did one or two a night like that. They never left when you asked them nicely. "Nicely" to them meant it didn't work.

I sat and drank with Tod and Rissy. Now and then I got up and pushed somebody out of the door. It worked. Soon there were just the three of us. At least Tod wasn't into the Arts. Too many people who fail at everything else turn to the Arts and then they just continue to fail there too. So Tod wasn't into that. One point for Tod. Two points for Tod: there was Rissy. A point against him: he was a *bland* mother. If he had any vibes, they were folded under his driver's license in his wallet. Now, *Rissy*, well, I hadn't been that near a woman-*woman*, well, for a decade. Like the *Grand-Dad*.

We drank and talked. The conversation wasn't particularly brilliant. Sometimes it even got Arty.

"You know Henry Miller?" Tod asked.

"Who's that?" I answered.

We finished the *Grand-Dad* and got into my cheap wine and they both started looking a bit sick.

"We've got to go now," Tod said.

He handed me a card. He ran a porno bookshop.

"Come on by some time," he said.

"No way," I said. "Lofty ideals."

"I'll bribe you."

"Like how?

"I'll drop my wife off tomorrow night."

"Rissy?"

"No, Rissy isn't my wife."

"I want to use the bathroom," said Rissy.

"Fine," I said.

Rissy walked off.

"Your wife," I asked, "is she anything like Rissy?"

"Really, she's a better number."

"What's the downer then?"

"She's crazy. She's been in and out. She commits herself."

"I don't need it that bad. I've lived with too many crazies."

"She's beautiful. Wild eyes. Long hair. Perfect body."

"Like I said. . . ."

"You won't know she's crazy. She's a clever crazy when she needs to be. She can hide it perfectly. You'll mistake it for soul. It's only when she gets to know you well, then she'll dump on you."

"All right, drop her off."

"And you'll come to the bookstore?"

"Yeah. . . ."

Rissy was back.

"My God, that bathroom is a *terrible* place! It's caked with all manners of deathly things!"

"Sorry," I said, "my maid ran off with the garbage man."

With that they left and I poured my nightcap, ale with white wine, as I pondered my future. . . .

Actually, I didn't expect anything to materialize. Humanity has many weaknesses, but two of their main ones were: the inability to arrive on time *and* no sense of follow-up on promises. There was also a wretched lack of loyalty, but here we were concerned with the Promise. Tod's Promise of the Deliverance of the Flesh.

Anyhow, I installed the closed-door policy that evening. As the drunks and suckerfish and pretenders and sharks and misshapen and soulless arrived I sent them each on their way. Some needed specialized treatment, which I then applied with gusto. Others, having learned at other moments, left quietly, seeking newer, if lesser, havens.

Tod arrived on the dot. In the middle of the dot. I saw his headlights dip, then rise, as he drove onto the lawn in front of my court and cut his motor. He exited from his door, cigarette dangling, and out of the machine came sliding the Flesh, high-heel, ankle, glance of knee and the eternal maddening thigh, she stood straight in the moonlight and shook a long glorious mane of hair. She was thin-hipped, neat, lank . . . she came striding toward my front door . . . along with this Tod. . . .

There was a tiny rap . . . hers . . . I opened. . . . Tod vanished into the night. All I heard was. . . .

"This is . . . Ingrid. . . ."

Fuck.

She walked on in. Shining gold. Flare of eye in wild painting. Centuries of men killing and dying for the like. I mean, you know, I was at last overcome. I attempted to counter with dim realities—strings of intestine, excreta, the tonality of mirage children without arms, broken garbage lids upon the streets of nowhere. It flashed like that. Then broke. She was still there, more than ever.

"Sorry," I said, "this is not a nice place."

Ingrid laughed.

"I like it."

"Sit down. I'll get something to drink."

I walked off to the kitchen. I even washed a couple of glasses, carefully. I had some vodka. I brought the set-up and put it on the coffeetable.

I had been drinking since noon, although mostly beer. I peeled the bottle and poured a couple of drinks.

"Have you eaten?" I asked.

"No . . ."

"Let's drink this. . . . I know a place. . . ."

I drove her up to Sunset, to *Antonio's*. I told the valet fellow, "Be careful. Don't strip the gears."

"Oh, no sir," he answered glancing at my twelve-year-old car, "I wouldn't strip *anything* on this machine. . . ."

Well, I thought, there goes your fucking tip, buster. . . .

Inside we got a table. She ordered a porterhouse. I ordered a porterhouse. Over drinks she started talking. She spoke in a soft voice and I couldn't quite follow it, nor did I care to. She looked fine, though. She seemed gripped by the edge of some panic. I was fucked-up too. I couldn't cure her. I couldn't cure myself.

Then I made something out: ". . . and while I was pregnant Tod moved this other woman in and we all lived together. . . ."

"Listen," I said, "I'm sorry for your troubles. But I'd like to know something. How does Tod get all these beautiful women? What does he have?"

"He doesn't have anything."

"That doesn't seem to be true. I mean, how does he do it?"

"He just *does* it. He doesn't have *doubts*, that's all. Most men are hindered by what they think they can't obtain."

I ordered a couple more drinks. She lifted her drink and stared at me as she had a hit. The eyes were blue and the blue went way back and in. I was hypnotized. I just dropped out of myself and swam in that blue.

"I've got the baby; she's cute," Ingrid spoke. "My divorce is final at the end of the month. I want you to marry me."

"I'm honored, you know. But I've only known you 30 minutes."

"I've known you many lifetimes. I was once a swan and you were an eagle and we mated, splashing and thrashing."

The steaks came and sat before us. I ordered two more drinks. I wasn't hungry. I guess Ingrid wasn't either. She picked up her plate and hurled it into the air.

"I don't want to eat this fucking steak! They killed some poor POOOOR ANIMAL to do this! I HATE IT!"

"Me too, baby. . . ."

The waiter came out and stared. I gave him a little wink and a wave. When the busboy came out to pick up the mess I slipped him a five. I carried my steak over to another table and sat back down. I nodded the waiter over for the bill. It would take the last of my resources and I was already three days late on the rent.

It had better be a good fuck because I was really getting fucked. . . .

Back at my place we got into the vodka and Ingrid seemed reasonably calm. I hoped for the best because the landlord told me one more police raid and that was it.

Halfway through her drink Ingrid said, "Let's do it. Where's the bedroom?"

"Well," I said, "sure. . . ."

The bed slanted to the left and down. Sometimes you had to hold on or you'd roll off.

Ingrid shook out of her dress and things and there we were. . . . Dear reader, why waste your time? I couldn't make it. . . .

"I'm too drunk," I told her.

We walked back into the front room and had some more vodka. Then I got mean.

"Put your dress and high heels back on!" I commanded.

She marched off and did it. She marched back in.

"Now sit down!" I commanded.

Ingrid did.

"Now cross your legs and pull your skirt back to your ass!"

Ingrid did.

"YOU WHORE!" I screamed.

"Yes," she said, "I suppose that I am."

"NO! NO! NO!"

"What?"

"Don't *admit* that you're a whore. That *spoils* it. *Deny* that you are a whore!"

"O.K. I'm no whore."

"Yes, you *are* a whore!"

"No, I'm *not* a whore!"

"You whore, you whore, you WHORE!"

I got up and pulled her from the couch by her hair. I slapped her across the face. I slapped her again.

"SUCK MY DICK, YOU WHORE!"

I had it out and she bent over and got it. She was good. Her madness whirled her tongue like a fantail of a snake burning in fire. I pumped it through her jaws like a male pig.

I never saw her again.

But I still kept my promise to Tod. I located the porno bookstore. It wasn't far from where I lived. I walked in. There was a homosexual sitting in a high booth at the entrance. He seemed very mean and superior. I don't mind homosexuals as long as they don't move on me. Being an ugly critter, I seldom had to face that problem.

This one just said, "A dollar for a token, sir. Then you can stay until closing."

"Look, I'm just paying off a debt. I told Tod I'd come on in here."

"Tod is busy now, sir."

Sure enough, Tod was busy. He had some scrabbly-looking creature dressed in rags by a head of hair and was leading him toward the exit with some force and venom.

"YOU DEMENTED ASSHOLE!" Tod screamed. "DON'T EVER COME HERE AGAIN! IN FACT, IF I EVEN SEE YOU IN THIS NEIGHBORHOOD I'M GOING TO BLOW YOU AWAY!"

Tod kicked this unblessed individual in the ass, hard, very hard, then reached up into the pulpit where the homosexual stood guard, reached and got out a .45.

"I'LL BLOW YOUR FUCKING MOUTH OFF!"

The guy blew at the door. I never saw him again.

Tod replaced the .45.

Then he took me into the back of the bookstore. He showed me the movie machines.

"These guys watch this shit and then they JACK-OFF right against the viewer! Sometimes I'm busy up front. And I come back here and there's just this STINK of COME! Nothing stinks worse than come, even shit! Sometimes I come back here and I catch them. Sometimes I don't. Then, you know what I've got? This hardened come! Goddamn, man, it's too much."

All that broke off. I didn't see Tod, or his wife, for some while. I got the rent up because the checks for the dirty stories started arriving. There were a whole string of publications on Melrose Ave. that went the dirty story route and they had a whole string of sub-publications. I'd get $375 for a suck-fuck story and then they'd write and ask me if they could republish same in some throwaway rag for $75 or $50 and I'd say fine, go ahead. That bit kept me from going back to the factory or trying another run at suicide. Bless all those wonderful bastards.

Anyhow, Tod came back. I had stopped the party nights and was just seriously drinking alone. There he was at the door, along with another beautiful female.

"Ooh, Mr. Chinaski!" she said, "I am so *thrilled!*"

"Me too, baby, what are you drinking?"

Tod, the ladies man, had him another number.

"This is Mercedes," he told me.

She voluted on in like a snake from heaven.

Over libations, Tod broke it to me.

"There's a vacancy over at our courtyard but nobody knows it yet. This guy is moving out and it's really a deal. He's already moved out but some of his stuff is still in there. I'm in with the landlord and I've got the key. Why don't you come over and look at it?"

Well, I did. I looked. It was a better place, much. And 50 bucks a month cheaper. Plus a glance at Mercedes now and then.

"O.K." I said to Tod. "One condition. You won't bother me, will you?"

"No way, man. . . . Your place is yours. You want to see me, I'm there. We damn well won't bother you."

"All right," I said, thinking that what a man said he meant. Well, not *all* that, but at least *some* of that.

So, there I was in the courtyard of Tod the Ladies Man. . . .

It was all right for a week. He didn't bother me. I got the phone put in, found a new liquor store. There was a place for the typer on the breakfastnook table. With the cheaper rent I had a chance to write the poem. I was tired of writing fuck stories even though I wrote them better than anybody else. What I did was to write a realistic story and just insert a bunch of fuck-suck and yet still go on with the story. With the poem you could write the way you wanted to because nobody paid for poetry.

Then it was a Wednesday night. I had just gotten in from the track, really tired. I drank until 2 or 3 A.M. each day. But I thrived on all that, it created a good tight line.

I got into the tub and stretched out. I always had the water sizzling hot and seldom used any soap. I had a can of cold beer. I let the cold run inside of me while the hot was on the outside. Then the phone rang.

I was no longer on the steady. I had given my number to maybe 5 that I had fucked once or twice. Dumb fucks. Useless fucks. But one still likes to ring the bell now and then for the sake of some sick glory.

I clambered out, long balls dangling, wondering which of those low numbers was calling.

"Yeah, Chinaski," I answered.

"Hey, man, this is Tod. What're you doing?"

"I just got in, Tod. My ass is on the floor. Really beat."

"Come on down. I wanna see ya."

"Hey, man, when do you think I *write*?"

"Don't give me that shit about *writing*, man. You can write *any* time."

"You write when it hits you. It's hitting me now."

"I've got a lot of good stuff down here. Take the night off. I want you to meet my roomy, Laura. I had to dump Mercedes for her. This Laura, you'll cream just glancing at her silhouette. She wants to meet you."

"All right, Tod, I guess I can spin the ribbon tomorrow night. Be down in ten. . . ." I hung up, thinking, who cares about that eunuch they call Immortality? . . .

There she was, there was Laura. Tod had done it again. Each one a bit better than the other. And intelligent. His women all had a bit of humor, albeit a bit worldly, a touch hard, but not too hard, not so hard that your feelings dropped away in spite of the body. Tod chose a nice blend. But where did he *find* them? All I ever saw were lonely vicious numbers, darkened in spirit because they had not been endowed as well as some others. As one of the creatures dumped upon the earth, I was ugly myself but I rather liked it. But being a woman in America was harder: an ugly woman was looked down upon, where if you looked down upon an ugly man, he was apt to beat the shit out of you and usually did.

Tod had music feeding through the room from a record player. Laura was mincing across the room, smiling a bit, singing words, looking fine. She seemed a bit high. But she worked away without crass flash. Or flash crass. How would Hemingway say this? Not very well, I think. Come join me.

Tod spread the coke upon the glass of the coffee table. The snow was encircled by a bevy of dildoes from his porno store.

He laughed. "You know some of the girls, white girls, come in and they only want black dildoes. So we sell them to them."

"Big ones?"

"Yeah. Right along with the myth."

"Is it a myth?"

"I hope so. . . ."

Laura sat down and we nostriled in the snow. I never much cared for it. The non-lasting qualities of it pissed me off. Coke was for chicken shits who wanted to get on and off real fast so they wouldn't get nailed. It was like fucking 8 or 10 times a night but never really coming. Maybe *real* coke was another number but it would never find me.

Tod looked up.

"I deal. Since you're my friend, I can get you down for half-price."

"You're on."

"Tod loves you," said Laura. "I mean in spirit. He's got all your books!"

"Yeah?"

"Yeah."

"Yeah, man, how about autographing them?"

"What do I get?"

"You can touch Laura's knee. . . ."

"Yeah?"

Tod went into the bedroom and brought out 6 or 7 paperbacks. *The Night I Fucked a Chicken with My Mother in the Bed. Your Water-Resistant Pussy Belches Coors. Limp in Nirvana with Greta Garbo. Suck Me, Suck You, Suck Suck.* Others of the same ilk. Ink.

"I can't sign this shit. I mean, Shakespeare wrote lousy but he never knew it. I know it when I do it."

"Let me bribe you. I deal grass. . . ."

Tod threw a packet down, mostly seeds and stems.

I began inscribing.

We went 3 or 4 more coke rounds and then I went back to my place. I sat down to the typer and the keys just looked at me and I looked at them. Fucking Tod, the ladies man. What did I have? He had coke. I got down to my shorts and rolled a joint of seeds and stems. It was funny. The seeds got red hot and dropped out of the paper and fell onto my undershirt, and beneath it, burning me. I ripped them out. I had to drink 5 or 6 cans of beer to come around and walk into the bedroom and sleep. . . . The next morning I had these little red burn-dots all over my chest and gut. . . .

This night I was sitting with one of my numbers, Ursella. Ursella had long red hair which came down to her ass. She was a pill freak. She had a sharp mind but a vicious one. I just liked to look at all that long red hair and drink. We had some sex but it wasn't major. With Ursella I just liked to relax and try to figure out how she had gotten so goddamned *hard*. I *never* wanted to get *that* hard and I thought that maybe by studying it I might avoid it. And not become something that hardly added to the little joy that there was in the world.

She had met Tod Hudson, The Ladies Man of East Hollywood, one night when Tod had come down with Laura. That night I had been very conscious of Tod's perfectly-fitted clothing. I mean, each piece of material gripped to his tiny ass. And his little knit shirts had clung to him. The belt fitted nicely into the notch. My belt dangled out, warped. I had buttons missing from my shirts. Cigarette holes therein. I forgot to comb my hair and I had an untrimmed beard. My pantlegs were either too long or too short. My shorts slipped up into the crotch of my ass and my face was red and puffy from the booze. Tod was like a paper cut-out. Even his farts were probably vanilla-scented.

The phone rang. It was Tod. It was a Thursday night. Laura was a nudie dancer at a nightclub on Tuesday, Thursday, and Saturday nights. Like I said, it was a Thursday night. Tod was lonely.

"What are you doing, man?" he asked.

"I'm tired."

"Why don't you come down here?"

"No, man, I don't want to."

"Oh, come on, man!"

"No, man. . . ."

"Well, FUCK YOU!" he said and hung up.

I walked back on into Ursella.

"That was Tod, wasn't it?"

"Yeah."

"He wanted to *see* you, *didn't* he?"

"Yeah."

"You hurt his *feelings*!"

"Jesus Christ, his woman's working tonight. He can't handle it. . . ."

"When's she work to?"

"Two A.M."

"You hurt his *feelings*! I'm going to *see* him!"

"That's up to you."

She grabbed her purse, opened the door, slammed it, and was gone.

How about my feelings? I thought.

Then, feeling that was not a rational thought, I went in and poured a tall scotch from the hidden fifth in the broom closet. It was always nice to have an ace. Sometimes without the ace it was over for you.

I finished the drink, then took my shoes off, and toed on down to Tod's court. I peeked between the blinds and saw the mound of coke spread between the dildoes. Ursella was going to get fucked by the Ladies Man. Frankly, it hurt me. Then I remembered the boxing matches were on at the Olympic Auditorium. I went back to my place, had a half-glass of scotch and beer chaser, and drove out there. . . .

I went down to Tod's court a couple nights later for my discount coke. I also purchased the usual bag of grass that was mostly stems and seeds. Tod was dressed in his usual clean fashion, the usual tailor-fit. The guy never had any dirt on him, never a spot. He never needed a shave, there was never a hair sticking out of his nostril. He was Mr. Cool. The only time I had ever seen him pissed was the time that guy had come on his movie machine. He was reading a copy of *New York*. Laura was practicing one of her dances. She danced into the other room to do a change of costume.

Tod looked up. "Hey, man, you should have been with us the other night. We went to see these cartoonists. I phoned you but you weren't in or didn't answer. . . . Those cartoonists are something else. Damn near everybody was there but Crumb. Anyhow, I made some sales. They started snorting. Then the guy's house we were at, I went for a walk with his wife. I brought here over here and fucked her, then brought her back.

"Did you know her very well?"

"Met her about 5 minutes once. . . ."

"How do you do it?"

"What?"

"Fuck at the drop of a leaf. . . ."

Tod smiled. "Hey, man, it's no *problem*. . . ."

Around then Laura danced back in and Tod spread some coke. He always spread better than he sold so I decided to stay. There was also beer and gin. Besides, I was making a study of the Ladies Man. One thing I knew: it wasn't his conversation, *that* was pretty dull. Maybe it was the things he *didn't* say. I had this habit of putting people off for life with just a simple sentence. Not that I minded so much but it had cost me a great deal of ass. And maybe that wasn't so bad either. Then maybe too, that's what guys like me pretended to think.

The night moved on. Not much said. Tod suggested that I give a reading, a poetry reading at his porno shop.

While we wasted the hours I got thinking on Tod. All the fucks he told me about, he never mentioned that *one* of them was exceptional or that *one* of them was bad, and he never spoke of *caring* for a woman. Maybe that was his style, not mentioning it. Some women revved on indifference; they took it as worldliness. But whatever he did, whatever he had, it was working for him. The Fuck Master of East Hollywood. And he wasn't that hung. Or so Ursella had claimed when I had phoned her in curiosity, and asked what he carried. "He shoulda used a dildo," she told me.

The night went on. Gin, snow and beer, grass. Laura talked about the freaks at the nudie dance place. She claimed they were jack-offs, they really tipped, and they fell in *love*. I talked a bit about the racetrack. The other came about a bit suddenly. Tod leaned forward with this sneer on his face and said, "Hey, man, you are always talking about how good you can eat pussy!"

"Ah, come on, Tod. . . ."

"No, man, every time you get high you brag about how good you eat pussy!"

"He's right, Hank," Laura said.

I always remembered what this guy big Tommy had said one day at the factory I was working down on Alameda when the guys were going on about how good they were at eating pussy: "Hey, any guy who eats pussy will suck a dick!"

Somehow that lasted on in my brain. I got to eating pussy at the behest of this young number who claimed she would leave me if I didn't. Well, after 4 years she did, but I had really sharpened my technique and somehow when I got high I got on to what a master I was, although in truth I had no great taste for it.

"I thought," Tod said, "that you might watch me eat some pussy and tell me if I'm any good or not."

"Ah, hell, man. . . ."

"No, I mean it."

Laura marched off to the bedroom. Tod followed her. I poured a gin and seltzer. *The March to the Gallows* played on the overhead.

"Hey," Tod yelled, "come on, man!"

I walked on in. They were both nude. Laura had her legs spread. Tod looked up. "Now, watch me, man!"

He went at it. It was too bland, like him.

"Jesus," I said, "show more *passion*! Go *mad*! Let *go*!"

Tod tried. He was very bad. It was like a dull joke. It really hurt my senses, all that waste. Laura just stretched there like a cardboard cutout.

"Christ, man, let me show you how!"

Tod pulled out. "O.K., show me!"

I downed my gin and leaped in. I pulled at my memory and got out my old Van Gogh strokes. I teased, plunged, relented, attacked again, let off, continued, finally staying, destroying. Laura was out of it. I decided to get off and let Tod go at it but I found I couldn't and next I knew one head was out and the other was in, my cock was driving home, Laura was ripping my back with her nails, then I heard Tod:

"O.K., YOU SON OF A BITCH! GET OUT OF HERE! NOW!"

I looked up. There was Tod standing there nude pointing the .45 at me.

"GET THE FUCK OUT OF HERE!"

I heard the safety catch click off. He had the .45 pointed at my bellybutton. I climbed off the bed.

"Hey, *cool*, Daddy Tod! You've lost your *cool*, daddy!"

"I SAID, 'GET THE FUCK OUT!' NOW!"

I picked up my clothes and put them over my arm. I walked out of the bedroom with Tod following me with the .45. I opened the front door and walked out into the night. I didn't look back. I walked down toward my court in the back. It was early morning and there wasn't anybody around. My dick was limp, quite. I reached into my pants for my keys and they were gone. Shit. They had dropped out of my pants somewhere along the way. I got into my shorts and started searching the walkway. I re-traced my steps all the way but I couldn't find the keys. The morning was getting cold. I walked back to Tod's door and knocked. There was no response. They were probably fucking. I had certainly warmed her up for him.

I knocked again.

I heard Tod: "GIVE THE SON OF A BITCH HIS KEYS!"

The door opened. It was Laura in the nude. She just handed me the keys. Then she closed the door.

I walked back to my place, keys and balls dangling. Inside, I drank two cans of ale and slept. . . .

Nothing was ever mentioned about that night. It were as if it had never happened. Meanwhile, my coke habit, even at cut-rates, was cutting into my resources. I forgot the poem and went back to the dirty story. Most of my dirty stories were funny, like there was one where this guy gets his balls nailed to the headboard of the bed while his man-hating lady slowly sprays him to death with cans of roach poison while she talks to her girlfriends on the telephone telling them that no man is ever going to fuck her over again.

Anyhow, I was back at Tod's this night. Laura was at her nudie dance spot. It was a slow night. We were on the beer. Tod said he wanted to open a string of porno shops and he wanted me to manage one of them. He claimed that I was one of the few guys he could trust. I told him I'd brood on it. Then there was a knock on the door. A knock could tell you much if you could read it. This was an *ugly* knock, somehow like bad darkness knocking. I mean, the read on that knock wasn't a good read. Not at all.

Tod went to the door. He had two chains on the door. He dropped one of the chains off, slid the door open a chink, looked out. Then he turned to me.

"It's my supplier, my main man."

"I'll leave then, right now."

"No, stay, it's all right."

"Jesus," I said.

Tod opened the door. First, this thin guy moved in. His little rat's eyes checked the room. He slid into the bedroom. He checked the can. The walls, under the rugs. He took off lampshades. He even opened the refrigerator. After this, in walked the Big Guy. Big and fat. Dressed in a dirty black cheap suit. He was sweating. There was probably no such thing as *evil* but if there was, there was most of it: *Mr. Evil*. He reeked of murder. He was like a guy who wanted to kill just to get rid of a nervous itch. I felt all that, plenty. And I felt fear because it was catching: it was coming off of him, waves and rolls of it. I had never seen a guy like that in the movies or in life or anywhere else. You couldn't invent anybody like that. He was just there.

He looked at Tod. "WHO'S THIS GUY?"

"He's all right. . . ."

"What's he want? What's he do?"

"He's a writer. He was just having a beer."

"Tell him to clear out!"

The sweat was rolling from Big Guy's forehead and it was running down his face. The thin guy came around and stood next to him. What would Clint Eastwood do?

I drained my beer, looked at Tod: "I need an ale."

Tod walked toward the kitchen.

"Hey, what the fuck is this?" said the big man. "He needs an ALE? What the *fuck* IS this?"

Tod came back with my ale, my favorite kind in the green can. I tore the clip and had a hit.

"Who is this guy? What the fuck does he want?" the big guy asked Tod.

"I told you," said Tod, "no problem." Then he smiled weakly, "I even let him eat Laura's pussy."

"That don't cut no fucking ice with me! My brother was killed by a sack of shit who looked just like this guy!"

I took a good hit of the ale. Frankly, I was scared, not of death, just of this Big Guy. I could understand most people no matter how much I disliked them. But with the Big Guy, there was no understanding. It just ran off the edge and vanished. You think, you know, after you've been around 5 or 6 decades that you've met them all. But there's always that one extra that they work in on you and nothing you've ever known or experienced helps at all.

"I'm going," I said, "one more gulp."

"Gulp it fast," said the Big Guy.

"Yeah," the thin guy finally spoke.

This pissed me off a little, not much, but a little so I didn't gulp the ale as fast as I had intended. They just stood there, Tod, the thin boy, the Big Guy, and they watched me as I drained the can.

"O.K." I said, "I'm leaving."

Then I stood up and pulled out a cigarette and put it to my lips.

"Anybody got a light?" I asked.

Big Guy walked forward, took the cigarette out of my mouth and crushed it, then this big hand came out and grabbed my jaw and my mouth opened and he threw the cigarette shreds into my mouth and slammed my mouth shut. My tongue came down on some of my teeth and I felt the blood almost immediately. And the pain.

"Now, you leave, huh?" asked the Big Guy.

I did. And as I went down the walkway I could hear Big Guy asking Tod, "Who the FUCK was that guy? . . ."

Well, we talked a little bit about that afterwards, Tod and I, that is, but not too much. Meanwhile, Tod scored on another of my numbers but I almost expected that. But he *did* fail on another who told me, "That guy reminds me of a jelly doughnut." But for my money he was still the fuckmaster of East Hollywood and *all* those girls just weren't coke-whores. I mean, I would really ponder it: did they like the way his pants fit so tightly against his tiny crotch? Or was it his always-shined shoes with the pointed glistening toes? Or his gartered stockings? Or his white-eyed face with windswept hair touched with a yellow almost borrowed from the sun? Or was it that he smelled like a man who would never grow old? Always cool, lazy, knowing . . . knowing something that the rest of us would never know? Generally, I thought of him as an Advertisement of what a Ladies Man *should* look like. And he wasn't dumb; he was bland but not dumb. Many things that fooled other people didn't fool him. He had some fucking perceptions. In fact, take 5 or 6 men, Tod would still be the best to talk to a bit some night. It was easy enough that way. But what bothered me was how he so *quickly* got into bed with almost any strange woman that he desired. I felt that there was some password, some words he must have said, so I stayed around trying to key in, like pretending to be a writer, I wanted to know the *essence* of his fuck-secret, I felt it was all a little bit beyond the obvious. Maybe something I could use, or maybe something we could all laugh at. . . .

Well, I think it was a Thursday night, maybe a Friday, I had been to the harness races and I was driving in, fairly drunk. I seldom drank at the races but this night I had. One of my numbers had started cranking down on me demanding that we go to Vegas and get married. It just came out like that and she just kept demanding. Some madness. It upset me. It couldn't have been my money. In fact, she had been one of those who had fucked the Ladies Man of East Hollywood. She kept saying, "Let's get married right now before we change our minds!" And worse, this number was one of those who fucked everybody: pizza delivery boys, religious fanatics, symphony orchestra violinists, termite men, mayors, carwash boys. My life was already hell, top-grade hell. I had failed at suicide 4 or 5 times but I still had hope. But married to this number I knew I would be in a triple Dante's *Inferno*. So, I escaped her by driving off to the harness races.

So I drank at the bar out there, trying to erase all her bullshit and I lost on top of that, maybe a couple of hundred. . . .

I drove in slowly. I was trying to contemplate where I was in Existence and I didn't arrive with very much. I even ran out of cigarettes. Things got bad, but there was no place to go when they got bad. If you went to a shrink, he just read to you from the book but when you looked at him, you knew he didn't know what you were talking about. You were just talking to a contented person. When what you really needed when you were going crazy was another crazy who read exactly what you were saying, but not from the book, from the street.

Parking was always tough around the court but more so this night. There was a large crowd about the front of the court and I thought, oh-oh, shit.

I had to park way around the corner and walk back in. The crowd was still there, larger than ever. I never liked crowds of people. People never made sense and the more of them you got into one area the less sense you had. Crowds were just Death with a lot of feet and heads and so forth.

I had to get to my court. Which, like I told you, was in the back. As I got closer I heard one guy say to another, "Somebody shot the shit out of him. The guy ran out and was gone. Nobody knows where he went. I don't think they know."

The lights of the police cars whirled. There was an ambulance. The cops kept pushing people back.

"Move back, buddy, or I'll crack your fucking nuts!"

"Don't shove me! This is a Democracy!"

"Move back! One more fucking word and you got no teeth!"

Plainclothes men were moving in and out of the front court. There were camera flashes from inside. Then they pulled Laura out of the door. They had her *cuffed*, for Christ's sake. They stood with her there outside the door for a moment. The moonlight and the whirling lights showed her face. She was silent but tears were all about her face. I don't suppose she'd ever felt that *nude* even before a Saturday night club full of jack-offs. I knew she could use me. I knew she needed help. But I was pretty fucking drunk. I knew I'd get the drunk tank, maybe worse. I watched them lead her off to a squad car.

Then they came out with the body. The crowd creamed on that. It was better than anything they'd seen on TV since its inception.

He was in a black sack, and he almost looked good in there: his feet lined up perfectly, his head straight, he was still neat. That was it. They carried him down to the wagon, the doors were open, they rolled him in and moved off, siren even going as if there were a hurry. I never knew what they did that with dead meat. I had learned something. I learned one thing each day and forgot two.

The crowd still lingered, talking more now, matching notes and thrills. "Shit, I was sitting there listening to Johnny Carson when. . . ."

I circled around the back of the court, went down the apartment house driveway next door, came up the back, climbed the little chain link fence, walked maybe 30 feet, and I was at my front door.

Inside, I took off my things, got down to my shorts, went to the refrigerator, and there I had a six-pack and a half of ale. I got out a can, came back, cracked it, found an old cigar in the ashtray, lit it. It occurred to me that Big Guy might be after my ass just for the hell of it. But having that old suicide inclination it didn't mean that much. Except it did. I preferred my own way out. It was degrading to be killed by somebody you didn't like except if it were yourself.

But I felt cheated by the murder of Tod. Perhaps I never would have gotten to his secret, I mean how he did it with the ladies so *easily*. It *was* an Art even though most men in the field were not artists. Tod just fucked away in an unmolested and almost boring manner. Why the women just fell and spread their legs for him by the dozens of dozens I would never know.

I drank four cans of ale, I drank five sitting there in my shorts, alone. In fact, I sat there drinking all of the ale that was left. The sun was up then; it was sliding through the dirty blinds.

Tod, I thought, you son of a bitch, why didn't you tell me? One more would hardly cut down on your score. Don't you realize that there are millions of people upon the earth that go from life to death without even fucking once? And there you go dropping panties and spreading beaver like it's all a matter of nonsense, on and on and on. . . . And you're probably fucking the first thing that crosses your path in hell. . . . Why didn't you tell me? Or, is there nothing to tell?

I walked to the bathroom, pissed, threw some water upon my hands, then my face, then my hair. I picked up the toothbrush, looked at it, dropped it into the sink. I walked into the bedroom, fell flat upon the bed, face upwards, the legs of the bed rattling and crackling once again to the familiar crash, yet, along with the grace of the Universe, holding but for another morning.

I would awaken very sick and unknowing, once again.

# THE BULLY

Harry managed to get in one more drink before the landing. Facing Tina again didn't exactly delight him. She'd come to that desert town after their split. She was living with her married sister, Ann, who didn't seem to like Harry too much. Ann was a failed writer and Harry was a lucky one. And he was lucky, too, that he had never married Tina. Tina was a nympho, always had it on her mind; sex was the only ultimate truth for her and Harry had tried every trick in the book and some out of the book in an attempt to appease her constant lust. But his drinking and gambling had often gotten in the way of her needs and one day she put it to him: "You either give up drinking and gambling or you give up me."

Of course, only a damn fool would give up both drinking and gambling and so that had ended it for them.

Yet, Tina was a looker: fine ass, legs, hair, breasts, wild eyes, and there was Harry, on a flight, going to see her. She had badgered and pleaded with him so constantly over the phone that he had given in, figured he would fly in, engage in four or five sessions (two days?), and then get out. Besides, he needed a rest from another woman back there, a woman who wasn't a nympho but who ate at his mind and his feelings by her need to play him against other men. Within that context he'd just as soon the other men had her completely. And by flying out he was giving her the open road. The problem with women was that as soon as you broke with one, another arrived to take her place. They never left you any areas to regroup in. . . .

As usual, Harry was the last one off the plane. It was a habit he had never analyzed. But it probably had something to do with egomania, oversensibility, plus a dislike of having to stand in an airliner aisle while looking at the backs of heads, and the ears and the elbows and the butts and all that.

It was a small airport compared to LAX and as he came down the runway, he spotted Tina standing behind a screen fence in the parking lot. He had his flight bag and went on through the exit and there she was. Harry grinned and she ran up, they hugged, kissed, and there was her tongue flicking in and out of his mouth. No commonplace greetings from Tina. Looked like those cowboys had her in fine tune. It was 9:35 P.M. in that desert town.

And there in the car was the dog. Tina knew he liked Jock. And Jock remembered him, was all over him in the front seat—leaping, twisting, his tail fanning wildly. Harry hugged, petted, talked to Jock, then put him in the back seat along with his flight bag.

The car was in motion and they were off to the sister's house. Tina had a slight smile on her lips. To Harry it looked like a smile of victory.

"You're looking good, Harry. I'll bet it's because you've cut down on your drinking."

"You look fine, Tina, maybe better than ever. But no, I still drink about the same. . . ."

"I just wish you'd hold it down while you're here."

"All right, Tina, drive me back to the fucking airport!"

"What is it?" she asked.

"Jesus Christ, I mean, you're starting in already!"

"I only mean it for your own good, Harry; you're not a young man anymore. That drinking is going to kill you."

"*Not* drinking is what will kill me! Now, tool this thing around and drive me back!"

"No."

"'No,' my *ass*! yelled Harry. He cut the key off on the steering wheel and pulled the emergency brake on. The car ran off the road, crashed through a mass of tall shrubbery, and there they sat.

Tina looked straight forward for a while, then she said, "All right, Harry, there's a pint of scotch in the glove compartment."

Harry ripped the compartment open, saw the bottle, unpeeled and uncapped it and had a good hit.

He noted that the headlights were still on, reached over and shut them off.

"You're a sweetheart, baby."

"Listen, Harry, why don't we live together again?"

"People don't live together, they die together and at the same time they die separately."

"You're a cynical prick, Harry. . . ."

"Reality is a cynical act."

"And you've got this *humor*. . . ."

"Tina, there's nothing funny about me. You give me too many credits. I don't know what the hell I'm doing . . ."

"You turn me on, Harry. . . ."

Harry took another hit of the scotch.

One thing about drinking: you didn't have to talk to the bottle.

Then—she was bending over him—unzipping his fly.

"What the hell you doing?"

"Hey, look: my *little* friend!"

"Don't be kind to me, Tina. . . ."

"What's he been doing lately?"

"Attempting to avoid the obvious."

Harry felt her tongue flick over the mushroom helplessness of his penis, up there, *flick*, and *flick* again. He took another hit of the scotch.

That was the main trouble with Tina: she gave the best head west and south of Boston. She reached down into his pants and yanked everything up and out of there. He felt that tongue roll up from his balls and then roll and whirl further up the vein snake madness to the head, then circle and circle the head in a fathomless and ultimately conquering ingenuity.

Harry decided to ignore it.

He looked out of the car window at the low-slung and arid hills. But she was getting to him. He tried to think of eating a bucket of shit, spoonful by spoonful.

No good. She was getting to him.

Jock had both paws up on the front seat, was looking over and whimpering. Dear Jock smelled the heat of it all. Harry reached over, pushed him back down, and had another hit of the scotch. After doing that and looking forward, he noticed that the moon was watching also.

Then, Harry began groaning and then—she bit him *hard*, right at the center of his cock—

"You fucking whore!"

He slapped her—hard—right on the top of her skull and that did it: she began working in immaculate and ultimate fury. Harry could no longer hold back: he ejaculated right into the middle of the desert among the 412 rabbits and 672 snakes and the 10,687 etc.

Tina then sat up, flicked on the overhead light and began applying lipstick with the aid of the rearview mirror, her slight smile of victory reappearing.

Then she started the car, got the headlights on and roared away, a large leafy branch of the brush still clinging to the top of the hood. She drove on peering through the obstruction. She'd had electro-shock treatments at the age of 22. . . .

As they parked outside of the ranch, Harry could see that the lights were on. Ann and her husband, Reddough, were waiting for him. Harry had never met Reddough. Tina filled him in at a rather late stage.

"I've seen you lose some good fights, Harry, but Reddough is another matter. He's the number one bully in this town. He's filled more hospital beds around here than cancer."

"I don't want any trouble, Tina; I'm working on a novella and I'd like to finish it."

"*Any* excuse is all this guy needs. I don't want you busted up until we've worked out a few times."

Harry took another hit: "Your concern for my well-being is appreciated, Tina."

They got out of the car and walked in there.

Reddough and Ann were sitting waiting for them at a table in the kitchen. They appeared to be well into their drinking. And there was a fifth of whiskey on the table. A radio was on, playing country and western. Reddough snapped the radio off: "Sit down, city boy."

Harry stuck out his hand. Reddough reached over as if to shake, stuck a beercap into Harry's hand.

"What am I supposed to do with this?" Harry asked.

"I don't know. Stick it up your ass for all I care."

Harry looked around at Tina who was still standing behind him: "I know I've said this before but, again, will you please drive me back to the fucking airport?"

"What's the matter?" Reddough asked. "Scared?"

"A little, not much."

Reddough pushed the fifth toward him: "Drink?"

Harry sat down: "Sure."

"Harry," Tina said, "*please* don't drink with him!"

"It tastes the same to me, no matter who's around. . . ."

Ann got up, came back with a water glass.

"How much?" Reddough asked.

"Topside."

"Beer chaser?"

"Thanks."

Harry sucked off half the glass of whiskey and took a hit of the can of beer before him.

Reddough watched: "Drinking doesn't make the man."

"What does?"

"Some things are just born in a certain way and that's it."

"You mean, like a skunk?"

"Hey!" Reddough looked up from lighting his cigar. "What have we here? This guy wants to play, huh?"

Reddough wasn't as big as all that, maybe 5'10" but he was blocky, very; he looked almost like a square but of course, he wasn't. But he was *wide* and stocked with muscular bulges—and some fat—but it almost looked as if the fat were stacked in the right places, if that were possible. And, his head was too small.

How the hell you going to beat on a head like that? thought Harry. It's going to be like trying to crack a walnut shell with your knuckles. Definitely unfair. And his wife, Ann, sitting there overweight and more than frustrated, hating herself and hating the world because she kept getting rejects from the massive novels she mailed to the New York City publishers every other year.

Harry always hoped that she would hit so that she would get off his case. And he had read some pages of her output—pages of humorless self-yearning and falsified sex-excursions. Her driving desire to be a great writer only seemed to drive her straight toward mediocrity.

Now she glared at Harry: "You still writing that shit and getting paid for it?"

"Oh yes, regularly."

"We got one of your books here," said Reddough. "We hang it from a string in the henhouse. There's one story in there where a man rapes a little girl. You call that writing?"

"Yes."

Tina came around and sat down. She had a Pepsi-Cola. She poured it into half a glass of ice.

"Listen, Harry, let's sleep now. We can talk in the morning."

"I'm a night creature, Tina. Mornings are bad for me."

"I don't want any trouble between you and Reddough."

"I'll chance that for a few more drinks. . . ."

Reddough blew a blast of cigar smoke across the table at Harry. "Don'tcha think you're a little *old* for Tina?"

"'Old' is just a word in the dictionary."

"No, 'old' is sometimes something that happens."

"You might be right there."

Ann had left. Then she was back. She had a sheaf of paper in her hand. She tossed it in front of Harry.

"First chapter of my new novel. Give it a read."

Just like that. But they all did it—just like that.

Harry drained his glass, looked at Reddough: "How about a refill?"

"Well, looky here!" said Reddough, filling the glass.

Harry began reading, hoping for the best. It wasn't there. Where did that urge toward dullness come from? There wasn't a writer in the world who thought they couldn't write. But it took more than one vote. And many crappy writers were published. And maybe he was one of them. But Harry didn't like Ann's writing. It just bogged and bawled and bitched—a tedious drumming of ineffectiveness.

He handed the sheets back to Ann. "There are some good parts, but all in all, I don't care for it."

"What do you find wrong?" Ann asked.

"I don't know. It's kind of a cross between Faulkner, Thomas Wolfe, and an ordinary soap opera."

"Maybe," said Reddough, leaning forward against the table, "maybe she ought to write about some man raping a little girl?"

"She can write about anything she wants as long as she does it truly."

"'*Truly*'? What kind of word is that? You think you've got the inside to truth? I don't think so."

"Drink up and calm down."

"Don't tell me what to do in my own house!"

"Look, Red, we can get along. Let's just relax. They might drop the Bomb at any minute. We're all trapped in this shit. What's the need for us to destroy each other? We should be laughing through our last moments. Wouldn't that be best?"

"Hey, fucker," said Reddough, "lemme tell you something: God is going to protect His *own!*"

"Red, maybe there isn't a God."

Reddough stood up. "THAT'S IT!"

"What?"

"NOBODY SAYS WORDS LIKE THAT IN MY HOUSE!"

With that, he came flying across the table, a big wingless sodden thing. Harry ducked to the left and the mass of muscle (and fat) fell face forward across the floor, skidded against the wall, then rose, puffing, chest out, eyebrows twisted. Reddough moved toward Harry who had rolled under the table and had come up on the other side.

"Red, I was just kidding. I'm sure there's a God somewhere. Right?"

Reddough wavered there across the table. "You're a coward!"

"Right. And listen, it might make you feel better to know that I don't even *want* to fuck your sister-in-law. She wants to fuck me."

Tina screamed and threw her Pepsi-Cola bottle at Harry. It bounced off his head, fell to the floor. There was a tiny ringing sound inside of Harry's skull.

Reddough moved forward a couple of steps as if to circle the table.

"Listen, Red, all men are brothers. Similar blood, similar fingers, similar bungholes, similar sorrows. Think about it!"

"Huh?"

Reddough stood there, seemingly unsure then of what to do and why. He wavered forward, then backward, then sat back down at the table. Harry sat down across from him. Ann and Tina stood watching.

"Pour me a good one, Red."

"Yeah."

He filled both water glasses to the rims. The fifth was empty.

Harry raised his glass. "Here's to us!"

They clicked glasses and each drained about half a glass.

Red looked at Harry. "You know, city boy, I kind of like you. You say what you think even if it is fucked-up."

"You say what you think too, Red."

"That's important, isn't it?"

"Yeah."

"You don't want to fuck my wife, do you?"

"No, Red."

"Anyhow, you're ugly. You don't worry me."

"Thanks, Red."

Suddenly Red put his head down on the table, knocking over his drink as he did so. He was out. . . .

Harry finished his drink, stood up, looked around, saw Ann.

"Goodnight, Ann."

Then Tina was leading him by the hand. Then they were in the guest bedroom. Nice place.

Harry sat on the edge of the bed, taking off his shoes. Tina was disrobing near the closet.

"You had a lucky night, Harry."

"I prey on good luck. It feeds me."

"I know. You're lucky to have me, Harry."

"Sure, Tina."

Harry got his clothes off and put himself down under the cover and between the clean sheets. Life was not so bad. Now, if he could get rid of that number in L.A. he could start all over again. He evolved off into sleep. . . .

It could have been 3 A.M., 4 A.M., one of those—anyhow, he was awakened to find Tina riding him topside. It startled him that he was hard. Her head was bent back and she was groaning. He played along with it.

"O.K., baby, ride the bronco!"

But all he wanted to do was to be back in L.A. watching the Johnny Carson monologue on TV and not liking it at all. But it was a place to be. A candy-cotton numb dream of isolation. And no trouble, no trouble at all.

Harry reached out, grabbed the cheeks of Tina's ass and said, "Work it, baby, you beautiful fucking whore. . . ."

# THE INVADER

It was a hot Saturday night, late. There had been nothing worthwhile on cable TV but they had watched it anyhow, relentlessly, and without hope. Harry had drunk a bottle of red wine and Ann about a half.

Now they were in the bedroom attempting to sleep but it was difficult: bad TV only put you to sleep while you were watching it. But their dog, Redeye, was asleep. In fact, he was snoring. Down there on the rug. No bad memories of rotten TV for Redeye.

The minutes rolled into a half-hour . . . then into almost an hour . . . and . . . at last Harry felt himself slowly easing into sleep. . . .

Sleep . . . ah, sleep. . . .

Then Ann was shaking him . . . "HARRY! HARRY!"

"Huh? What is it?"

"EYES!"

"What?"

"EYES! I SAW THESE EYES STARING THROUGH THE WINDOW!"

"What window?"

"THAT WINDOW! THE ONE TO THE RIGHT! THERE BY THE BUSH! THE EYES WERE LOOKING AT ME RIGHT OVER THE TOP OF THE BUSH!"

"Are they gone now?"

"Yes. . . ."

"Then let's go to sleep."

"HARRY, YOU FIND OUT WHAT THOSE EYES WERE! I'M TERRIFIED!"

"All right, all right. . . ."

Harry wandered through the yard in slippers, pjs and robe, along with a flashlight and the baseball bat. He could see Ann watching from the window. He poked through the brush with the bat, flashing the light.

"O.K., Peep freak, come on out! I won't hurt you too much! Come on out now, we'll talk the whole thing over! I'm a recovered peep-freak myself. Come on out and we'll talk about some of the good things I've seen!"

"Harry," Ann hissed from the window, "it's not funny! Be careful!"

Harry kept poking in the brush and flashing the light.

"Come on out, baby! We'll go inside and watch some porno movies!"

There seemed to be nothing about. Harry turned to re-enter the house.

It was then he heard *something* running behind him.

"SHIT!" Harry yelled.

He swung the bat at the thing and missed. The thing leaped high, quite high and landed on a small ledge that ran across the top of the back door. There wasn't much space on that ledge but the thing managed to cling there.

Harry walked closer and flashed the light upwards. And he saw the EYES. . . .

THE WILD, FEARFUL CRAZY EYES.

"Harry, Harry . . . what *is* it? Be careful! . . ."

Harry flashed the light fully upon the thing.

"Ann, it's a goddamned MONKEY!"

"A monkey?"

"Yes, a monkey. . . ."

"Oh, I'll be right out . . ."

"Don't come out the back door . . . it's hanging out there, over the top . . . on the little ledge. . . ."

"I'm coming out the window. . . ."

"Stay in there . . . it might bite. . . ."

"No, I'm coming out. . . ."

Harry heard the screen push open and there was Ann clambering out over the brush. . . .

"Oh, I tore my nighty. . . ." she was at his side.

"Where is he?"

Harry flashed the light. "Up there . . . look. . . ."

"Oh, the poor thing . . . he's *terrified*!"

Harry said, "I'm going to call the zoo or the fire department or Animal Control or somebody!"

"Oh, Harry, not at *this* time of the night!"

"I can't think of a better time."

"Harry, he's scared to death! Look at him!"

"Yeah."

"He only wants understanding . . . love. . . ."

"He needs the sanctuary of the cage . . . that will buck him up."

"No, wait, Harry, please . . . I'll be right back. . . ."

Ann was clambering through the window again.

Harry kept the light on the monkey. Actually the thing scared him, a bit. It moved too fast and it looked weak in the brain. A fucker like that could do anything. It could turn on you in a flash.

The EYES kept looking at him. There, they were red. Then a pale orange. Now they were lit by a long yellow inner glow, rather like an electric charge. All colors of danger.

Then Ann was there again.

"I've got some bananas. . . ."

"Bananas?"

"Yes, the poor thing is probably STARVING!"

Ann moved forward. She had two bananas. She dropped one to the ground. Then she half-peeled the other and held it up to the monkey.

"Come on down . . . Come on down, you poor thing . . . Come on down and get your banana!"

"Ann, that goddamned thing isn't going to come down! I'm going to phone the authorities!"

"Come on down, Bozo, and get your nice banana! Come on down, Bozo!"

"Bozo?"

"Bozo *loves* bananas, *don't* you, Bozo?"

"Ann, that thing is never. . . ."

Bozo leaped down in a forceful arc. He stood still there upon the ground. Then in a lightning flash movement he shot along the ground. But he didn't take the banana from Ann's hand. He grabbed the other one, ran off a short distance, peeled the banana, and gulped it down.

"Poor Bozo, he's *starving!*"

"All right, Ann, let's leave him the other banana and go on in."

"*What?* We can't leave that poor thing out there all night!"

"Why not? He's from the *jungle!* They *love* the night!"

"Harry, I won't be able to sleep while thinking about him out here all night alone!"

"And I sure as hell won't be able to sleep with him inside our place!"

The monkey just sat on the lawn, motionless, watching them.

"Besides," said Harry, "he won't come in. He's wild."

"Oh, the poor thing . . . he'll come in . . . watch. . . ."

Ann walked over, opened the back door, then moved toward Bozo, dangling the half-peeled banana before her.

"Come on, Bozo, come on inside. Lots of bananas inside, Bozo. Come on. . . ."

Bozo moved toward the banana. Ann backed up. Bozo followed. Ann moved up the steps of the house, going backwards. She dangled the banana. Bozo followed.

"Come on, Bozo. Good old, Bozo. . . ."

Ann backed into the house and the monkey followed her.

As Harry got inside, Bozo was finishing off the banana. Then he looked down at the skins, made a nasty sound, and threw them over his head.

Then he walked over to Redeye's dogfood dish. There was some dogfood in there. Bozo bent over, stuck his head in there, and began eating. He had his rump up in the air and it was ugly, red, and full of bloody scratches.

"I didn't think they ate meat," Harry stated.

"He's starving, poor thing. . . ."

"In the morning I'm going to phone somebody. This thing *belongs* somewhere. . . ."

"Harry, he belongs here. The Fates have sent him."

"Well, the Fates are out of luck. . . ."

"Harry, I've always wanted a baby. . . ."

"Oh, Christ! . . ."

Bozo finished the dogfood, then slowly walked into the front room. Ann and Harry followed.

"Look at him, Harry! He acts right at home!"

"Stuffed with bananas and dogfood. . . ."

Bozo leaped up on the back of the couch. There he slumped over and closed his eyes.

"Look, Harry, he's going to sleep!"

Suddenly . . . Bozo let it go: he defecated on the back of the couch. It was diarrhea-like, a large wet splotch of stringy material. It smelled similar to burning rubber and ammonia.

Bozo then reached down into it, got some on his fingers . . . then rubbed the fingers around his mouth.

Then, he screeched in joy, leaped upon the rug.

"That thing has got to go!" said Harry.

"I'll clean it up! Harry, the poor thing just couldn't help himself!"

Ann ran to the kitchen for her cleanup materials.

Just then . . . Redeye walked into the room. The dog. Redeye was an old swayback mongrel in his last years. In the old days he had been tougher than love gone wrong but Time had no consciousness: when the dog saw the monkey, the dog slowly walked backwards, whimpering. He slowly walked, crept backwards, low-down, low-born at last, he retreated, he vanished from the game.

Bozo gave a little Tarzan victory-call, beating his chest with one hand. Then he stopped, looked at the hand, sensed something in his fingers: a flea had exited in all the fury of this victory, got caught in a nail and Bozo bent down and ate one of his eternal enemies.

Well, thought Harry, now it's just me and the fucking monkey.

The next day, a Sunday, Harry was watching a professional football game on TV and drinking beer. Ann and Bozo were in and out of the house, playing. Nothing too untoward had happened. . . . Well, Bozo had shit on top of the refrigerator.

It was a good football game and Harry almost forgot about the monkey. Redeye was at his side, trembling but true, trying to gather in his lost past. Harry reached down, petted the old mongrel. . . .

"Don't worry, we'll get rid of that son of a bitch. . . ."

And he drained his beer can.

At least Ann wasn't trying to get him to take her to some movie. She had her movie: that red-assed subnormal hunk of fur.

Harry left the TV to go take a piss.

Then he had to come out fast to all the yelping and chattering: Bozo was dug into Redeye's back, riding him. The dog was running about the room, crazed.

Harry made a flying tackle and then they were all about the floor: dog, monkey, and man.

Redeye shot off into the other room.

The monkey leaped onto the coffee table, grabbed a banana, peeled it, and gulped it down. . . .

Late that night, Harry and Ann were in bed together.

They hadn't made love for about three weeks. Somehow, they got into it.

Harry worked away. For the first time in a long time he felt normal again. Sex wasn't terrible at all. It was quite interesting.

He had once been a hell of a lover. Or so it had seemed.

For it all, it was going well.

Then . . . Ann began giggling . . . wildly. . . .

"What the fuck?" Harry asked.

He fell out.

"Look! Quick!" Ann said.

Harry turned his head.

Bozo had been watching.

He was on top of the dresser, masturbating.

He had a long thin red string of a thing and he was beating at it. His eyes had a dumb blank look.

Bozo gave a little yelp. He was finished. He leaped off of the dresser and ran out of the room.

Ann was still giggling.

"That was really funny!"

"Yeah?"

"Baby, that fucking thing has got to *go!*"

Upon awakening that A.M. Harry grabbed the phone, phoned in sick.

"I'm not sure what it is," he told them, "but I'm coming down with *something* and I think it's something *bad.* . . ."

He slowly hung the phone up.

"What is it?" Ann asked. "What are you coming down with, Harry? What can I do?"

"Nothing. Where's that goddamned monkey?"

"He's in the house somewhere. I've got things locked up so he can't get out."

"I'm getting his ass out of here! We're harboring a wild animal! We're not equipped to do that! He has to go!"

"Oh, Harry, *please*! He's so *cute*! All he needs is love!"

"All he needs is a cage and a keeper!"

Ann got up and went to the bathroom. She closed the door. After a while he could hear Ann sobbing.

Harry walked to the door, spoke through it: "I'm sorry, Ann, I know that he has certain charming ways . . . but . . . he's destroying our lives! I have to get rid of him. . . ."

There was a wail from behind the door. It made Harry feel bad but he walked back to the bedroom, began dressing. First thing he had to do was find the monkey. Then he'd put him in that carrying-case they used when they took Redeye to the vet's. After he got him in there he'd phone Animal Control.

Harry went outside and got the carrying-case out of the garage. It was sturdy, built of plywood with large screen windows. It was big enough to carry Bozo. He brought it into the house, set it down in the kitchen.

Bozo was nowhere to be seen.

Harry found a couple of bananas.

"Bozo, baby, come on out from wherever you are! Come on and have your breakfast! Bozo! Nice bananas! Nice ripe bananas!"

Where was the son of a bitch?

Then he found him. He was asleep on top of the TV. He was like a little man covered with fur. There *was* some charm there, and a certain low-grade type of innocence.

Asleep like that, Bozo did score some points.

Harry walked up to him, touched him on the ear. Bozo opened one eye, looked at Harry. The monkey almost seemed to smile.

"How about a banana, boy?"

Bozo slowly sat up, got his haunches under him, then dangled his feet over the TV screen. He was still half asleep.

Harry peeled a banana.

"Come on, boy, have a bite. . . ."

Bozo took a small bite, chewed it down, scratched the back of his neck, and looked at Harry for more. Harry gave him the remainder of the banana. Then he peeled the second banana and fed it to him.

The monkey appeared to be quite relaxed.

"Bozo, come here to Papa. . . ."

Harry reached around and picked the animal up. Bozo's arms went around Harry's neck.

Harry walked the monkey slowly toward the kitchen, toward the carrying case.

Maybe we ought to keep him, Harry thought.

No, I've got to be strong. This is like something that came in the night to tear our hearts out. It can destroy our lives. It doesn't mean to, of course . . . but. . . .

He placed Bozo on the floor in front of the case. The door was open.

"Come on, Bozo . . . you just walk in there and look around. It's a little playhouse for you. . . . And we'll all be happier when you get in there . . . yeah. . . ."

Bozo stood there and looked at the opening. He wasn't moving. . . .

Harry reached down to that red ugly ass and gave Bozo a gentle shove.

The monkey was almost in. . . .

"NO, NO, BOZO! DON'T GO IN THERE! BOZO, RUN! BOZO, LOOK OUT! RUN!"

It was Ann, standing behind them.

The monkey was startled. It twisted as if to leap away. . . .

Harry grabbed Bozo hard, he had him in his grip. He held him there. Bozo wiggled, kicked, screeched but Harry had him in a good hold.

Harry moved him gradually toward the door of the case. The monkey was strong and making a good fight of it but Harry was jamming him forward through the door. . . .

Then Ann had her arms about Harry's neck, pulling him backwards from Bozo. . . .

"NO!" she screeched, "NO, NO, NO! HE'S NOT GOING IN THERE!"

Then Harry was struggling with the monkey and with Ann.

He encircled Bozo with his left arm and fought Ann off with his right.

The monkey was wiggling free from his left arm and Harry relented from fighting Ann in order to get better control of Bozo.

Harry brought his right arm around, took his right hand and pushed against the animal's head, against the top of the head to push Bozo back down into the grip of his left arm which had been encircled about the waist but the monkey had wiggled upwards and almost out. . . .

In the struggle, Harry's right hand slipped from the top of Bozo's head and down the face, down to the nose, the mouth. . . .

The monkey bit through Harry's index finger . . . completely ripping through the finger and the bone. It sheared the finger off just below the knuckle.

Harry rolled to the floor . . . YOWLING IN WORLD-ENDING TER-ROR AND PAIN . . . as the monkey ran out through the back door which had been left open. . . .

Bozo ran out into the world with the finger in his mouth. . . .

Harry sat on the floor, pressing his hand against his stomach.

"GET A TOWEL! GET A TOWEL! GET SOME HYDROGEN PEROXIDE!"

He inhaled heavily, exhaled.

"CALL A FUCKING AMBULANCE!"

Then, curiously, the pain almost stopped. It just felt as if some-thing were still taking small bites from the finger stub. There was an odd coldness too, as if the finger were in freezing weather, yet it throbbed.

Ann came running in from the bathroom with the materials, which included a small first-aid kit and the instruction booklet.

"OH, MY GOD, HARRY, IT'S ALL MY FAULT, ALL MY FAULT! I LOVE YOU, HARRY, I LOVE YOU! OH, THAT STUPID MONKEY! WHAT HAVE I DONE?"

"It's O.K., baby, don't blame yourself, it's just rotten luck. Here, give me some peroxide!"

Harry pulled the hand away from his shirt, looked at it a mo-ment . . . so *odd* to see that missing part . . . and he doused the finger-stump with the peroxide.

"Give me some cotton, baby, and some bandage-wrap. . . ."

Harry felt fairly calm about it all and his mind asked him, why are you so calm about all this?

And then his mind answered, I don't know.

"Adhesive, please. . . ."

Harry bound the clumsy affair. . . .

"Scissors, please. . . ."

"OH, HARRY. . . ."

"Phone for the ambulance, Ann . . . I have to go to Emer-gency. . . ."

Ann moved toward the bedroom to get at the telephone. Harry ran past her toward the front door. . . .

"HARRY, WHERE ARE YOU GOING?"

"I'VE GOT TO GET THAT MONKEY, THAT MONKEY HAS MY FINGER!"

"HARRY, WHAT DO YOU MEAN?"

He paused at the doorway.

"THEY SAY THAT IF YOU CAN GET A PART BACK SOON ENOUGH THEY CAN SEW IT BACK ON!"

Harry ran out into the yard.

"Bozo, baby, where are you, Bozo? I'm not mad, Bozo! Bozo, baby, come on, come on, plenty of bananas and you can ride the doggy, you can crap all over everywhere, I won't care. . . . Bozo, here Bozo!"

Harry ran about the yard searching . . . the blood was beginning to seep through his makeshift bandage. It was like a white mitten which was gradually turning red. The hand had stopped throbbing. The throbbing had gone up to his temples. . . .

Shit, he thought, maybe the son of a bitch has rabies. . . .

"Bozo, come on, Bozo, we all love you!"

The yard appeared to be vacant of the animal.

Harry hurried up the driveway, stood out front a moment, took a gamble and turned right, walked toward the Johnson house. Mrs. Johnson, a grey lady with a fat white face, thick legs, and eyes like faded pearl buttons, Mrs. Johnson just stood there watering her lawn. The water from the hose just arched out and splattered against the same area of grass. Mrs. Johnson was consumed with the sound and the action of the water.

"MRS. JOHNSON!"

"Oh, good morning, Mr. Evans. . . . Nice day, isn't it?"

"Mrs. Johnson, have you seen a monkey?"

"What?"

"Have you seen a monkey?"

"Oh, yes, I've seen them."

"I mean, right now! Around here! NOW!"

"Why?"

"Why? MRS. JOHNSON, THAT GODDAMNED MONKEY HAS MY FINGER!"

"Please don't use vulgarity around me, Mr. Evans!"

"OH, MY GOD!"

Harry ran past her and down her driveway.

"Where are you going?"

She dropped her hose and ran after him.

"YOU GET OUT OF MY YARD!"

Harry ran about her yard, searching, searching. . . .

There was nothing.

He turned and ran back up the driveway past Mrs. Johnson.

"I'M GOING TO TELL MY HUSBAND HOW RUDE YOU WERE TO ME! HE'LL KICK YOUR FRIGGING ASS!"

My god, thought Harry, as he ran out of there, she didn't even notice my bloody hand. . . . Oh, it's useless, I'll never find that beast. . . . He's probably tossed my finger away by now . . . but I've got to keep looking . . . not much time left. . . .

He saw Ann standing in front of their house.

"HARRY, I CALLED THE AMBULANCE! THEY'RE ON THE WAY!"

"THANKS, BABY, TELL THEM TO WAIT! I'LL BE RIGHT BACK!"

"I LOVE YOU, HARRY. . . . I'M SO SORRY, OH MY GOD, I'M SO SORRY!"

"IT'S O.K., BABY, I'LL BE RIGHT BACK!"

Harry ran further left down the block. He ran down the drive of the Henderson house. The hired yardman, a thin and rather contented fellow, was using his leaf-blower to clear away various debris. As Harry ran up the yardman saw this *thing* running toward him, this thing with a bloody white arm-end. He screamed, lifted the blower and shot a blast of air at Harry.

"Shit," said Harry.

He turned and ran back up the driveway and out into the street.

He stood in the street center, looking about, thinking, I must be just about out of time on that finger.

Then, to the left, about a half a block down he saw a crowd

gathered about an icecream truck. There were mostly children and a few adults.

And there on top of the icecream truck was some small type of creature.

Harry ran down the street.

When he got to the crowd, there was Bozo . . . just sitting on top of the ice cream truck.

And, hanging from the edge of his mouth was the end of Harry's index finger.

Bozo just sat there, almost in a dream-state.

"O.K.," said Harry, "that's my monkey. Now, just stand back. . . . Don't frighten him, please. . . ."

"I'll give him my ice cream if he'll come down," said a little boy with just a touch of snot dripping from his left nostril.

"Thank you, son, but please let me handle this. . . ."

"Hey, mister, what's that thing hanging out of his mouth?" asked a little girl.

"Never mind what that is. . . . Whatever it is, I want that and I want him. . . . All right?"

"Sure, mister. . . . How come your hand is all bloody?"

"It's nothing. . . . Now, everybody, please step back. . . . You are frightening him. . . ."

The crowd was quite nice. Adults and children all, they stepped back. Not too far, but they did step back.

Harry looked up at the top of the truck.

"Bozo, it's me. . . . Remember me? Come on down . . . and bring that . . . thing . . . you have in your mouth with you. If you do, we'll be friends forever, I promise you! Bozo, are you listening?"

"What's that thing in his mouth, mister?" asked the same little girl.

"GODDAMN IT, IT'S MY FINGER! NOW, DO YOU UNDERSTAND?"

"What's he doing with your finger, mister?"

Harry looked at Bozo just sitting up there in the same dream-like trance.

Harry turned to the driver of the ice cream truck.

"Get me something, Something luscious! Something that . . . if you were a monkey . . . you'd come down and eat!"

"Huh?"

"All right, forget it . . . get me an ice cream bar!"

"What flavor?"

"Banana."

The driver worked his way toward the back of the truck.

Harry looked back up at the monkey.

"BOZO! YOU MUST BE HUNGRY! WE WANT YOU TO EAT! UNDERSTAND? WE'RE GOING TO GIVE YOU SOMETHING TO EAT, UNDERSTAND? EAT!"

Bozo made a little sound.

Harry smiled.

Then Bozo took the finger out of his mouth, looked at it, put it back into his mouth, and started chewing.

"OH SHIT! NOT THAT! STOP STOP STOP!"

Bozo kept chewing. The driver came up to Harry and attempted to hand him the ice cream bar, saying, "We're outta banana. . . ."

Harry slapped the bar to the street. Harry tried to climb the side of the truck but the side was smooth, had no grips.

Harry stopped.

His bloody hand had left ugly and strange smears against the truck side.

Harry put his head there, rested.

"Oh shit . . . oh god. . . ."

Then he pulled his head from the truck side. He looked back to the top of the truck.

Bozo was giving it a last munch. . . .

Then he rounded his mouth and spit. . . .

A little bone flipped through the air and landed upon the asphalt. Harry looked at it, then turned away.

He began walking back down the street toward his house.

Then he heard a voice.

"HEY, MISTER, WHAT ARE YOU GOING TO DO ABOUT YOUR MONKEY?"

Henry turned.

It was the little boy who had the snot emanating from his left nostril.

"You can have him. . . ."

"OH BOY! OH BOY, OH BOY, OH BOY!"

Harry began to walk toward his house again.

He could see the ambulance in the driveway. There were two or three figures . . . maybe four . . . waiting there. . . . Maybe more. Things were beginning to blur. One of the figures that he could distinguish was his wife.

"HARRY, THE AMBULANCE IS WAITING! SHOULD WE COME DOWN THERE?"

He waved his arm over his head, the one with the bloody hand. . . .

"NO, NO! I'LL BE THERE SOON!"

Strangely, he felt as if not much had happened.

But he knew that *something* had happened.

As he walked along he held his hand down to his side, *that* hand, and he didn't look at it.

Mrs. Johnson was still watering the same spot on her lawn as he walked by.

"MY HUSBAND," she screamed upon seeing him, "IS GOING TO KICK YOUR FRIGGING ASS!"

There was nothing else to do but walk toward the ambulance.

# PLAYING AND BEING THE POET

4/12/92    11:42 P.M.

Where to begin? Well, it was Nietzsche who, when asked about the poets, responded, "The Poets? The Poets lie too much."

As one reads the poetry of the past and of our time, this criticism seems damned apt. There seems much posturing, prancing . . . playing at being the poet, this select messenger from the gods. I believe that if the gods selected most of our poets, then they did, indeed, select badly. Of course, there is much con and chicanery in all the Arts, but I believe the poets are the best at besmirching their particular field.

And I will grant you here that it's much easier to criticize poetry than to write it. When I was a very young man, I enjoyed reading the critical articles in the *Sewanee* and *Kenyon Reviews*, in regard to poetics. Those critics were such darlings, such snobs, so protected, so inbred, and they were amusingly vicious—at times—toward other critics. They neatly sliced each other to pieces in the finest of language, and I admired that, for my own language was rather coarse and direct, which I preferred, yet their way held much wonderment for me. Ah, such a gentlemanly way of calling each other assholes and idiots. Yet, beyond this, they had some insights on what was wrong with poetry and what could possibly be done about that. But, look here, when I turned to the actual poetry within the pages of those magazines, it was very bad poetry—pretentious, pale, in-conclusive, muddied, boring. . . . It was an insult to the pages. The fight was gone, the gamble was gone. It was stale milk. It was the wretchedness of being all too careful. And when the critics them-selves tried the poem, it had none of the bombast and fireworks of their critical pieces. It was as if moving to the poem form, they left what there was of their souls someplace else. Poetry is the final testing ground and very few practitioners in our time or in centuries past have passed the test.

Poetry comes from where you've lived and how you've lived and from what makes you create it. Most people have already entered the death process by the age of 5, and with each passing year there is less of them in the sense of being original beings with a chance to break through and out and away from the obvious and the mutilating. Generally, those who do have had life experiences and continue to have life experiences that set them aside, isolate them in such a manner that they become beautiful freaks, visionaries with their own visions. Perhaps there is some luck involved here but not exactly, for daily we are given choices, and if you choose wrong too often, anti-life, then you will soon be dead long before burial.

Those who are best at poetry are those who have to write it and will continue to write it no matter the result. For, if they don't, something else will happen: murder, suicide, madness, god knows what. The act of writing the Word down is the act of miracle, the saving grace, the luck, the music, the going-on. It clears the space, it defines the crap, it saves your ass and some other people's asses along with it. If fame somehow comes through all this, you must ignore it, you must continue to write as if the next line were your first line.

Also, there *are* other writers, though very few of them. But for me, there were maybe 6 or 7 who kept me going when all else said stop.

And although we must ignore praise, there are times when we might allow ourselves to feel good for just a bit. I received a letter from a prisoner in a jail in Australia who wrote me, "Your books are the only books that pass from cell to cell."

But, I've talked enough about writing poetry here; there is still time tonight to write some. A few beers, a cigar, classical music on the radio. See you later.

—Charles Bukowski

# SOURCES

"The Reason Behind Reason," *Matrix*, vol. 9, no. 2, Summer 1946. "Love, Love, Love," *Matrix*, vol. 9, nos. 3–4, Winter 1946–47. "Cacoethes Scribendi," *Matrix*, vol. 10, nos. 3–4, Fall-Winter 1947. "The Rapist's Story," *Harlequin*, vol. 2, no. 1, 1957. "80 Airplanes Don't Put You in the Clear," *Harlequin*, vol. 2, no. 1, 1957. "Manifesto: A Call for Our Own Critics," *Nomad*, no. 5/6, 1960. "Peace, Baby, Is Hard Sell," *Renaissance* 4, 1962. "Examining My Peers," *Literary Times (Chicago)*, vol. 3, no. 4, May, 1964. "If I Could Only Be Asleep," *Open City Press*, vol. 1, no. 6, January 6–13, 1965. "The Old Pro," *Ole*, no. 5, 1966. "Allen Ginsberg/Louis Zukofsky," *Ole*, no. 7, May 1967. "Notes of a Dirty Old Man," *Open City*, no. 32, December 8–14, 1967. "Bukowski on Bukowski," *Open City*, no. 92, February 23–March 1, 1969. "The Absence of the Hero," *Klacto 23/International*, Frankfurt, 1969. "Christ With Barbecue Sauce," *Candid Press*, December 27, 1970. "The Cat in the Closet," *Nola Express* no. 51, March 20–April 2, 1970. "More Notes of a Dirty Old Man," December 6, 1970, *Candid Press*. "Ah, Liberation, Liberty, Lilies on the Moon!" unpublished ms, UCSB, 1971. "Sound and Passion," *Adam*, vol. 15, no. 3, March 1971. "I Just Write Poetry So I Can Go to Bed With Girls," *Rogue*, No. 29, April 1971. "The House of Horrors," unpublished ms, 1971, University of Arizona Library. "Untitled essay on d.a. levy," *The Serif*, Vol. VIII, no. 4, December 1971. "Henry Miller Lives in Pacific Palisades and I Live on Skid Row, Still Writing About Sex," *Knight*, vol. 9, no. 7, 1972. "A Foreword to These Poems," *Anthology of L.A. Poets*, eds. Charles Bukowski, Neeli Cherry & Paul Vangelisti, Laugh Literary/Red Hill Press, 1972. "*The Outsider*: Tribute to Jon Edgar Webb," *Wormwood Review*, vol. 12, no. 1, issue 45, 1972. "Vern's Wife," *Fling*, vol. 15, no. 2, May 1972. "Notes of A Dirty Old Man," *Nola*, No. 104, April 14–27, 1972. "He Beats His Women," *Second Coming: Special Charles Bukowski Issue*, vol. 2, no. 3, 1973. "Notes of A Dirty Old Man," *L.A. Free Press*, June 1, 1973. "Notes of A Dirty Old Man," *L.A. Free Press*, June 28, 1974. "Notes of a Dirty Old Man," *L.A. Free Press*, August 22, 1975. "Notes of a Dirty Old Man: Notes of a dirty old driver of a light blue 1967 Volkswagen TRV 491," *L.A. Free Press*, Nov. 7, 1975. "The Big Dope Reading," *Hustler*, March 1977. "East Hollywood: The New Paris," *Second Coming*, Vol. 10, no. 1/2, 1981. "The Gambler," *High Times*, November 1983. "The Ladies Man of East Hollywood," *Oui*, February/March 1985. "The Bully," unpublished in English, 1985. "The Invader," unpublished in English, 1986. "Playing and Being the Poet," *Explorations '92*, 1992.